'Balchin has done so much to raise the standard of the popular novel' *TLS*

'A superb storyteller' *Sunday Times*

'Balchin can tell an exciting story as well as any novelist alive' *Sunday Chronicle*

'Mr Balchin is a writer of such considerable and varied gifts ... He is certainly one of the most intelligent novelists' *Time and Tide*

'To some good judges, Balchin, rather than C. P. Snow, was the novelist of men at work' *Guardian*

'He can always be relied on to give us the set-up magnificently' *BBC*

'A little masterpiece like Nigel Balchin's *The Small Back Room* speaks to our own time, but with so much literary experience behind it' Shirley Hazzard

'One of the best writers, and certainly one of the best stylists, to come out of the war years' Michael Powell

'Perhaps the most successful British author to emerge during the war' *Saturday Evening Post*

'*Mine Own Executioner* is a triumphant success'
L. P. Hartley, *Sketch*

Nigel Balchin was born in 1908 and graduated in Natural Sciences from Cambridge University. During the Second World War, he worked as a psychologist in the personnel section of the British War Office, before becoming Deputy Scientific Adviser to the Army Council. His novels enjoyed great critical and commercial success during his lifetime, and he also wrote pieces for *Punch* magazine as well as screenplays for cinema. In 1957, he was awarded the BAFTA for Best British Screenplay for *The Man Who Never Was*. Four of his novels were also adapted into films, most recently by Academy Award-winning writer Julian Fellowes, who filmed *A Way Through the Wood* as *Separate Lies*. Balchin died in 1970, in Hampstead, London.

Fiction by Nigel Balchin

No Sky
Simple Life
Lightbody on Liberty
Darkness Falls from the Air
The Small Back Room
Mine Own Executioner
Lord, I Was Afraid
The Borgia Testament
A Sort of Traitors
A Way Through the Wood
Sundry Creditors
The Fall of the Sparrow
Seen Dimly Before Dawn
In the Absence of Mrs Petersen
Kings of Infinite Space

A WAY THROUGH THE WOOD

NIGEL BALCHIN

WEIDENFELD & NICOLSON

A W&N PAPERBACK

First published in Great Britain in 1951 by Collins
This paperback edition published in 2016
by Weidenfeld & Nicolson,
an imprint of the Orion Publishing Group,
Carmelite House, 50 Victoria Embankment,
London EC4Y 0DZ

An Hachette UK company

1 3 5 7 9 10 8 6 4 2

A CIP catalogue record for this book
is available from the British Library.

ISBN 978-1-474-60120-7

Printed and bound in Great Britain by Clays Ltd, St Ives plc

The Orion Publishing Group's policy is to use papers that
are natural, renewable and recyclable products and
made from wood grown in sustainable forests. The logging
and manufacturing processes are expected to conform to
the environmental regulations of the country of origin.

www.orionbooks.co.uk

'When the Citie of Nola was over-run by the Barbarians, Paulinus Bishop thereof, having lost all he had there, and being their prisoner, prayed thus unto God: "Oh Lord deliver me from feeling of this losse; for Thou knowest as yet they have touched nothing that is mine."'

MONTAIGNE, *Of Solitariness*

Foreword

I first came across Nigel Balchin's novel, *A Way Through the Wood*, from which *Separate Lies* was made, thanks to an old friend, Jenni Hopkins. She knew I had been looking for a 'moral maze' story and one day she telephoned suggesting this one. I wanted a subject where you are never quite sure whose side you are on. Where good people do bad things. Where bad (or baddish) people do good things. Where the reader changes his or her mind. I enjoy American films enormously but I am sometimes unconvinced by their polemic; the heroes are invariably heroic and one is told who the 'bad guys' are right from the start. Life, it seems to me anyway, is a little more complicated than this. In *Separate Lies* we have a couple, James and Jill Manning, who are apparently leading the dream life. He has an important job in the City, they live in a charming house. Their childlessness is the only clue to the fact that all may not be as perfect as it seems. Then comes a chance meeting followed by an accident, and everything is changed, or rather unravelled. On the face of it, the story may appear to concern itself with the events of one unfortunate night, but much more than this, it is a study of an apparently flawless relationshp that is, in reality, deeply flawed. The novel is a study of the couple's journey towards that bitter truth.

Of course the Mannings are very fortunate – the settings in which they lead their lives are glamorous and beautiful and, as such, it might seem that their problems belong to the few rather than the many – but I would like to think that their story resonates at a more universal level. The Mannings' problems are not, after all, unique to the privileged. Anyone who has ever lost themselves in a relationship because it seemed easier than fighting, anyone who has ever had to choose between their own misery and lack of fulfilment and bringing unhappiness to those they love, will understand the quandary that Jill faces. And anyone who has discovered that the love they had based their lives on was a fiction of their own imagination will understand James.

As for the accident that does so much to destabilise their lives, who has never chosen badly in a moment of panic and then lived to regret that unwise choice? If you have, then you will be able to sympathise with the predicament of all three main characters. Lies are reproductive. One lie, told in a guilty hurry, will soon spawn others until a sticky, dishonest web engulfs the teller. On some level or other, most of us have done it and regretted it. Which of us is really entitled to condemn these characters for doing the same?

At any rate, these were the themes that interested me when I read the book. Just as they are the themes that interest me in much of Nigel Balchin's work. Widely recognised and praised in his lifetime, Balchin has been absurdly overlooked for too long. If this edition of the novel, if my film, can help to restore him to his proper place among the great masters of English fiction, then I could not be happier. He certainly belongs there.

Julian Fellowes
July 2004

'In the middle of the way of life, I found myself in a dark wood.' This is the only way in which I resemble Dante. No one looks at me as I pass and whispers, 'There is the man who was in Hell.' If they say anything it is, 'Old Jim Manning's had a rough time lately.' And they don't say it with awe.

Very properly. For there is nothing awe-inspiring about a personal mess. It is a thing for the sensible man to forget, rather than to try to remember.

But though it is all over now I am still desperately confused; and I am tired of confusion. There is still a great deal about the whole business that I don't understand, and it is very important to me that I should understand it; for not to do so is not to understand people – how they will think and feel and act. Until this happened, I thought I understood people tolerably well. Now I am in the dark wood, in which it seems that anything might happen. I know that there must be a logic – a justice – even an inevitability, about what has happened to me in the past year; and Heaven knows, it is a thing that happens to plenty of people. But knowing that there is sense in it somewhere, I still can't see it or feel it.

So I shall write it all down, hoping that as I do so, some pattern will emerge, and I shall see the shape of my dark wood, and how it came to be planted – and even perhaps a way through it. Somebody once defined insanity as 'remembering everything at once.' I have seen for months exactly what he meant. But if that is insanity, perhaps sanity is remembering things in order. I hope so.

J. L. Manning

1

I suppose the psychologists would say that this story has its real beginnings before I was born. Or thirty-seven years ago when I was two. Alternatively, you could say it began eleven years ago when I married Jill. Or after the war when we moved to the country. Things like this don't begin neatly any more than they end neatly.

But for practical purposes it began in the early spring of last year, and I always tend to date it from Easter Monday. I'm not quite sure why, except that that was the day of the fête, and I can remember it better than other days round that time.

I don't know who first thought of having the annual fête in aid of Maidley Village Sports Club on Easter Monday; but by the time I knew the place it was a tradition, and nothing could alter it. It meant that about two years out of three it was a showery day, and the organisers had to decide whether to go on with it on the Manor lawn and let everybody get wet, or move into the village hall, which made it dull and pointless.

But last year it was a lovely day right from the start. I got up about half-past seven and went and walked round the garden. There was a brilliant sun, and I stood and looked at the house, and thought again that Crossways had the most beautiful Queen Anne façade I had ever seen. There was a nip in the air, and I was afraid there might have been a frost which would have messed up the outdoor peaches. But the maximum and minimum thermometer had never gone below thirty-four.

It was so lovely that I decided to go and rout Jill out and make her come and look. I went back to the bedroom, and she was still asleep, looking about seventeen and rather grave. I sat on the bed and looked at her for a few moments and then kissed her and said, 'Come on, hog. Wake up.' She half-opened her eyes and said, 'Oh – hallo. What time is it?'

'About quarter to eight.'

She said, 'Oh. That's all right,' and shut her eyes and curled up again.

I said, 'No, it isn't all right. It's Easter Monday and I've got to be Queen of the May, and it's lovely outside. So wake up, or I shall pull the bedclothes off and smack you.'

Jill said, 'You wouldn't do that, darling. That wouldn't be kind.' She grinned and stretched and said, 'Do you *really* want me to get up. *Now?*'

'Yes. Now. Come and look at the house with the sun on the front. It's lovely.'

'Can't I say it's lovely from here?'

'No.'

She shook her head and said resignedly, 'All right. If that's what life's like, then that's what life's like.'

When we were having breakfast Jill said, 'I've got a conscience about to-day. I ought to have looked after the catering. The President's wife always looks after the catering.'

I said, 'Of course you ought. But it's no use having a conscience about it now. Anyhow Mrs Milray loves doing it. You look after your nice darts and make a lot of money. Did you fix up with Harry about the stand?'

'Yes. And I got the board and a thing to put the money in, and a book to enter the scores. I don't want anything else, do I?'

'Well, you want some darts, but I assume you've got those.'

There was a moment's silence and then Jill said, 'My God . . . !'

I said gently, 'Do I take it that you *haven't* got any darts?'

'I clean forgot about them. Darling, what on earth am I to do?'

'Well, as it happens, you can borrow them from the pub. But *really*, Jilly . . .'

'I know. I'm so sorry. I had a sort of idea that people brought their own. They do in the "George". Still it was inefficient of me. Sorry all.'

I said, 'I've always wanted to know *what* it is you think about all the time.'

'How d'you mean, darling?'

'The thing that takes your mind off the matter in hand.'

Jill said, 'Just a blank, darling. Just a blank. Where d'you think I'd better try for them? The "George" or the "Sisters"?'

I went down to the Manor immediately after breakfast. There was still a lot to do, but most of the stalls and sideshows had been put up on the Saturday, and it wasn't too bad. There were about thirty people there, milling about, a dozen getting on with the job and the rest wandering about looking for something they had lost, or asking everybody how they could possibly be expected to do X if nobody would provide Y. As soon as I got there they stopped asking one another and came and asked me. Jack Early and Teddy Wigan were driving in the posts for the coco-nut shies with sledges. The vicar came teetering over, with those very small steps which always make him look as though he is walking on something very slippery and dangerous. He said to Jack and Teddy, 'I wonder if you fellows would be good enough to help me over to the Jumble Stall with this?' 'This' was a very small light form, about three feet long. I said, 'No – don't take them off the job, padre. I'll bring it over.' I picked the thing up and put it under one arm and said rather pointedly, 'Is there anything else to come?'

'No, no,' he said blandly. 'Just that. It's very kind of you, Mr Manning. Only I find it tiring standing up all day . . .' He teetered along beside me quite happily as I carried the thing over to his stall. I got a broad grin from Jack and Teddy as we went off. The vicar is famous for calling for volunteers even if it is to walk ten yards and post a letter. When we got to his stall he looked carefully over my head, as he always does in conversation, and said, 'Where is your lady? Is she here?'

I said, 'No. She's coming later. She's running the darts.'

'Oh,' he said, obviously disappointed. 'I had wondered whether it might be possible for her to have come and relieved me later on. I have several things to . . .' I put his form down and said firmly, 'I'm afraid she'll be pretty busy herself.'

He said, 'Oh, well – at least we've been blessed with fine weather. Last year I caught a chill that hung about me for months.'

Prior, the schoolmaster, who was running the concert, came up and said, 'That man Payne, who was coming to sing, has cried off. Sprained his ankle. D'you think we dare put in George Wade?'

I said, 'Not if you can possibly help it. Surely there's somebody else who can do something?'

'It looks like George or Miss Radley singing.'

'Oh God – then make it George.'

Phyllis Gouldy said, 'Mr Manning – there isn't a bucket for throwing the tennis balls into the bucket.'

The whole morning was like that. My worst trouble was Hunt, the head gardener at the Manor. He always hates the fête, and you can see why. It takes him the whole summer to get the lawn back into shape. Old Lady Freeth, who owns the place, is nearly ninety, and she will insist on having the show on her lawn, and then forgets it has happened and grumbles at Hunt about the state of the grass. About every quarter of an hour he came up to complain that people were wrecking the place, and I had to go and smooth things over.

Jill turned up about half-past twelve. She had borrowed some darts from the 'George' but had forgotten the box to put the money in. We set up her stand with the dart board on it, and after that I was uncommonly glad to go and have a glass of beer and a sandwich in the tent.

Jill said, 'Anyhow, Mrs Milray has forgotten the teaspoons.'

'How d'you know?'

'I went and asked her if everything was all right, hoping she might have forgotten something, and she said she'd forgotten the teaspoons. So it isn't only me.'

I said, 'Not a comparable case. You can have tea without teaspoons but you can't play darts without darts.'

Doc Frewen was in the tent, drinking a glass of stout. He came ambling over looking as huge and pink and shining as ever and said, 'Hallo, Jill. My, you look pretty. Doesn't she look pretty, Jim?' He always greets Jill like that. I said, 'She may be pretty but she isn't at all good.'

Jill said, 'I'm in disgrace for forgetting the darts and leaving the money-box behind.'

Doc put an arm round her and said, 'Never mind, my

dear. We can't all be efficient, and some of us can't even be nice to look at.'

It was rather pleasant standing there looking out at the Manor gardens and drinking beer. I was just thinking that I was rather happy when Jill said almost crossly, 'I can never see why all this has to happen on Easter Monday.'

I said, 'Why not, honey?'

'Well, it completely mucks up Easter, which is the only time when you get a long week-end.'

'It's fun in a way.'

'Some bits of it are. But I've hardly seen you since you got home on Thursday night. And now to-morrow will be Tuesday and you'll be going back to the office. Do we *have* to go to the dance to-night? It's always a bit grim, and I shall have to dance with Dicky Lewis and he treads on you.'

I said, 'I don't suppose you *must* come if you don't want to. But I shall have to go, being President of the thing.'

After a moment Jill said, 'I tell you what we shall have to do soon, and that's have some people in for drinks. We owe drinks to every bore in the district.'

The people started to come about two o'clock, and by three everything was in full swing. I went over to Jill's stand. She had two small boys and was letting them throw from half-way and putting in the money for them herself. I said, 'That's a profitable operation. How are you doing?'

'Not badly. Bit slow.'

'You want to yell "Warkup warkup," or have a rattle or something. Salesmanship – that's what's needed. There's the Honbill. Let's make him have a go.'

The Honourable William Stephen Fitzharding Bule had just come in sight, looking very country gentleman in a Harris Tweed suit and a red waistcoat with brass buttons. I called, 'Hey – Bill. Come and win a pig.'

He came over with his long-legged lounging walk and said, 'Hallo, my dears. I say – this is an event, isn't it? Is it always like this?'

Jill said, 'Yes. Except that it usually rains as well.'

'Well, I was in the refreshment tent a minute ago and a completely strange character with a bow tie and a whisky breath came up to me and said "You're Bule." I said "Yes" and he said "Do you shoot?" I said "Only if someone else starts something," and he nodded and said "Ah" and went away quite satisfied.'

I said, 'That'll have been Eastman.'

'It may have been Eastman or it may not, James. I don't *know* Eastman. But it struck me as a nice piece of dialogue.'

'He probably wanted you to go and shoot at his place. It's a very good shoot too.'

Bule shook his head and said, 'I once shot at a chaffinch with an airgun when I was ten, and hit it. I've never cared for shooting since.'

Jill said, 'Have a go at this. Three darts for threepence. You might win a pig.'

Bule threw and scored about twenty. He turned to Jill and said, 'Pig?'

'Not a hope. I've had somebody already who's scored a hundred and ten.'

'In that case I shall have another three-pennyworth with the object of scoring a hundred and eleven.'

He spent about half a crown and never scored more than fifty. As I left them he was saying to Jill, 'I tell you what – *you* have a go. Only costs you threepence. You might win a pig.'

The afternoon was hard work but fairly uneventful, except that the small tent in which Miss Armitage was telling fortunes blew down on top of her. About half-past four Jill handed over the darts to somebody else and we went and had tea with Doc Frewen and his wife. Mrs Doc had been helping with the Jumble Stall and apparently the vicar had been complaining all the afternoon that most of the stuff was 'very inferior jumble.' We spent quite a long time working out our various ideas of what would be superior jumble. To everybody's great pleasure Phyllis Scott, wearing a bow tie and a man's trilby, stopped at our table just long enough to say to Jill, '*Marvellous* tea, Jill darling. You must have *slaved* over it,' and then went away before anybody could disillusion her. Jill said, 'That's another of the people we owe drinks.'

I looked round for Bill Bule, but he wasn't in the tent. Doc said he had gone but that he was coming back for the concert. I asked Jill if he'd won the pig, but apparently though he'd spent nearly ten shillings at threepence a go he had never scored more than eighty. Mrs Doc said in her simple way, 'You know, I think Mr Bule rather *laughs* at village things like this.'

Doc said, 'So do I. What are we supposed to do? Cry at them? Anyhow he's been very good this afternoon going round and taking part in things.'

Jill said, 'I think he's been enjoying himself. He and Mr Evans and Jack Millett have been the backbone of the darts' takings.'

I said, 'I should think he'll like George Wade, if he comes to the concert. He won't have heard George before.'

Jill said in horror, 'George Wade? Jim – he isn't going to recite?'

'Yes, he is.'

'Then, darling, I mustn't come. I can't take it. Last time I heard George I felt sick from not giggling.'

'Oh, come – George is fine as long as you don't *look* at

him. Keep your eyes on the floor and think about something else and you'll be all right.'

The concert was at five-thirty. As President, I had to sit in the front row. When we got in we found Bule already there in the seat next to ours, and like a fool I put Jill next to him so that she was between us.

The next hour or so was one of the most agonising I have ever spent. I have been to a few village concerts in my time but this will always be the one that sticks in my memory. It began perfectly normally with Mrs Prior, the schoolmaster's wife, playing a couple of short pieces by Chopin quite competently, and then she and Prior played something by Corelli for piano and violin. It was then that the trouble started. The next performer was a visitor – a stout woman with one of those plummy contralto voices, and for some reason she chose to sing *I'm Seventeen come Sunday*. It was funny, but no funnier than many an Isolde that I have heard at Covent Garden, and hardly funny at all as village concerts go. But it started Jill giggling, and after that she just giggled more and more the longer it went on. During George's recitation she got her head well down and stared at the floor, but her shoulders were shaking, and I was afraid not only the audience but George himself would see, because we were slap in the middle of the front row. I must say that Bule behaved beautifully. Throughout the whole of George's performance of 'He fell among thieves,' Bule sat and looked at him, with his head slightly on one side and an expression of mild concern, as though somebody had just told him their aunt had died. But Jill was so bad that I was rather cross with her, and when George had finished I said, 'Look, darling, if you're going to laugh as much as that you'd better go out. People must be able to see . . .'

She sat up and said, 'I'm sorry. I've stopped now. I just got ...' She blew her nose and I could see her deliberately pursing her lips into shape, and she looked round with a sort of guilty dignity, with the tears still in her eyes. Bule said without a flicker of a smile, 'Of course, it isn't really easy, James. I'm feeling a certain sense of strain myself.'

'So am I if it comes to that. Never mind. We don't have George again.'

After that we got through two more items and all would have been well if it hadn't been for old Stuart's announcement of his cornet solo. He is very old now, and I believe he was a very good bandsman in his day. Anyhow, he always plays a cornet solo at all these things, and he was greeted with loud applause. He is a rather odd-looking little man with pince-nez, and stepping forward he said confidentially, 'Ladies and gentlemen, some of you know what's happened to my teeth, but I'm going to try *The Lost Chord*.' Before the applause could come and drown her, Jill let out a loud resounding snort and dived into her handkerchief. I saw old Stuart's eyes come down to her for a second in surprise, and then he looked round with a rather wistful smile and stepped back and lifted his cornet. I think Jill realised she had gone a bit far, because she stopped laughing and sat and listened quite seriously. But I knew the old boy had seen her and been hurt, and I didn't like it.

Jill knew I was angry. As we came out she said, 'I'm awfully sorry about that. I couldn't help it.'

I said, 'Darling, if you must behave like a giggly schoolgirl I suppose you must.'

Bule said very solemnly, 'Bad show, Jill. Bad show.'

'Well, it was the bit about the teeth and then *The Lost Chord* ...'

'I dare say, but you must learn to control yourself. After

all, I was remembering that Dan Leno used to begin that song "Seated one day on the organ . . ." but *I* didn't snort. And *I'm* not the President's wife.'

I said rather curtly, 'Are you coming to the dance?'

Bule said, 'No, James. That I can't do. I must go home and rest after this whirl of pleasure-seeking. Good-bye, my dears. See you soon.'

After he had gone Jill said, 'Are you angry with me, Jim?' And I said, 'No, of course not. But you are an old ass sometimes. Now what are we going to do about this dance? There's no need to come if it's going to bore you.'

She looked at me anxiously with big mud-coloured eyes and said very solemnly, 'But I *want* to come – if you'll take me.'

Jill being repentant is always too much for me. So I grinned and said, 'All right. Then you damned well *shall* come, and be trodden on by Dicky Lewis, and be bored stiff, and have to do a lovely President's wife act, and serve you right, awful.'

I think Jill must really have thought I was angry with her, because at the dance she was very good, and I knew it must be an effort for her. She is too shy to be a good mixer, and this makes the village boys shy of her. She is about as far from being a snob as anybody could be, but she has never picked up the knack of living in the country, and at this sort of show she is still liable to act like a very polite but shy nineteen-year-old. I should think Jill is the only person in the district who addresses old Peter Fenn as 'Mr Fenn.'

But this evening she really set out to do a job, and danced all the time, and went and sat with her partners instead of coming back all the time to me or to Doc and Mrs Frewen or the Marriots. And when it came to a 'Ladies' Choice' dance she made a bee-line for poor little

Dicky Lewis, who has one leg shorter than the other and is about five foot high. I danced with her myself soon after and said, 'Now that was a nice girl.'

'Who?'

'You. Choosing Dicky.'

'Oh, yes,' she said rather bitterly. 'Hell of a nice girl.' After a moment she said, 'He's sweet really, is Dicky. Very gentle. I wish I wasn't such a bitch, darling.'

I said, 'You're not a bitch.'

She shook her head moodily. 'Oh, yes, I am . . . Look – you haven't danced with Miss Lovett and she'll be hurt if you don't.'

We had to stay to the end, because I had to make a speech winding up the whole thing and thanking everybody who had helped and announcing that the fête had raised over fifty pounds for the Sports Club and so on. It was after two when we got home. It had been a long day and I think we were both very tired. We sat and drank a cup of tea for a few minutes before we went to bed. Jill said, 'Oh – by the way – I've asked a few people in for a drink next Friday. Is that all right? We do owe it them.'

'Friday's my Board day. But I should think we shall be through all right. How many?'

'Only about a dozen. Just the usual people . . .' She sat for a moment in silence. I thought she looked depressed and said, 'What's the matter, darling? Tired?'

She said listlessly, 'I'm not a good wife for you, you know. I wish I was.'

I grinned and said, 'You seem pretty good to me.'

'Oh, yes – I dare say. But I'm not really. And you know it. Take to-day. Almost anybody else would have been more – more help. More what you want. Even Mrs Doc.'

I said, 'I should love to be married to Mrs Doc.'

'Well, at least she wouldn't giggle about in public and . . .'

I said, 'Oh – *that's* it? Still got a conscience about that?'

To my surprise, she suddenly burst into tears and said, 'Well, he *saw*, and it hurt his feelings and – and . . .' I put my arms round her and said, 'Oh, come on, honey. It didn't matter. And it *was* funny . . .' But she pulled away and said, 'But it *did* matter. It mattered a hell of a lot. You were furious with me, and so I should darn well think. And I didn't do anything all day and I forgot the darts and I forgot the bloody box and I can't *do* it!' She ended in such a wail of woe that I couldn't help laughing, and seeing me laugh Jill started to giggle too, slightly hysterically. I took her in my arms and said gently, 'Now stop being an ass and listen – you were very sweet at the dance and you looked perfectly lovely and I was very proud of you, and I know this isn't particularly your sort of show and so what?' She looked at me for a moment but didn't say anything. I kissed her and said, 'Come on – bed. There's been quite enough of to-day and I've got to get up in the morning.'

Jill said, 'Oh God – I wish you hadn't got to go to the office.'

'So do I. But there it is. Come on.'

The last thing I remember about that Easter Monday is being half-asleep and suddenly hearing Jill say, 'Jim – will you tell me something? Truthfully?'

'Yes, honey?'

'Is it a hell of an effort to be as nice to me as you are?'

I squeezed her and said, 'Of course. It strains every fibre of my being.'

She sighed and said, 'Well, I'm not worth it, you know. I'm not really any good to man or beast.'

I said sleepily, 'Useless Jilly. Not any good to anybody. Darling Jilly.'

It seems unbelievable, but that was a year ago, almost to the day.

2

I usually reckoned to get the five o'clock train from Charing Cross, which meant that I got home just before half-past six. But on that particular Friday the Board Meeting went on and on all day, and by about three o'clock I could see that I should never make it. So I sent a note out to my secretary telling her to ring Jill up and say that I should have to come down on the 7.30, and that I would have dinner on it. It was particularly irritating, because of the people she had invited in for drinks.

I have seen Jill standing on the platform as my train drew into Knowsley Station so many times that the recollection may be a composite one. But I seem to remember that she was wearing a camel-hair coat and that her hair was smooth and shining in the lamplight like the skin of a chestnut. I don't quite know why, but it meant a great deal that she should bring the car to meet me herself; and on the odd occasions when she couldn't come, the platform always looked cold and empty and unwelcoming.

Anyhow, she was there that evening. I kissed her and said, 'I'm awfully sorry about this evening but I just couldn't make it.'

She said, 'Darling, it didn't matter in the least. It was rather dull anyway.'

I put my hand through her arm and squeezed it and said, 'Well, now we've got all the week-end anyhow.'

I remember that she squeezed back with her arm. As we were going through the subway she said, 'Look – we shall have to go out with the Honbill. I couldn't get the car to start. Battery's flat. So he said he'd bring me to get you in his.'

'That was nice of him. Was he at the party?'

'Yes.'

Bule was sitting in his big dark green Lagonda in the station yard. He leaned out and grinned and said, 'Hallo. Return of tired business man.' I said, 'Hallo, Bill. This is very kind of you.'

'No, it isn't. It's a cunning tactical move to get myself offered another drink.'

Jill opened the back door of the car and said, 'I'll pile in here,' but I said, 'No – you go in front with Bill,' and shoved her in.

There is a long straight outside the station and as we accelerated along it I said, 'This is a very grand motor-car, Bill. How long have you had her now?'

'Six months.'

'Like her?'

'I like her fine.'

I noticed that even when we were out in the country he didn't use his headlamps, but drove on a big spotlight that was set so that it showed the left-hand verge. I was sitting behind Jill and I could see her silhouetted against the lighted road. I was slightly disappointed that Jill had had to come with Bule, because I always enjoyed that ten minutes' drive in the dark with her, and getting home and going in to the fire. And now the Honbill would have to come in and have a drink, and probably wouldn't go. He lived by himself, and I think he was rather bored and lonely. Anyhow, he usually liked to stay on pretty late.

I don't think anybody said anything until we got home. Bill only took about seven minutes to get to Maidley, which is our village. He drove exceptionally well, sitting right up to the wheel with his elbows well in, never taking his eyes off the road. I had never been in a car with him before. As we turned into the drive of Crossways he said, 'Do I get my drink?'

I said, 'Sure. If the party hasn't drunk the place dry.'

He didn't go into the garage, but stopped outside the front door. The outside light was on. We got out and Jill went in. I was just shutting the nearside rear door when I noticed that it had a bad scratch right across the paintwork. I said, 'What have you been doing to your door?'

Bule said, 'Door—?' and came round and looked at it. I said, 'Didn't you know it was there?'

He didn't answer, but looked at it and then said, 'Damn that man. I shall have to fire him. He *is* the worst chauffeur in the world, bar none.'

I said, 'Touched it coming out of the garage I should think.' It looked like that – a long narrow scrape that had gone through to the metal in places.

We went in and I went to drop my coat and bag. When I got back Jill was sitting on the floor by the fire. She nearly always sat on the floor. Bule was leaning against the big beam that goes across the open fireplace, looking down at her and talking. His body looked curiously slack and boneless. He is six feet three and very slim, and though he is a handsome chap in most ways, being so tall gives him a habit of bending his head and shoulders down, so that he looks as though he is stooping.

When I came back he stopped talking to Jill and said, 'It's a pity you weren't here this evening, James. There was a political debate between Phyllis Scott and old Chivers that was worth every penny of the money.'

'Phyllis was selling him Socialism?'

'She was. Phyllis inherited about half a million and she's all for Labour; and old Chivers is solvent for the first time in the last thirty years because of Government subsidies, and he's all for going back to a sound Tory Government. And there were you wasting your time making cigarettes.'

I said, 'I doubt if I missed much. I've heard it all before.'

Bule looked down at Jill and said, 'What does James really *do* in London, Jill? I always visualise him as literally making cigarettes – you know, with one of those little gadgets.'

Jill grinned and said, 'That's right. You put the paper in and spread the tobacco on it and roll . . .' and they chorused, 'and lick the paper . . .' and giggled.

Bule said, 'Don't you run short of lick, James? I always run out of lick if I have to lick more than two stamps.'

I said, 'What I am short of at meetings like that is patience. This one went on from ten till six-thirty, and the whole thing could have been over in an hour.'

Bule shook his head and said, 'I don't see how you do it.'

'Do what?'

'This captain of industry stuff.'

'It's quite fun.'

Jill was staring into the fire. She said, 'You always say it's quite fun, and yet you're always coming home and telling me how boring it's been.'

Bule said, 'Perhaps James likes being bored.'

Jill looked up at me thoughtfully and said, 'Perhaps he does.'

I said, 'Did old Snead come?'

'He certainly did.' Bule looked at Jill and said, 'I'll bet James likes Father Snead.'

I said, 'I do like Father Snead. So do you, don't you? I think he's rather a good bloke.'

'I don't like parsons at all, of whatsoever denomination,' said Bule. 'Particularly parsons who drink whisky in large quantities and are all boys together.'

'*Was* he all boys together this evening?'

Jill said, 'He was a bit.'

'He put his arm round Jill and I thought he was going to offer to be an uncle to her.'

'Well, damn it, the old boy nearly has been.'

'Not in the way I mean. At least I hope not. I don't mind if Jill embraces the Catholic faith, but I don't like seeing it embrace her.'

I said, 'Old Snead's all right,' and let it go at that. One of the pictures was a bit crooked and I got up and put it straight. It was nothing much – a small eighteenth-century portrait of a soldier in uniform, slightly Lawrencish that had belonged to my mother. As I came away from it Bule said, 'James, for one glorious moment I thought you were going to take it down. You shouldn't raise my hopes like that and then disappoint them.'

I said, 'Why should I take it down?'

'Why shouldn't you? There's a perfectly pleasant piece of wall behind it.'

'It's quite harmless.'

'Don't you believe it. Bad pictures are never harmless. You see them, whether you know you do or not. And they eat into your æsthetic sense and corrupt it.'

'I haven't got that sort of æsthetic sense. It would take more than that to hurt it. Anyhow, I think it's rather pleasant.'

Jill looked at the thing and said, 'I wouldn't mind if he were a *handsome* man. But he's got such a queer nose.'

I was surprised and said rather curtly, 'Well, darling, as far as I remember you put him there.'

'Oh, yes. He's all *right*. Anyhow he's an ancestor or something, isn't he?'

Bule said, 'Oh, a family portrait? I didn't realise that. Jolly interesting picture, old man.'

There was nothing in all this, superficially. They had

been at a cocktail party and I hadn't. And anyhow the Honbill was always like it. But I hadn't wanted him there in the first place, and the 'poor old James' stuff was a bit irritating. So I just smiled and said, 'Listen, Bill – you're obviously in a thoroughly carping mood, so drink up your drink and go. Otherwise you'll be telling me I mustn't wear this tie next.'

He said, 'Well, you mustn't. Of course you mustn't. It's an offence, that tie. Look at the smooth decency of the thing – its sleek, smug self-satisfaction. There ought to be a law against it. In fact, I'm not sure there isn't. The Offences Against Innocent Bystanders (Foul Ties) Act. Ah, well—' He shook his head sadly and finished his drink and said, 'Sent away, turned out into the snow, with my infant in my arms. And after I'd been a good Samaritan too. There's no gratitude.' He picked up his cigarette-case and put it in his pocket. Then he looked from one to the other of us and said, 'Am I going to see you over the week-end?'

Jill said, 'How about coming in for a drink before lunch on Sunday?'

Bule said, 'I shall do that. 'Night, Jill.' He turned to me and said, 'Good-night, James. Thanks for the drink.' On the way to the door he stopped and looked at the picture again and gave a little moan and shook his head.

When we got out to the car I said, 'Thanks very much for picking me up.'

'That's all right, James. Pleasure. See you Sunday.' He took the Lagonda off very smoothly and quickly, and I saw him switch on the big spotlight as he went down the drive.

Jill was still sitting on the floor in the lounge staring at the fire. She looked up and said, 'Wasn't that rather beastly of you, darling?'

'What?'

'To chuck the Honbill out. After all, it was nice of him to come and get you.'

'I know. But he irritates me. And anyhow I wanted to be alone with you. Incidentally. I wish you wouldn't play that game with him.'

'What game?'

'The "poor old James" game. First it was my job, and then it was Father Snead, and then it was the picture. I get tired of it.'

She looked rather startled and said, 'I don't see what you mean, darling.'

'Well, the Honbill is always being clever and critical about somebody or something. I don't mind its being me. But I don't think you ought to gang up with him against me.'

Jill said, 'Darling, I'm sorry. We were only fooling. I . . .'

'I know, honey. But it's all rather smart undergraduate stuff, and very boring. And anyhow, most of it's complete nonsense as far as you're concerned. You know old Snead's a dear, and you know you've always rather liked that picture. I don't think you ought to play disliking things just because Bill Bule does. Otherwise you'll soon find yourself not liking anything.'

Jill hesitated and then pursed her lips slightly and said, 'I'm sorry,' and stared into the fire again.

I knew she was cross, and I felt that perhaps I had been making rather a fuss about nothing, so I stroked her hair and said, 'It's a pity old Bill does that. Otherwise he's an amusing cuss.'

Jill was silent for a moment. Then she said suddenly, 'But does it *matter* anyway? All this mild cattiness about things and people? It's quite amusing and it doesn't do any harm.'

'Of course it doesn't matter – as long as it doesn't

become a habit. But I've never heard the Honbill say a nice word about anybody yet. It gets so dull.'

'He was very funny at the party. The one bright spot in fact.'

'Who else came, apart from Phyllis and old Chivers and Father Snead?'

'Doc Frewen was on a case, but Mrs Doc came. She was in fine form. Wearing *all* her pearls.'

'Who else?'

'Oh, the Margetsons and Henry Riley and a vague man he brought. You didn't miss anything.'

'I rather like Riley.'

'He was all right, but a bit agricultural. The market for pigs is weakening. Did you have a horrid day with your Board?'

'Average. Never mind, we've got the week-end now.'

We sat in silence for a while and then Jill got up and took a cigarette out of the box and sat down in the arm-chair opposite. I looked at her and thought how attractive she was. I said, 'You're very pretty to-night, aren't you? What are you being so pretty about?'

She smiled at me and said, 'Am I? I thought I was looking rather a hag.' She seldom smoked, and she still tended to puff at a cigarette all the time, as she had when I first saw her. After a while she said, 'Look, the Duke's giving his Spring Ball at Lowood Castle the week after next and the Honbill's been asked to take a party. He wants to know if we'll come. I said I'd ask you. What d'you think?'

I said, 'I don't know, darling. Would you like to go?'

'I would, rather. I've never been to Lowood.'

'Yes. It might be fun. What day?'

'Thursday.'

I looked at my diary and said, 'Oh God, I've got to be in town that night.'

'What for?'

'I'm dining with old Arthur Maitland. You know – I told you about it.'

'So you did. I'd forgotten it was that night. Can't you put him off?'

'Darling, I don't see how I can. I've put him off twice already.'

'Couldn't you have an awful cold or have broken your leg or something?'

'Well, you see, it's a bit difficult. The old boy's very hard up now and very sensitive about it, and I'm afraid he may think I don't want to go.'

'Do you, anyhow?'

'Heavens, no. It's a penance. He's practically stone deaf. But I don't see how I can get out of it, all the same.'

Jill said rather crossly, 'Well, surely it doesn't make sense to miss something you want to go to, so that you can go and bawl at poor old Arthur?'

I grinned at her and said, 'You've no social conscience. You never have had. Never mind. I'll try and fix something.'

'But I said we'd let the Honbill know to-morrow.'

'Well, if the worst comes to the worst, and he's taking a party, there's no reason why you shouldn't go without me, is there?'

She turned the mud-coloured eyes full on mine and said, 'But I wanted to go with you.'

The next morning just after breakfast I was out in the garden walking round the peaches, when I heard Claude, my bull mastiff, barking his head off. This could only mean that somebody very respectable had arrived. Claude is one of those dogs who only bark at respectable citizens, and fawn all over tramps, gipsies and other dubious types. I went round the house, and sure enough it was Eddie Cator, our local bobby, on his motor-bike.

I said, 'Shut up, Claude, you old fool. 'Morning, Eddie. Want me?' He propped his bike up and said, 'Well, it was really Mrs Manning, sir. Elsie asked me to come up and give her a message and say she's sorry about not coming.'

Elsie was our charwoman and Eddie is her brother.

I said, 'All right. I'll tell my wife. What's up? Isn't Elsie well?'

'Oh, *she's* all right, Mr Manning. It's her husband.'

'Joe? What's up with him?'

'He got knocked off his bicycle by a car last night. They've took him into hospital. Elsie's in there now.'

I said, 'I'm sorry about that. Is he badly hurt?'

Eddie shook his head. 'They reckon he's pretty bad. Fractured skull, they say.'

'How did it happen?'

'Right outside his own gate. 'Bout half-past six. It seems Joe got home, and Elsie was getting his tea, and Joe found he hadn't got any fags. So he says to Elsie, "I'll just pop up to Thomas's and get some fags. Shan't be a minute." So he must've gone out and jumped on his bike, and just as he came out of the gate a car came along very fast round that bend there, and caught him.'

'What car was it?'

Eddie shook his head. 'I don't know, Mr Manning. I wish I did. It didn't stop, see.'

'Just drove straight on?'

'That's right. Just drove straight on and left him there as though it'd run over a rabbit.'

'D'you think the chap who was driving knew he'd hit him?'

'I don't know, sir. Maybe. Maybe not. Elsie saw it all out of the window. 'Course, it was half dark, getting on for

26

half-past six. But Elsie says it seemed to catch the bike more than him. She says he was just getting on, and this car came along and seemed to catch the bike and sort of threw him and the bike across the road. Doesn't seem the sort of thing that could happen and a chap not know he'd done it.'

'Elsie didn't get the car's number, of course?'

'Well, no sir. She was inside, and it was all over in a second.'

I said, 'What a rotten business. He's a nice chap too, is Joe. Do they think he'll pull through?'

Eddie had put a hand down and was stroking Claude's head. Claude had now decided that Eddie was a tramp, and lovable. Eddie said, 'They won't say. They seem to think there's a chance, but not much of one.' He looked down at Claude and said quietly, 'Joe was in Crete. He came all through North Africa and all through Italy and never got a scratch. Then he comes back and some silly fool mucking about goes and does this. Married man with three kids.'

He shook his head and gave Claude a gentle cuff. 'Well, sir, I'd be obliged if you'd let Mrs Manning know. Elsie was worried about not coming.'

I said, 'I'll certainly tell her. And don't let Elsie worry about that. It doesn't matter at all. You say she's at the hospital?'

'Yes, sir. He's still unconscious, but she wanted to be with him.'

'I'll try and slip in this afternoon and see if there's anything that – that wants doing.'

Eddie said, 'That's very kind of you, sir. She'd like that.' He pushed his motor-cycle off its stand, got on to it rather slowly, and started the engine. Just before he started to move he turned his head and said, 'Now I'm going to find that car.' He had queer, rather angry-looking blue eyes and lashes that were nearly white. It wasn't a pleasant face.

The noise of the engine was too much for Claude. Tramps don't have motor-cycles. So he stood and barked until Eddie was out of sight. He was still barking at the distant noise when I went into the house.

I knew Jill would be upset. She was very fond of Elsie. Jill is very bad with most sorts of servants, and doesn't handle them well, but she always gets on well with charwomen. I can never remember the time when we hadn't some charwoman, usually with a lot of children, whom Jill liked, and who adored her. The only way in which Elsie was different from all the others was that she was thirty and had three children, instead of being forty-five and having seven; but to make up for it, she was cross-eyed.

Jill was making out a shopping list, but as soon as I told her that Joe had been knocked down and was in hospital she said, 'Oh, poor Elsie! I must go down and see her,' and was for rushing off at once.

I said, 'It's no good going down there. Eddie says she's at the hospital. I thought we might have gone in after lunch.'

'Well, but how about the children? Who's looking after them?'

'Eddie will have fixed that. I expect they're with their grandmother.'

She hesitated for a moment and then said, 'I think we ought to go and see. You know what the Cottage Hospital's like.'

'It's all right.'

'Yes, but you know how it is. They won't call in specialists or – or do anything unusual unless there's somebody to make them . . .'

In matters of this kind Jill is and always has been the complete one-man Salvation Army. I remember thinking,

'Here goes our week-end.' But I knew from experience that there was nothing to be done about it, so I just said, 'All right, darling. What do you want to do?'

She said, 'Couldn't we go into the hospital right away? I think we ought to, Jim. Or look here – I'll go, if you can start the car for me. There's no need for you to come.'

I said, 'No, that's all right. We'll both go this morning, if you'd feel happier about it.'

I suppose there will come a time when Aldingly Cottage Hospital will begin to feel like a proper, impersonal bit of the State Medical Service, but it hasn't happened yet. Matron told us that Doc Frewen was handling the case and that she'd see if he could come and have a word with us. While she was gone I said to Jill, 'I suppose this was why Doc wasn't at your party. What time did it start?'

'Just before seven.'

'Well, this happened about half-past six, so that'll be it.'

Doc Frewen came out, looking very happy. I can never quite get over the medical profession's cheerfulness on these occasions. I know perfectly well that Doc Frewen is the gentlest and most compassionate person imaginable, and that in his job if you didn't go on being cheerful you'd die. But even so I am still impressed and slightly shocked every time.

Doc said to Jill, 'I'm sorry I couldn't get to the party. My wife says she had a most enjoyable time.'

Jill said, 'We've come about Joe Pearce. How is he?'

Doc Frewen said, 'He's alive.'

'Is he going to pull through?'

'Well – people always may pull through until they're actually dead.'

I said, 'As bad as that?'

Doc pushed the glasses back on his nose and said, 'It's a

piece of very bad luck really. The man's got an abnormally thin skull. As far as I can see it was the road that he hit his head against – not the car. If he'd had a normal skull he might have got away with nothing much – or a slight fracture. As it is . . .' He shrugged his shoulders.

Jill said, 'Is there anything possible that we can do, Doc? Specialists or . . . ?'

He waved a hand. 'I've had Hagood already. Excellent man. Specialist on head injuries. Came, stayed a quarter of an hour, agreed with me and went away again.' He tapped a finger on the side of his bald head. 'There's a lot of laceration. As I say, he may pull through. I've seen people survive as bad – and worse. But not often.'

Jill said, 'Does Elsie know?'

'She knows he's in danger. No point in trying to keep that from her.'

'Is she here?'

'Yes. Been here since they brought him in. Won't go in case he comes round. Very natural. I don't think he will, but I let her stay. I think the police are here waiting to see her. Apparently she saw it happen.'

I said, 'Who's here from the police?'

'Her brother Eddie, and Sergeant Groves from Monckton. You know Groves?'

'Yes. I've often met him at the court. Where are they? I'd like to have a word with Groves.'

Jill said, 'And I'd like to see Elsie.'

Doc hesitated and then said, 'All right. I'll take you in. Probably be a good thing. She's shaken up, of course, but she's taken it very well on the whole. Groves is in the end waiting-room if you want him, Jim.'

Groves and Eddie were sitting at a table in the waiting-room with a lot of photographs in front of them. I said, 'Have you got any further over the car?'

Groves said, 'Well, no, Mr Manning – that's what we're on now. It's just possible that if the boy comes round he may be able to tell us something, but I doubt it, because it seems the car came from behind him. The only person who saw it was Mrs Pearce, and she doesn't seem to be able to help much. So I was just setting these out, and then I was going to get her in, and see if she could pick out anything that looked at all like it.'

I looked at the photographs. They were all silhouettes of cars, rather like the aircraft silhouettes that were used for training in spotting during the war. Groves said, 'Of course, it was getting dark and it all happened pretty quick . . .'

Eddie said, 'Elsie says it was a big car.'

I said, 'I tell you what's rather puzzling me, Sergeant – and that is what a big car was doing along that road by the Pearces' cottage. It's very quiet, and except for tradesmen, I shouldn't have thought you'd get three cars a day down it. It doesn't go anywhere much.'

Eddie said, 'You can get through to Stapleton that way.'

'I know. But it's a longer way round than the main road.'

Groves shrugged. 'Maybe somebody who didn't know the district lost his way. After all, Friday night – you begin to get the traffic from London.'

'But not along there.'

'No. I see what you mean, Mr Manning. But there it is – it *did* come down there, worse luck.' He paused for a moment and then said, 'Well, look, Eddie – will you go and see if your sister'd like to come and have a look at these? Because the longer we wait the more difficult it's going to be.'

When Eddie had gone I said, 'What chance have you got of tracing a car in a case like this?'

Groves shook his head and said, 'It depends on a lot of

things, sir. If the chap who was driving knew he hit him – if he's a real hit-and-run bastard who'll keep his mouth shut, and his passengers do the same – then unless the car's badly damaged, it's like looking for a needle in a haystack. He might be in Scotland by now. The best chance is that he *didn't* know, and that if we appeal to the public to help, he'll come forward. I've known that happen. But...' He shook his head again. I nodded towards the photographs and said, 'I doubt if those will help you. I've been trying to pick out our own Daimler from them, and got it wrong.'

'I doubt it too, sir. But we've got nothing else to start from but Mrs Pearce. And at least she may be able to give us a line on what general sort and size of thing it was.'

Eddie came back with his sister and Jill. Elsie was a very tall, raw-boned woman with hands and feet like a man's. She was one of the strongest women physically I have ever known. She had a face that might have been handsome in a big-featured masculine way; but you didn't notice that easily because she had a bad squint. She had been crying, and her eyes and nose were red. She looked incredibly ugly, and I think that made her a good deal more pathetic than as though she had been some pretty little thing.

I said, 'Hallo, Elsie,' and she said, 'Good-afternoon, sir,' almost in a whisper. She was always very polite.

Groves said gently, 'Now, Elsie, I got all these pictures of cars. What I want you to do is look at them, and pick out the one that's most like the – the one you saw.' When Groves was talking to Elsie he had much more Sussex accent than when he talked to me.

Elsie nodded slightly and went over to the photographs. A thought struck me and I said, 'These are all saloons, Sergeant. I suppose you're sure it was a saloon – not an open car?'

Eddie said, 'Elsie reckons it was.'

Elsie stood looking at the pictures in silence for a while. Then she said, 'It was big – not like that little one,' pointing to a Morris Minor. There was a long pause. Then she said rather helplessly, 'There's a lot that's rather like it. That – and that – and that.'

Eddie said, 'Humber Pullman. Humber Snipe. Sunbeam 90.'

I said, 'All post-war and made by the same group of companies.'

Elsie said, 'Or that.'

'That's a Yank,' Eddie said. 'De Soto. That isn't much like the others, Els.' He said it slightly crossly. She turned and looked at him nervously and her lips trembled. She said rather tremulously, 'It was dark, see, Eddie . . .'

Jill said quickly, 'Of course it was. And she only saw it for a moment.'

Elsie said in a low voice, 'See, I heard it coming and I looked out of the window but the light was in my eyes an' it was only as it passed I saw it, and it was going fast.'

I saw Groves shake his head slightly. I said, 'Try to think if there's *anything* you remember about it, Elsie. The noise it made, loud or quiet?'

She shook her head. 'I didn't notice, sir. It was just – the noise a car makes coming.'

'No impression of colour, of course?'

'No, sir. It was dark, see. I reckon maybe it was black or some dark colour.'

'Nothing at all that you can remember?'

She said, 'No sir . . .' and then added, '. . . not except the light. It was very bright – white like – and it sort of swept across my face.'

'As the thing came round the bend?'

'Yes, sir.'

There was a long pause. Then Groves said without much enthusiasm, 'Well, let's have one more go with these. Other way round this time. You just put aside the ones you're pretty sure aren't like it.'

It was hopeless. She put aside half a dozen confidently enough, but then she was obviously lost. After a while she even threw out the De Soto that she had picked out before as being like it. Eddie saw this and gave an irritated growl, but I caught his eye and shook my head at him and he kept quiet. When Elsie still had about fifteen left, she hesitated for a long time, and I could see her hand clenching and unclenching on her handkerchief. I thought she was going to cry. Jill thought the same and said, 'That's really as close as you can get, isn't it, Elsie?' She nodded silently. Groves said quickly, 'That's all right, then. That's been a real help, Elsie,' and got up.

Jill said, 'Have you finished with her now, Sergeant?'

'Only one other thing, Mrs Manning . . . Look, Elsie – I want you just to think about this for a minute. Do you reckon whoever was driving saw Joe? I mean – *must* have seen him? Or might be that he never saw him at all? Did he seem to swerve or anything?'

She was standing looking down at her fingers but at this her head came up. She squinted across at Groves and said, 'He saw him.' Her voice was quite different from what it had been before – cold and hating.

'What makes you so sure? *Did* he swerve or . . . ?'

Elsie said, 'I don't know. I never saw whether he swerved or no. But he saw him. An' he didn't care.' Her voice cracked slightly. Groves hesitated for a moment and then said, 'All right then, Elsie. That's all, and thank you very much.'

Jill went out with her. After they had gone Eddie said bitterly, 'Don't seem she saw much. Of course, she *can't*

34

see very well, with only one eye that works.' He nodded towards the picture. 'All we can tell from that's that it was something over about fourteen horse. And I wouldn't trust that far.'

Groves sighed and said, 'No. Nor I.'

I said, 'What can you do now?'

He shrugged. 'We can ask anyone who was driving along there about that time to come forward. Apart from that we can check with our chaps, and A.A. Scouts, and people like that if they saw anything like it round about them . . .'

'Like what?' said Eddie curtly.

Groves scratched his chin and said, 'That's the trouble.'

After about a quarter of an hour Jill came out and said, 'Doc Frewen's going to get her to bed here for a bit. It's the best thing. She's been up all night and she's all in. I've told her I'll go down and see that the children are all right. They're with Joe's mother, but she's pretty helpless.'

As we were driving home she said rather crossly, 'What was the good of all that? It's quite obvious that she didn't see anything useful. She's as blind as a bat anyhow. And that fool, Eddie, snapping at her . . .'

I said, 'Eddie wants to find that car. So do I, if it comes to that.'

'Why you?'

'I just don't think people ought to get away with that sort of thing.'

'Oh, I see. Yes. Still, it won't bring Joe to life again, and it's no good bullying her when she's in that state.'

After a while I said, 'There's still a thing that's puzzling me. That's what a big car was doing down there. Where was it going?'

Jill said, 'I'm still not sure what really happened. Where was it? They were out together, were they?'

35

I said, 'Oh, no. It was just outside their cottage – you know – down in Tarrant's Lane. Joe was just going out on his bike to get cigarettes. Elsie saw it happen out of the window.'

After a pause Jill said, 'What time was this?'

I said, 'Around half-past six.' As far as I remember she made no reply, but I can't be sure, because at that moment a tractor came out of a side road, and I had to brake hard and squeeze round it. Jill went down to see Elsie's children in the afternoon.

3

I had forgotten that Jill had asked Bill Bule in for a drink before lunch the next day, and I didn't come in from the garden till about half-past twelve. He and Jill were in the lounge looking as though they had been there some time.

As I got myself a drink Bule said, 'I hear you won't be able to make the Duke's party, James?'

I said, 'I shall try. But I don't see quite how to put old Arthur off again. He might be hurt.'

'But if you don't come *I* shall be hurt. And so will Jill. Who is this old Arthur who can't be put off? And why?'

'Well, he's old and poor and deaf as a post and a bore.'

'All perfectly good reasons for not going to dinner with him. If he were young, rich, and acute of hearing and wit, I should see your point of view. As it is, I think you'd better come to the Duke's. Don't you, Jill?'

Jill said, 'I'm coming anyhow.'

'What – even if James doesn't?'

'Mm.'

'Ah,' said Bule, 'I misunderstood.' He turned to me and said solemnly, 'I entirely see your point about Arthur, James. Nice Arthur. Dear old Arthur. One could hardly put old Arthur off.'

I said, 'I couldn't understand why you felt so strongly about my coming. Have another drink?'

'Thank you.' Bule tipped himself back in his chair until his weight was well on his shoulderblades, and his very long legs were half-way across the hearth-rug. 'You know,' he said reflectively, 'it must be very hard work being a nice type. A decent chap and so on.'

I said, 'I don't know. I seem to remember that when I was an undergraduate it was pretty hard work trying to be a bounder.'

'Ah, it would be for you, James. But for me it's easy. It's all a question of one's natural instincts.'

Jill said, 'What is a bounder?'

'Someone with weaknesses different from one's own,' said Bule promptly. 'If you're a sober type, a man who drinks is a bounder. But if he happens to cheat widows and orphans and so do you, then he's just a smart business man.'

I said, 'Oh, come. That's a bit too easy. There's such a thing as absolute bounderdom surely?'

'Such as what?'

I thought for a bit and then said, 'Well – current example. The chap who knocked Joe Pearce down last night and drove on, seems to me to be a bounder absolute. Have you heard about that by the way?'

'Yes. Jill was telling me.' Bule looked at me reflectively with his peculiarly wide open blue eyes. 'Well take that, James. You say the man was a bounder. Supposing he didn't know he'd done it?'

'Well, of course, that alters the whole thing. As long as he comes forward when the police broadcast for him.'

'On the general principle that the whole school will be kept in if he doesn't?'

'No. On the general principle that if he doesn't, Mrs Pearce won't get a cent out of anybody for the loss of her husband.'

He hadn't thought of that and it stopped him for a moment.

Jill said sharply, 'Is that really so, Jim?'

'I should think so. Drivers have to be insured against third party claims. From what she says she would have a claim against the driver. No driver – no claim.'

Bule said, 'I wasn't really thinking in financial terms, James. If anybody paid, it would be an insurance company, which means a pure matter of book-keeping. But I was beginning to suspect that you wanted somebody *punished*. Decent chaps usually want bounders to be punished.'

'You think that's unreasonable?'

'I don't know, James. I tell you – I'm not a decent chap. I just want to be happy, and on the whole I prefer other people to be happy too. Punishment never made anybody happy – except certain people who like administering it.'

'So you think people should be allowed to get away with anything, because it would make them unhappy if they were stopped?'

Bule said, 'Oh, no. You can *stop* them if you like – and can. But once a thing is done, I don't see much point in revenge – either by individuals or society.'

Jill said something about lunch and got up and went out. I said, 'I seem to remember this conversation from some years ago. When I was at Oxford in fact.'

Bule smiled rather frostily and said, 'And none the worse for that, James. Some of us are at our best when we're at Oxford. We're still asking questions then.'

I was getting bored by all this so I just said 'Maybe,' and looked at my watch pretty pointedly. I was afraid that if I didn't shift him, Jill would have to ask him to lunch, and I didn't feel like any more of the Honbill just then. But he finished up his drink at once and said, 'Well, well – brother, we must away.'

It was a lovely sunny morning and the Honbill's Lagonda was standing outside the door looking very handsome and shiny. I don't know what we were saying –

something about the Duke's party I think – as he got into the car. But anyhow, just as he started the engine I happened to notice something about the paintwork on the nearside rear door – some break in the smoothness of it – and then I remembered the scratch. I looked again, and saw that it had been painted over, and I was just on the point of calling out 'Quick work' or something of that kind, when Bule let the clutch in and the car went off. He waved a hand as he turned out of the drive. I stood there and watched him swing her out on to the road, and then I stared hard at the gravel for a few moments. It was then that the idea first occurred to me.

Lunch was ready when I got inside, and all through the meal I thought about it, and the more I thought about it, the more sense it seemed to make. We took our coffee into the lounge, and I suppose I must have looked a bit abstracted because Jill suddenly said, 'Is something up, darling? You're very quiet.'

I said, 'I've been thinking. And if what I've been thinking happened to be true, something would be very much up.'

'What?'

I lit a cigarette and said, 'Jill – you know him better than I do. Just how unscrupulous a character *is* the Honbill?'

'Unscrupulous?' she said slowly. 'I don't quite see what you mean?'

'He always makes himself out to be utterly selfish and so on.'

'Oh, yes. But I don't think it means anything. It's all fooling, really.'

'That's what I've always thought.'

'Why, Jim?'

I thought a bit and then said, 'Your party last night – what time did the Honbill turn up?'

'When everyone else did. About seven.'

'He wasn't early?'

'No. There were several people here before he was. It must have been after seven. Why?'

I said, 'Well, this may be complete nonsense, but think about it. Joe Pearce was knocked down about six-thirty by a big car. The thing that has always puzzled me is what a big car was doing in Tarrant's Lane, which doesn't really go anywhere. But you just imagine coming from Bule's place to here. You *could* come that way.'

'You could, but why should you? It'd mean driving right round us. It's miles quicker along . . .'

'I know. But at least there's a big car that *might* have been on that road.'

'Yes, but . . .'

'Wait a minute. That night when you came to fetch me, there was a long new scratch on the near side of the car.'

Jill didn't answer. She had gone rather pale and was staring at me in a startled way. I said, 'Elsie says that the car seemed to catch the bicycle. What she means is that it was a glancing blow – a scrape. If that had happened to Bule's car it's a perfectly possible sort of mark to find on it.'

Jill said, 'But that might have been done in scores of ways.'

'Of course it might. But it also might have been done that way.'

'But even so . . .'

'Let me finish. Elsie said the lights of the car seemed to go right across her face. Now, normal headlights wouldn't. But if you remember, Bule has a big spotlight trained on the left hand verge, and the light from that *would* . . .'

Jill suddenly laughed and said, 'Darling – Sherlock Holmes—!'

I said, 'Don't fool, Jilly. This is serious. Do you realise that he's already had that scratch painted out?'

'Well, why not?'

'No reason why not. But it's pretty quick work, isn't it? On a Saturday night or Sunday morning?'

There was a moment's pause, and then Jill said, 'Look, Jim, are you seriously saying that you think it was the Honbill who knocked Joe down?'

'I wouldn't go as far as that. But I must say it all seems to fit together rather uncomfortably well.'

'But . . .'

'But what?'

'Well, damn it – he's a friend of ours. He . . .'

'Up to a point. But what's that got to do with it?'

Jill hesitated and said, 'Anyhow, it seems to me absolute nonsense. The place isn't five minutes away, and Bill didn't get here for another half-hour at least and anyhow he'd never come that way. Phyllis Scott came in a big car. It might equally well have been her. His car had a scrape on it, but cars are always getting scraped. As for getting it painted over, who wouldn't?'

I said, 'I don't suggest that it proves anything. But . . .'

'Anyhow, if he had been on that road anywhere near that time, surely he'd have said so when we were talking about it?'

'That's what I'm wondering. You see, I think you trust him. I don't.'

'Why not? Because he pulls your leg?'

'No. I just don't think he's much good. That's all.'

Jill shrugged her shoulders and said rather contemptuously, 'Well, if you feel like that about it, the only thing to do is to ask him straight out. It'll be a pretty nasty thing to do, but . . .'

'And then he'll say "No" and how much further on are we?'

'Well, what are you trying to *do*, darling? You're not a policeman.'

I said, 'No. But I'm a magistrate. And I want to find that car.'

'I dare say. But what good does that do anyhow? I should have thought it was better to spend your time worrying about what's going to happen to Elsie and the kids if Joe dies.'

'I think both things are important.'

Jill shrugged and turned her head away. I was rather irritated and said, 'Look, Jill – it's all very well, but if Joe Pearce dies through somebody's criminal negligence and leaves that poor devil Elsie as a widow and those kids without a father, we can't just shrug our shoulders and say it's too bad and leave it at that. Don't let Bule's stuff about "decent chaps" and "good citizens" sell you that attitude, for God's sake.'

She said sullenly, 'Well, what are you going to do about it?'

'I don't know; because it's all circumstantial evidence and guess-work. You may be quite right and it may be nothing to do with Bule at all. What I'm talking about now is the principle. And there I'll tell you flat what I would do. If I knew for sure who was responsible for a thing like this I'd give him the chance to go to the police, and if he wouldn't I'd go to them myself. And if that's pompous or sneaking or priggish or any of the other prep school phrases, then I'm pompous and a sneak and a prig.'

There was a long silence and then Jill looked up and smiled and said, 'All right, darling. Sorry. You're right, of course. But seriously, I am worried about Elsie and the kids, if Joe pegs out. She can't earn enough to look after all of them.'

I said, 'No. We shall have to think about that. Is there any news of Joe?'

'I rang Doc Frewen this morning and he sounded pretty gloomy. Joe's never come round.'

Looking back, I fancy that one of the reasons why I was irritated by this talk with Jill was that, when one came to discuss it, there really didn't seem to be much in my idea that Bule might have knocked Joe down; and though I might lecture her about it, the suggestion that I was sneaking about playing detective got under my skin. But chiefly I think what I resented was that once again I felt, as I had several times lately, that Jill and I were on opposite sides of the fence about Bule. We had only known him for about six months, and though he was good company at times and I quite liked him, I had never reckoned him as an intimate friend, and was irritated to think that Jill did. I rather wished I'd never mentioned it to her.

I don't know what I should have done about it – whether I should have gone on suspecting the Honbill, or forgotten all about it or what – if I hadn't happened to run into Eddie in the village that evening. He came by on his motor-bike just as I was getting into the car outside the Post Office. He pulled up when he saw me. I asked him if there was any news of Joe and he said, 'Doc doesn't reckon he'll last the night. If he does, Doc reckons he may have a chance.'

I said, 'Got any further over the car?'

He shook his head. 'There's nothing to go on, see, Mr Manning. I been down and had a look at his bike, but it doesn't tell you anything. Hardly touched it is. Crank bent, but that's most likely where it hit the road. I reckon it must just have touched his handlebar. There's a mark on that, a chip out of the grip – but you can't even be sure that wasn't there before.'

'Elsie hasn't remembered anything else?'

'No. She just keeps saying it was big and going fast and she saw this one bright light and that's all. I suppose he was driving dipped and it was one of those dippers that switches off the offside light.'

I was startled. I said, 'Hey – half a minute. Surely she said *both* headlights were on?'

'No, sir. Only one.'

'She didn't say that when I was there.'

'No. It was before you came. But she told Sergeant Groves and me that it was only one very bright one, and she's always stuck to that.'

I said, 'So it was either somebody driving dipped, or with one headlight not working – or driving on a spot-light?'

'That's it, sir. The chances are he was driving dipped.'

It came back again – that curious sense of 'hunch' that I had had before I talked to Jill. I said, 'Eddie – just one more thing. What sort of handlebars has Joe got on his bike? What shape?'

Eddie said, 'Oh – sporting sort. You know – dropped a bit. 'Bout like that.' He pointed to a bicycle leaning against the front of the Post Office. I reckoned that the grips on its handlebars were about two feet six off the ground. It all tied up.

I said, 'Then you'd expect that the car that hit Joe would have some mark at about that height?'

'I should reckon so, Mr Manning. But maybe quite small, see. Nothing to notice, most likely.'

There was a pause, and Eddie put his foot on the kick-starter.

I said, 'So it looks a pretty hopeless job, eh?'

Eddie turned the angry, bloodshot light blue eyes on me.

'Hopeless, sir? I'm going to find that car if it's the last thing I do.'

'But how?'

'I dunno, Mr Manning, but I am.'

When I got home Jill was in the rose garden. I went out and said to her, 'Look, Jill darling, will you try to be very patient with me if I ask you about something?'

She grinned and said, 'I'll try, honey.'

'Well, it's about this damned car business. I know you think I'm playing detectives, but I can't get this idea about the Honbill out of my head. And the more I hear about it the more it fits.' Then I told her what Eddie had said. When I finished she sighed wearily and shook her head.

I said, 'I know what you're going to say – that it doesn't prove anything. And of course it doesn't. But all the same I'd be prepared to bet a small sum that I'm right about this. It – it *feels* true. And what I want to know is – feeling like that, what can I do about it?'

Jill said, 'I've told you. Ask him. I don't suppose he'll be very pleased, but if you've got to the point where you must sacrifice his friendship to – to . . .' She turned away.

I said, 'Is his friendship as important to you as all that?'

Jill said, 'As all what? After all, darling, I'm down here most of the time by myself. I haven't got many people that I like. The Honbill happens to be one of them. He's always been very nice to me, and I think he's rather fun. You can't expect me to be very pleased if we can't know him any more because you've got this damned silly suspicion about him.'

I thought for a bit and then said, 'All right – then how about this? If I can find out where the Honbill was at the time this happened, I should be perfectly satisfied. Is there any way that I can find that out without – without being a sort of Inquisitor?'

Jill pulled off a dead rose leaf and threw it away rather viciously. She said, 'Well, if *that's* all you want, darling, I can set your mind at rest. He was at the Cannings'. I know, because he told me at the party that he'd come on from there.'

'Well, why on earth didn't you say so before?'

'I'd forgotten till you asked me. And anyhow, what difference does it make?'

'Simply that if he was coming here from the Cannings' it would be absurd to go along Tarrant's Lane. And anyhow, presumably he was with them when it happened.'

She turned and grinned at me and said, 'Fine. So now you know what you want to, and now please may we go to the Duke's party?'

I said, 'Oh, I see. It's the possibility of missing the Duke's party that's made you so cross about this? Jilly, you *are* awful.' I put an arm round her and she squeezed it and said, 'Well, a girl can't miss a good party because her husband wants to go arresting her host.'

I must have disliked Bule a good deal more than I realised, because I went straight away from Jill and went indoors and rang up Henry Canning. I had meant to chat about something, and in the course of conversation to ask if he'd seen Bill Bule lately. But I was saved the trouble, because the Cannings were away, and had been away for three days. Like most other people who try to vamp up a quick alibi, the Honbill hadn't checked up on his facts. I can remember thinking, 'Poor Jill. She's going to miss her party.' I was sorry about that. The rest I think I was glad about.

My first instinct was to go and tell Jill that Bule had lied to her – to show her that I wasn't being such a fool as she seemed to believe. But on thinking it over it seemed best to keep her out of it. So I just rang up Bule and said, 'I'd like to come and have a word with you. Will you be in any time to-day?'

I very seldom went to Bule's place. He usually came to us. But he didn't seem surprised. He said, 'Sure, James. How about coming in and having a drink about six? That'd be fine.' He said it as though he was pleased, and I remembered that I quite liked him in some ways, and though by then it was important to show Jill that I was right about him, I didn't feel very happy about it.

The Honbill's place, Motley Court, was a very beautiful Queen Anne house on the ridge about two miles away. What he wanted with a house that size I had never understood, since he was a bachelor and didn't seem to entertain much. When I arrived, he was sitting in the drawing-room with a jeweller's glass in his eye, examining a coin. He collected coins. It was an odd room, but rather effective. The Honbill had a theory that rooms should not be furnished in the style of any particular period. 'Periods' were invented to make things easy for people with no eyes of their own. One should just buy the bit of furniture one wanted, to produce a certain effect, irrespective of when it was made. So in his drawing-room there was a bit of everything, from Queen Anne to contemporary. It looked pretty good, too, even if it did remind you slightly of a very high-class second-hand furniture shop.

Bule got up – all the six feet three of him – looking more

like an ivory carving than ever, and said, 'Hallo, James, this is nice. Have a drink?'

I had meant to stay completely formal – to refuse a drink, and just come right down to the unpleasant brass tacks. But those very wide-open blue eyes and the grin were so obviously friendly that I couldn't very well do it that way. So I said, 'Thank you. Sherry I think, please,' and took a cigarette and tried to think of another way of tackling it. Bule gave me my drink and sat down and said, 'Where's madam?'

I said, 'I didn't bring her because I wanted to have a word with you alone.'

The Honbill looked slightly startled and said, 'Oh!' so blankly that I couldn't help smiling, and that helped. I just said bluntly, 'Look, Bill – was it you who bowled over Joe Pearce?'

There was just a fraction of a second's pause. Then he said, 'You mean knocked him down the other night?' It was well done, but not quite well enough, and from then on that awkward feeling of dealing with a friend was gone. I said, 'Yes.'

Bule was staring at me with his eyes even wider open than usual. He shook his head in silence for a couple of seconds. Then he said, 'No. It wasn't I. Was it you?'

'No.'

'Then it was some third party,' he said solemnly. 'That's the answer, James. As Holmes always used to say, "Eliminate all the other possibilities and the one that remains, however improbable, must be correct."'

I said, 'All right. Then I'm going to ask you a question. You don't have to answer it if you don't want to, but it would help me if you would...'

'Help you to do what?' he put in gently.

'Set my mind at rest, say. Joe was knocked down at half-past six on Friday. Where were you then?'

'Half-past six on Friday,' he said reflectively. 'Surely I was at your place? Your party?'

'No. You didn't get there until after seven.' As he still hesitated I said, 'Jill says you told her that you'd come on from the Cannings', if that helps you.'

'Well, if I told Jill that I'd come from the Cannings', then I'd come from the Cannings'. I'm a truthful type, really.'

'You can't have, because the Cannings have been away since Thursday evening.'

He shook his head slowly and said, 'Then I got it wrong. Or Jill got what I said wrong. Or you got what Jill said I said wrong. Or something like that.'

'You admit that you *weren't* at the Cannings'?'

'I can't very well do that if Jill says I was, can I? I mean to say, surely, James, this is simply a Manning family dispute? Jill says I was at the Cannings' and you say I wasn't. You must fight it out between yourselves.'

'Never mind what we say. Where do you say you were?' He said, 'I'll give you a clue, James. Wherever I was, I was minding my own business.'

'Fine. Now we know where we are. In other words you lied to Jill and you refuse to tell me where you were?'

'If you like.' He raised an eyebrow. 'Does that – er – help, or set your mind at rest?'

I leant forward and said, 'Look – Joe Pearce was knocked down by a big car driving on a spotlight, in a place where through traffic has no reason to go, but where a local resident might. The car seems to have scraped his handlebar, which is about two feet six from the ground. You have a big car. You often drive on your spotlight. You might conceivably use that road in coming to our place. That night you had a fresh scrape on your car about

50

the right height from the ground. You told Jill, quite gratuitously, that you'd come from the other direction, which was untrue. You had that scratch painted out very quickly the following morning. I don't suggest that any of this proves anything. In fact you've only got to prove that at half-past six you were somewhere else, and the whole thing is settled.'

Bule nodded. 'Yes, I see.' He thought for a moment and then said, 'But supposing I *was* somewhere else but just preferred *not* to prove it to you, James?'

'Then you can't complain if people suspect you.'

'I don't complain. I don't mind in the least, my dear chap.'

'. . . or if the police ask you the same question.'

'Ah – I thought we should get to the police soon. In fact, if I don't explain my movements to you, you'll go to them and say you suspect me?'

I said, 'I shall.'

Bule said reflectively, 'The trouble about being a good citizen is that it sometimes lands you in making an abject ass of yourself.'

'Of course it does. But I'm prepared to risk that.'

'I'll bet you are.' Bule sipped his drink and stared at me. 'I wonder why you're so anxious to prove that I did it? After all, we may not like one another much, but it wouldn't give me any particular fun to put *you* in a mess.'

I said, 'I don't particularly want to prove that you did it. But I want to know who did. And having got this idea into my head, I must get it settled one way or the other.'

He nodded. 'Yes. I can see all that. But it isn't quite the whole story, is it, James?'

I knew it wasn't, but that was beside the point. I said, 'I told you the other night how I felt about this, before I ever suspected you. You didn't understand then and probably you don't now. But if I can find the driver of that car I shall do so – whoever it is. If it wasn't you, prove it, and I'll apologise and go.'

Bule stared into the fire for a moment. Then he said slowly, 'Well, will this do? For reasons which are neither here nor there, I don't want to describe my movements at that time. But I give you my word of honour that I did not drive my car or any other car along Tarrant's Lane that night, and I did not knock down Joe Pearce. Does that satisfy you?' He turned and looked full at me and I looked back at him for a moment and then said, 'No – it doesn't.'

He raised his eyebrows and said, 'Why not?'

'Mainly because I've heard you a dozen times saying that the truth doesn't interest you, and that you see absolutely no reason for telling it if it's inconvenient . . .'

Bule said crossly, 'Really, James, you are an ass.'

'. . . and partly because there's no real reason to ask me to rely on your word when you can prove it quite easily. I'm not interested in your private life. I don't care in the least what you were doing or where you were. But I'm not prepared just to be told you'd rather not say, when you've already tried to set up a false alibi about it through Jill.'

There was a long pause. Then Bule sighed and said, 'All right. I've done my best, but the good citizen defeats me. Supposing I *was* in Tarrant's Lane round about that time, what do you want me to do?'

'You admit that you did knock Pearce down?'

'I don't admit anything of the kind. But supposing it's all just as you suppose – what then?'

'Then obviously you go to the police.'

'And then . . . ?'

'Then it's up to them. The only person who saw the accident was Pearce's wife . . .'

'Who'll say I was doing ninety miles an hour. Yes?'

'Well – it was a bad show not stopping – if you knew you'd hit him. The police don't like hit-and-run. And if he dies . . .' I shrugged my shoulders.

'Then they run me for manslaughter?'

'Possibly.'

'And then I go to jail?'

'Possibly.'

He shook his head. 'Really, you know, James – but *really* – it won't do.'

'What d'you mean?'

'Well, think. Joe Pearce is killed. His wife is widowed. His children are orphans. Haven't enough people been made miserable by one bit of bad luck already, without wrecking somebody else's life by sending them to jail?'

That was a mistake. I got up and said, 'Are you going to the police or shall I?'

He said slowly, 'James, you don't think about these things, that's your trouble. Those really are the alternatives?'

'Yes.'

Bule sighed and said, 'Then you leave me no choice.' He suddenly smiled up at me that peculiarly sweet and boyish smile and said, 'All right, James. I'll go and own up. To-morrow morning. And then the whole school won't have to stay in.'

I suddenly didn't like it again. I didn't like it at all. I said, 'Damn the whole business. What on earth happened, Bill? Did you know you'd hit him?'

'Of course not.'

'Did you see him?'

'Yes. For a fraction of a second. But he was well clear of the wings then. I knew it had been fairly close, but that was all. I think he must have wobbled into the back of the car.'

'The scratch was on the back door. You just touched his

handlebar and that chucked him and the bike into the road. Doc says that if he'd had an ordinary skull he would have been all right.'

Bule said wearily, 'Yes, it was all very unfortunate. Who had I better go and see?'

'I should think Sergeant Groves. Take your solicitor with you.'

'Yes. That's an idea.' He got up and smiled again and said, 'Well, well, James – now your mind will be at rest and you'll be able to sleep soundly.'

I said, 'I'm sure it's the right thing to do, you know.'

'And I'm equally sure it's the wrong thing to do. But I don't doubt we shall see.'

I drove home slowly, not feeling very happy. As long as Bule was wriggling and prevaricating and generally trying to laugh it off, I could remember Elsie's face, and pinning him down was positively enjoyable. But once I had got him, the actual prospect of the Honbill landing in jail was much less so. It was only that facile old argument about punishment merely producing more unhappiness that had left me properly angry. It's a reasonable idea in the abstract, but hardly one to trot out if you're the person liable to be punished.

Moreover, I found that I didn't relish the job of telling Jill what had happened. I didn't want her to like the Honbill quite so much, or to trust him. I wanted her to see him as I saw him – amusing enough, but on no account to be taken seriously as a person. But I would rather have showed her in some other way. I wondered for a moment whether I could possibly just keep my mouth shut, and leave her to think, when she heard about it, that the Honbill had gone to the police by himself. I distinctly remember wondering that, so there is no question of my having gone back triumphantly to prove that I was right and she was wrong. But I decided that it wouldn't do. It would mean a lot of lying and acting, and I disliked that with Jill. It had always been a part of our relationship that apart from Jill-lies, a special sort of small-scale stuff which was a family joke, we didn't lie to each other about things.

Jill was in the hall when I came in. The telephone is there and it flashed across my mind that Bule might have rung her up while I was on the way home. But I couldn't see why he should have, and anyhow she greeted me with, 'Hallo, darling. Where'st bin?'

I liked it even less when I saw her, but I thought I might as well get it over, so I said, 'I've been up to Motley Court. Bill asked me in for a drink. Or rather I asked myself in.'

'Why didn't you take me, hound?'

I said, 'Come in here. I want to tell you something.'

We went into the lounge and I said, 'Look, honey – you're not going to like this, but I can't help it. I was right about the Honbill.'

'Over what?'

'It *was* the Honbill who knocked down Joe Pearce.'

She stared at me for a moment in silence and then said rather breathlessly, 'How could it have been? You said that if he was coming here from the Cannings' . . .'

'He didn't come from the Cannings'. I checked up, and they were away. He told you that to make an alibi. Anyhow there's no doubt about it, darling. He admits it.'

She said slowly, 'He admits that he knocked down Joe Pearce?'

'Yes. He denied it, but I nailed him on the fact that he couldn't say where he was at the time. And in the end he admitted it. Apparently he didn't know he'd actually hit

Joe, which I can quite believe. But he admits that he saw him, and that he knew it had been a near thing.'

Jill nodded. She was staring at me with the mud-coloured eyes and blinking slowly in a queer way. After a while she said very calmly, 'Well, well, well. What happens now?'

'He's going to see the police. I've advised him to take his solicitor.'

'Was going to the police his idea or yours?'

'Mine. What else is there to do?'

'I should have thought the Honbill would have favoured keeping his mouth shut.'

'He did, you bet. But I told him that if he didn't go to the police I would.'

She said quietly, 'You really said that, James?'

'Yes.'

'And you would have done it?'

'Yes, darling. I would.'

'Then you're crazy,' she said without heat.

'All right, darling. Then I'm crazy. But it's the sort of crazy I prefer to be.'

'D'you realise what'll happen? They'll . . .'

'They'll probably run him in for dangerous driving. If Joe Pearce dies, they may charge him with manslaughter. And if they think the charge is proved he may go to jail. Yes. I do realise it, and though you probably won't believe me, I don't particularly like it. But it isn't a question of what I like or what you like. It's a matter of common justice.'

'But, good God, Jim – the thing was an accident. You can tell from what he says that it was.'

'All right. If he wasn't to blame, then I don't doubt he'll get away with it.'

'Don't *you* ever make mistakes?'

'All the time. And pay for them.'

She opened her lips to say something and then changed her mind. After a while she turned her head away and said, not looking at me, 'Jim, darling – I'm going to ask you something. Something you're going to find it difficult to do. I think it's worth asking, because I know you're a generous person.'

I said, 'Well, honey?'

'I'm going to ask you to ring Bill up,' she said in a low voice, 'and ask him to come over. When he comes I want you to tell him that you won't force him to go to the police – you'll just leave him to decide for himself. I don't want it to be – to be *you* who makes him. See?'

I said, 'But don't you see, darling – you could do that with some sorts of people – people with some sense of responsibility. But with the Honbill it's hopeless. He wouldn't think about what was the right thing to do, or about Elsie and the kids, or about anything but what was convenient for him.'

'But don't you see *I've* thought about all that, God knows, and I think you're wrong – hopelessly wrong. I think what you're doing is – is just convention. I don't think you've thought about it at all – not at *all*, Jim. You've just put in a penny and pressed a button and out has come the answer.'

I shook my head and said, 'I'm sorry, darling.'

'You really won't do that for me?'

'No. Not even for you.'

'You really care more for your – your blasted principles than for anyone?'

'I certainly care more for them than I do for Bill Bule's convenience. And if you don't like that I'm sorry.'

Jill started to say, 'You haven't answered . . .' when the telephone rang. I went over to it. Doc Frewen was on the

57

line. He said, 'I thought I'd better let you know that Joe Pearce died half an hour ago. Never recovered consciousness.'

I said, 'How's his wife?'

'Oh, not so bad. She's got a lot of guts. Very hard luck. He was a nice boy.'

I said, 'Yes. Very. Well, thanks very much for ringing, Doc,' and hung up.

When I turned round Jill was standing in the middle of the room staring at me. She was very white.

She said, 'Joe?'

'Yes. He's dead. That was Doc.'

I walked back towards the fireplace but she only turned as I walked past her, and didn't follow.

I said, 'Well, that rather settles it, darling, doesn't it?'

'Settles what?' she said quietly.

'One can't play about with the truth when a man's been killed.'

Jill suddenly laughed. It startled me and I turned round quickly. She was standing in the middle of the room looking at me and laughing. She said, 'No. We must have the truth. You like the truth, don't you, Jim? Well, here it is if you're so keen on it. I was in Bill's car when it hit Joe, or Joe's bicycle, or whatever it was.'

I said stupidly, '*You* were in it?'

'Yes. And what's more I was driving it.'

I must have looked rather odd because suddenly her face seemed to crumple up and she had her arms round me and was saying, 'Darling, I'm so sorry – so *damn* sorry. Darling Jim . . .'

4

'On the Friday evening Bill came over about five to help me get ready for the party. When I came to look, I wasn't sure that we'd got enough gin. You remember – you were going to have brought a couple more bottles down with you from town, and I'd been reckoning on them. I'd forgotten that as you weren't going to be there, the gin wouldn't be there, either. So we decided we'd better go and get some. We went over to that pub near Levening . . . Well, while we were there we had a drink and sat and talked . . .'

'Were you tight?'

'Oh Lord, no. Of course not.'

'How many drinks did you have?'

'Oh – two, I think.'

'Quite. But how many drinks did you *really* have, Jill?'

'Well, as a matter of fact I think it was three. Anyhow, we certainly weren't drunk. But Bill suddenly looked at his watch and found that it was quarter-past six, and as these people were coming at seven, and we hadn't finished getting ready, we had to bolt back pretty quickly. I asked Bill if I could drive back and he let me.'

'Had you ever driven that Lagonda before?'

'Yes. Several times. She's beautifully easy to handle anyhow . . . Well, I didn't want to drive up to the front of the house with Bill, for obvious reasons. So we decided to go down Tarrant's Lane, and then he could drop me so that I could come in the back gate through the orchard, and he could go home and change, and come on to the party when the others came.'

'If you'd started off with him, I don't see why you shouldn't just have come back to the house with him.'

'I didn't start off with him. He brought the car round to the orchard gate then, too. I thought you wouldn't like me to go off with him in front of the staff.'

'That was a nice thought, darling.'

'Well, anyhow, we came along Tarrant's Lane. I wasn't going very fast. You can't. It's too narrow. I never saw Joe at all, first or last. Or felt anything. All that happened was that Bill suddenly said, "Whoops! That'll have put the wind up him!" I said, "What?" and he said, "Bloke with a bicycle. Nearly came out right under your wheels." That was all. Honestly.'

'Didn't either of you look back?'

'I think Bill did just glance back. But you see it was pretty dark. I never thought any more about it until . . .'

'Until I saw that scratch?'

'No – even that didn't register. You see I didn't know *where* Joe had been knocked down. It was only when we were coming away from the hospital, and you said it had happened in Tarrant's Lane, that it ever occurred to me.'

'But why on earth didn't you tell me then, Jilly?'

'I didn't want you to know I . . . I'd been out with Bill.'

'Why not? Hell, there's no harm in going out to buy gin.'

'I thought you'd be cross and – and be sure it was my fault and . . .'

'What did you do when you realised what had happened?'

'I rang up Bill. He said he thought it couldn't have been us and we agreed that we'd better keep quiet.'

'Was that when you decided to say that he'd been at the Cannings'?'

'No. That was just me. He never said he had. I just told

you that because then I thought you might stop suspecting him.'

'I thought that was a bit crude for the Honbill. Did he ring you up while I was on the way home? This evening?'

'Yes.'

I put my hands over my eyes and tried to think about it, but everything was all mixed up together and I couldn't seem to get started. There was something funny about the feel of the silence. I realised at last what it was. I opened my eyes and said, 'That damned clock's stopped again.'

Jill looked at it and said, 'Yes. I must take it and get something done about it.'

After a while I said, 'What I don't quite get is all this – this telephoning and picking up at the orchard gate and so on. How much have you been going out with Bule?'

'I've been out with him several times.'

'How much is there to it?'

'How d'you mean, darling?'

'Are you his mistress, Jilly?'

She looked at me in a startled way. 'Darling – of course not. It – it isn't like that at all. It's just that I've been a bit bored and – and have been making an ass of myself and – and kicking up my heels rather. You see I've been here by myself and . . .'

'And that's all there is to it?'

'Of course.' There was a pause and then she looked full at me and said quietly, 'You believe that, Jim?'

I said, 'Oh, yes. I couldn't really conceive that – that there'd be anything else. But I had to ask you because otherwise – I shouldn't know where I was.'

She said in a low voice, 'I'm most desperately sorry to have let you in for this.'

I said rather vaguely, 'That's all right. The thing we've got to decide now is what to do about it.'

Jill was sitting on the floor. She suddenly put her arms on my knees and put her head down on them and said, 'Think for me, Jim. My God, you always have to think for me. I'm a useless person. I'll do whatever you say.'

Her shoulders were shaking. I put my hand down and stroked the back of her head, where her hair was very smooth and shiny. I said, 'I dare say we can think of something.'

I went up into the rose garden. The pruning was all done now, and there was nothing but short stumps. It's always difficult to believe, when you see a rose garden in April, that the whole thing can happen in time for the June flowering. After a while I found that I was still thinking about that instead of the matter in hand, so I sat down and shut my eyes and tried to concentrate. I remember that I kept thinking. 'This is my nightmare. It's always exactly like this.' Ever since I had been married to Jill, I had had a nightmare at intervals, in which something was going to happen to her, and I was there looking on and couldn't stop it. Once I dreamed that we were prisoners of the Japanese and they were taking her away, and I was bound hand and foot, and she kept looking at me as though she thought I should save her. Another time we were in some sort of school or reformatory or something, and she had got into trouble and was going to be beaten. She was frightened and kept saying, 'Don't let them – don't let them,' and I couldn't think how to help her. Always it was that she had got herself up against some power that I knew I couldn't tackle, and I would wake up in a muck sweat. I sat on the seat in the rose garden and thought, 'It's exactly like that; except that this time it's really happened.'

After a while I began to be able to think a bit straighter, and I tried just looking at the facts. The thing was obviously a pure accident. If we got a first rate barrister, he could probably convince any jury that it was – that they hadn't even seen Joe, let alone knowing they'd killed him. And Doc would say that it was a pure piece of bad luck that a knock like that had fractured his skull.

But against that they'd been in a pub drinking. Three gins isn't a lot when you're drinking it and talking, but it sounds quite a lot to a jury, for a young woman who's going to drive somebody else's car in the dark. And probably when the police came to check up with the pub, it would really be more than three, knowing the Honbill. Tarrant's Lane was very narrow, and it was a fool place to take a big car, even if you didn't go very fast. And they were hurrying back. Elsie had already told the police that they were going fast.

Elsie might help. She loved Jill and wouldn't want anything to happen to her. But after all, she had loved Joe, and he'd been killed, and I hadn't liked the look on her face when she said, 'He knew – and he didn't care . . .' The hell of it was that we'd lost so much time. If the thing was to be represented as a pure accident that they hadn't known about, we ought to have gone to the police as soon as there was the slightest chance that it might have been Jill. Instead of which there had been all this telephoning and lying and backstairs stuff.

I suddenly found myself extremely angry about all that. I thought of my talks with Jill about it, and going to see Bule, and thinking I had him cornered. And all the time they were ringing one another up, and finessing against me. Jill had driven the Lagonda before. She had been out with Bule several times. I'd had the feeling on Friday night that she was ganging up with him against me. That was the idea about the Duke's dance. She knew I couldn't come that night . . .

63

I distinctly remember getting up from the seat and saying to myself, 'Snap out of it. This is Jill you're talking about. And Jill is an old ass and she tells Jill-lies and always has. But she doesn't do you dirt with characters like Bule – not serious dirt. She's just blundered into a mess in her cheerful way, and now you've got to get her out of it, which is what you're for anyhow.'

I can't say I really got it all worked out in the rose garden. But after a while I got tired of being there, and didn't seem to be getting any further, so I went inside – I think with some vague idea of telephoning Garry Petre, who is a K.C., and was at school with me. Jill met me at the door and said, 'Look, I've telephoned Bill and he's coming over right away.' I had had about enough of these telephone conversations and I said, 'What did you do that for?'

'Well, darling, I rather had to. He had to be told that – that you knew. Otherwise, as you'd left it, he was to go off to the police to-morrow and tell them some yarn about its being him. Surely we've got to see him?'

There wasn't much answer to this. I said rather bitterly, 'Well, you've got one satisfaction out of this bloody mess – Bule's certainly got the laugh on me.'

Jill said, 'I don't think he's doing much laughing. Anyhow, you were dead right, weren't you?'

'How?'

'About its being Bill's car. All that you were wrong about was who was driving it, and that you couldn't know.'

I said, 'Yes. It was a nice piece of observation and deduction, and it's giving me a lot of satisfaction. I think I'm going to ring up Garry Petre and see what he thinks.'

I went into the study and looked up Garry's number. But as soon as I'd found it I realised that I couldn't very well talk to him about it on the telephone. I could only make a date to see him, and I could do that better from London. So I just sat at my desk and stared at the telephone directory, until I heard Bule's car in the drive. I remember looking at my watch and seeing that it was eight o'clock, and wondering vaguely what we were going to do about dinner. I wasn't hungry, but if you don't have meals it's difficult to be sure whereabouts in the day you are.

I went into the lounge. Jill had been out to the car and she and Bule came in together. Bule said, 'Hallo, James. I gather madam hasn't been able to keep her big mouth shut.' He glanced at Jill and smiled, but she was looking down at her hands.

I said, 'I should have liked it better if she'd opened it a bit sooner. As it is, I'm not sure whether I owe you an apology, or you owe me one.'

Jill said in a low voice, 'The only person who owes anybody an apology is me.'

I said, 'Apart from apologies, we've now got to decide what to do. I've been thinking it over, and I think there's a chance that you might get away with it as an unavoidable accident. The snag is that the longer we wait, the less chance there is of that. But on the other hand I don't want to go rushing along to the police without having legal advice. I can get hold of Garry Petre to-morrow.'

Bule said, 'Well, I've been thinking about it too, James. And I can't say I feel very optimistic. Particularly now the lad has pegged out.'

'Nor do I. But ...'

'Wherefore,' said Bule slowly, 'I can't help feeling that we were in a stronger position when you and I parted this evening than we are now.' He was looking at Jill's bent head as she picked at a fingernail.

I said, 'Why were we?'

'Well, the idea then was that Bule goes to the police and makes a clean breast of it. "Sergeant, I cannot tell a lie. I *did* chop Joe Pearce," or words to that effect. Bule then takes the rap and goes up the river, or else is acquitted without a stain on his character. This didn't strike me as attractive, but there was at least some grain of satisfaction in it for Detective Inspector Manning. As it is, there doesn't seem to be anything in it for anybody.'

He had been looking at Jill all the time. Now she raised her head, and as soon as she did that he turned and looked at me. 'At least, James, I suppose being a decent citizen doesn't include enjoying your wife going to jail?'

I said, 'No. So what?'

Bule sighed. 'I was afraid it didn't.' He spread out his ivory-coloured hands. 'Then the only thing to do is to stick to the previous arrangement.'

'What arrangement?'

'The Bule-takes-the-rap arrangement. Obviously . . .'

Jill said without enthusiasm, 'Don't talk bunkum, Bill,' and looked into the fire.

'Bunkum?' said Bule indignantly. 'What d'you mean, bunkum? It's only what any decent man would do, isn't it, James?'

I said, 'Look, if you've got anything serious to suggest, let's have it. There's no time to waste playing the fool.'

'All right. Then I suggest just that. Perfectly seriously.'

I looked at the wide-open eyes with their fake solemnity and I knew he'd got me. Jill said, 'Don't be an ass,' but she smiled at him slightly.

I said, 'You know perfectly well that's out of the question.'

'But *why*, James? That's the trouble with you – so many things are out of the question. Here we are with three possibilities. The first is that I should say I did it. You say that's out of the question. The second is that we should all keep our mouths shut. You've already told me *that's* out of the question. The third is that Jill shall risk going to jail. And that seems to me to be – er – out of the question.'

Jill said, 'Why? It was my fault if it was anybody's.'

'Because I shouldn't like it, and neither would James. And neither would you, my dear.' He shrugged his shoulders. 'Believe me, what I'm proposing is purely selfish. *I* don't want to be a martyr. It isn't my game. But I should dislike even more to see . . .'

I said, 'Oh, shut up, for God's sake,' and walked over and looked out of the window. I have disliked Bill Bule a good many times, but I don't think I've ever disliked him more than at that moment. There was a long silence. Then Jill said wearily, 'Surely it's all perfectly simple? You get hold of Garry to-morrow morning. It'll mean another few hours' delay, but that can't make much difference now. We decide with him just how we're going to put it, and then we go along to the police. After that it's up to them. If I get away with it – fine, and if I don't, that's too bad.'

Bule said, 'My dear girl . . .'

I turned round to him and said, 'You know damn well I can't take you up on that, otherwise you'd never have suggested it.'

'Take me up on what, James?'

'The idea of saying that you were driving.'

He said, 'You're quite wrong as it happens. I should have been slightly surprised if you'd agreed, but no more than that. You see I don't understand good citizens. They're a closed book to me, like radio sets. They may do almost anything.'

'. . . you also know that you've got me in a corner and that I've *got* to agree to keep quiet.'

He spread out his hands. 'What can I say, James? *I*

haven't got you in a corner. You've got yourself there. I must say it's always seemed the most sensible thing to me. But it's for you to decide.'

I said, 'All right, then. And I wish us all joy of it.'

Jill said rather too calmly, 'Half a minute. As it happens it *isn't* for Jim to decide. It's for me. And I'm not having that.'

Bule sighed and said, 'Don't tell me we've got *another* good citizen in on this, or I shall cry.'

Jill had risen to her feet. She was looking at me. She said, 'You know you wouldn't like it. You know you wouldn't.'

Bule said, 'Of course he wouldn't. But he'd like it better than the other thing.'

Jill took no notice. She said, 'You know you'd never forgive me if – if I did that to you.'

I turned away and said irritably, 'Don't be silly, Jill. There's no question of forgiving you. It's the only thing we *can* do.'

She said, 'I won't do it.'

I had had rather a packet by then, and something cracked. I turned round and nearly shouted, 'Well, good God, isn't this just exactly what you've been asking for all along – telling me I was wrong and crazy and priggish and so on? And now I *do* agree, you start saying you won't do it. It's your old game. Even when you get your own way you won't take responsibility for it. All right. Then I will. You're the person who wants to tell the truth, and I'm the person who insists on lying. Does that fix it all for you?'

Bule said, 'Gently, squire. Moderate the voice. Otherwise whether we actually *tell* other people about it or not will be purely academic.'

Jill stood and looked at me for a moment. Then she said, 'I don't like it. I – I don't want it like that...' Then she turned suddenly and went out. We heard her running upstairs. After a minute Bule said, 'The social conscience seems to be infectious. Or perhaps contagious.' As I didn't say anything, he went on, 'I'm rather glad she's gone, James, because if you'll forgive me for saying so, a certain amount of quick thinking's got to be done.'

'Why? What about?'

'Well, if you could cotton on to the fact that it was my car that hit Joe, so may somebody else. Gradually, if not with your Holmesian speed. So we'd better get that possibility covered. What put you on to it in the first place?'

'The scratch. And its being at the right height.'

'That's all right. Nobody ever saw that except ourselves and my chauffeur. What else?'

'The spotlight. From what Elsie said it sounded as though the car was being driven on a spotlight, and I noticed you drove on yours.'

'Yes. It's a long shot though, isn't it?'

'They were all long shots, but they added up. The main thing was that I thought only a local car would use Tarrant's Lane, and yours fitted with what Elsie said.'

Bule nodded. 'Think she'd know the car if she saw it again in the same conditions?'

'She might. But of course there'd be nothing to prove that it was the same.'

'There never *was* anything to prove it, my dear chap. If only Jill hadn't tried to fix a fake alibi, bless her heart, you'd got nothing definite to go on.' He thought for a while and then said, 'You see, Jill's all right, whatever happens. Apart from people in a pub fifteen miles away, nobody knows even that she was with me that evening – let alone that she was driving. What's needed is an alibi for me. Or rather, for the car.'

I said, 'Is all this really necessary? The chances are . . .'

'The chances are that it'll never enter anybody's head. But it might. And if some keen-eyed type should suddenly turn up and ask me the questions you asked me to-night, I should prefer to know the answers – for all our sakes. At six o'clock I was in that pub. At quarter to seven I was at home. Where was I in the meantime, James? Why is it quite impossible that I should have been in Tarrant's Lane at six-thirty?'

He leaned back and smiled at me. I got the impression that he was enjoying himself.

I said, 'I don't care what you say. Does it matter?'

'Of course it does. Like Melbourne, I don't care what damn lie we tell, as long as we all tell the same damn lie. And some good citizen has got to confirm it . . .' Bule suddenly slapped his knee. 'Of course – I've got it. There's no problem. I knew I was going to your party and I'd sent everybody out. When I got back the place was empty. The story is simply that I went straight home from the pub, got home about six-twenty, which I should have; changed, and came on to you, arriving just after seven. In fact, at the time that matters, I was at home.'

'But you said it had to be confirmed.'

Bule grinned. 'It is, James. It *is*. Because just about six-thirty you rang me up from town and spoke to me at home. See?'

I said, 'For God's sake. That starts a lot of other complications.'

'Not at all. It's just formal confirmation of a perfectly ordinary story – just in case we need it.' He put his head on one side and looked at me solemnly. 'After all, James, if this whole production ever had to be staged, which is very unlikely, I'd like you to have *some* part, if only a small one. I think you've earned that.' I didn't say anything. After a moment he went on, 'So there it is. At six I left the pub and went straight home. At six-thirty you telephoned me there, and asked me to pick you up at the station later in the evening, because you knew Jill would have a busy time with the party. That is why I subsequently *did* pick you up. See?' He looked at me in silence for a few moments and then said gently, 'Don't look so – so *un-co-operative*, James. We criminal types must hang together.'

I went to bed early that night. It was only about half-past ten, but I was dog-tired. Jill had never shown up again and I guessed she had gone to bed. When I went into our room it was dark and she didn't say anything. I thought she was asleep, so I didn't switch a light on, but just undressed in the bathroom and went and got into bed as quietly as I could. I could just see the dark shadow of her hair on the pillow. After a moment I saw her turn her head restlessly from side to side, and realised that she was awake. I put my hand out to stroke her hair, and touched her cheek, and found it was wet. I said, 'What is it, Jilly darling?' but she didn't say anything. She never did say anything that night.

I said, 'It's all right, honey. You couldn't help it. Don't cry,' and put my arm round her. She was lying straight and rigid, and I could feel the little convulsive movements as she cried, though I couldn't hear anything. I said, 'Come on now – relax. Otherwise you'll never go to sleep.' I pushed her gently over on to her side, so that we were lying as we always did to go to sleep. For a little while she stayed stiff and straight. Then she heaved a deep sigh, and I felt her body relax in my arms.

I was very sleepy myself. I remember saying, 'It's all right, because you are my darling girl, and I love you, and it doesn't make any difference what you do, I always shall.'

She still didn't say anything, but I think she stopped crying, and the last thing I was conscious of thinking was that she seemed to have gone to sleep.

5

It is rather odd that though I can remember nearly every detail of what happened at that week-end, I am very vague about the next week or so. Of course, I was going to London every day, leaving the house at eight and only getting back about seven. One night I stayed in town, and two of the evenings we went out somewhere, so I didn't see much of Jill. But we must have been alone together at times, and we must have talked about the whole business. Indeed, I know we did. But we don't appear to have said anything that stuck in my mind. My general recollection is that Jill was rather silent and depressed, and that I was trying to cheer her up, and make her see that it was no use crying over spilt milk. I am pretty sure that during this time I didn't see Bule.

The next thing I can be sure about was that at breakfast time on the following Saturday Jill suddenly said, 'Look – something's *got* to be done about Elsie. Otherwise they're just going to starve.'

I said. 'Yes. I'd been thinking about that. Has she said anything?'

'No. She wouldn't. But there are herself and three kids and Joe's mother, and as far as I know all they've got coming in is the three pounds a week or so that we pay Elsie. Of course, I can give her a bit more – I did to-day. But the whole thing will – will have to be dealt with.'

I said, 'All right. I'll go down and see her to-morrow and arrange something. What d'you think would be best?'

'Well, Joe was earning about five pounds a week. I think

she'll get a widow's pension or something, but it isn't much and . . .'

'No. Well, I'll talk to her and see what's necessary.'

Jill fidgeted with her bread. She wasn't looking at me. She said, 'I don't want you just to do it. It isn't your responsibility. I'd like it to come out of my allowance or something . . .'

This was very typical vague good intentions, and I was at once amused and slightly irritated. I grinned and said, 'Well, since you've never been known to keep within your allowance yet, five extra people won't get very fat on it. I think you'd better leave it to me, honey.'

She frowned and said, 'No. It's always like that and it – it isn't sense . . .'

'Well – what d'you want to do then, darling?'

'I thought I could manage a hundred a year out of my allowance. In fact I darn well *will* manage it.'

'But that wouldn't be enough for all that lot.'

There was a long pause and then she said, 'No. But – but Bill says he'd like to help because – well, I mean it was his car, and he was there, and so on. He says he'd give another hundred or so, and I don't see why he shouldn't. It won't hurt him.'

I was a bit startled. I said. 'Have you talked to him about it then?'

Jill said quickly, 'Only on the telephone.'

'Well, for Pete's sake, *don't* talk about this on the telephone, or you'll have it all round the district. And anyhow, there can't be any question of Bule being in on this.'

Jill said, 'Why not?' She seemed genuinely puzzled.

I said, 'My dear girl, if this is anybody's responsibility it's yours. You happen to be my wife, and therefore it's mine. Bule can do what he likes, by himself. But I'm not going to have an arrangement in which you and he club together and say it's nothing to do with me.'

Jill just stared down at the tablecloth with the moody, sullen expression that I was getting to know. I said, 'Anyhow, I've told you before that I wish you'd cut out this telephoning business with Bule. If you want to discuss the thing with anybody, discuss it with me. I'll go down and see Elsie to-morrow.'

I didn't particularly want Jill to come with me, but she insisted that she must. As you drove down Tarrant's Lane you could see how the whole thing happened. With a car as big as Bule's Lagonda, there would be only about five feet to spare, and anybody coming out of the Pearces' garden gate, and perhaps wobbling a bit as he went to get on his bike, would be pretty difficult to miss. The Pearces lived in one of those cottages that are all right as long as you only have to see them from the road – thatched and built of lovely old brick, and with creeper over the front, like a sentimental chocolate box. Inside there are about four tiny rooms, very dark, with brick floors that are always damp, and ceilings so low that a tall man can't stand upright. Elsie had cleaned everything that could be cleaned, and polished everything that could be polished. But as the three kids were nine, five and two, and the old woman was over eighty, and they all had to live in one small room and the kitchen, the place usually looked a muddle, and it always smelt of Lifebuoy soap on top of another smell.

The two elder kids were playing in the front garden, loading stones into a wooden box on pram-wheels. The nine-year-old girl stopped as she saw us, and scampered off indoors shouting, 'Mum! Mum! Somebody's outside.' As we passed the small boy Jill smiled and said, 'Hullo, Martin,' but he just looked at her and turned back to his stones. Elsie was looking like a scarecrow. She usually looked rather neat if I ever saw her about the house at home, and I had never realised that she put on better clothes to come and char for us than she usually wore. She knew that both she and the place weren't proper for receiving visitors, and all the time we were talking, she kept dabbing at her hair, which was straggling all over the place, and pulling at the dirty overall affair that she was wearing, which hardly came together properly over her breasts and didn't seem to have much underneath it. The old woman was sitting close to the fire knitting. She knitted very fast, in a queer way, with the wool round her neck and the needles close up to her eyes. She was practically stone deaf. When Jill said, 'Good-afternoon, Mrs Pearce,' she nodded her head and smiled and mumbled something. But after that she went back to her knitting and never looked up again till we were going.

The baby girl was crawling about on the floor, but the older one came and hauled her to her feet and took her off without being told to. Elsie turned some odd clothes and a cardboard box with wool in it off a chair, so that Jill could sit down. She sat very upright herself, fiddling with her hair and her overall, looking incredibly gaunt and ugly. I told her we had been passing and had just thought we'd drop in to see how she was getting on. She said, 'Yes, sir,' very politely, and then, realising that more was expected, she said, 'He had lovely flowers, didn't he, madam?'

Jill said, 'Absolutely beautiful.'

Elsie said, 'People you wouldn't expect sent. Everybody's been very kind.'

I think I had rather been expecting Jill to do the talking. Elsie was less shy of her than of me. But she didn't say anything, and there was rather an awkward pause.

I said, 'What we really wanted to ask you, Elsie, was – how you'll be fixed now – over money, I mean?'

I think she guessed we had come about that, but all the same she went red and said, 'Oh ... I 'spect we'll manage, sir, thank you.'

'How does it work out?'

'Well, I get a widow's pension – I don't know how much. Mr Barnes is finding out. And then Mother's got hers; and then I thought if I could go out a bit more, Mrs Taylor wants somebody, and that would be so's we could manage.' She said it all with a curious dullness, as though she had been over it all before, and was tired of it.

I said, 'Even then it won't be a lot for five of you nowadays.'

'If I was to go to Mrs Taylor afternoons...'

'But how about the children?'

'They're not home till four except baby, and she's all right with Mother for little whiles.'

She said it not as though she believed it, but as though it didn't matter. I looked at the old woman and wondered which would look after which.

Jill said gently, 'Look, Elsie – you can't do it all by yourself. You must let us help.'

Elsie said, 'You mean – come more often to you, madam?'

As we were sitting, her squint made it seem that she was looking at me with one eye and Jill with the other. Jill said, 'If you like. But anyhow you must have enough to live on and – and we'd like to see to it.'

Elsie just looked puzzled. I said, 'What we mean is that we don't want you to be worried about money, and that we should like to arrange for you to have what you need to live on.'

She understood that time and for a moment the listlessness vanished. She went still redder and said, 'Oh ...

it's very kind of you, Mr Manning, but I shouldn't wish that.'

'Why not?'

'Well, you and madam's always been very good and . . .' The oldest child opened the door and looked in. Elsie turned and said sharply, 'Now you go along, Maureen, and see after Sheila.' The child shut the door quietly and without a word, but something in this upset Elsie. Up till now she had been shy but quite calm – it seemed almost bored. But when she turned back from speaking to the child I thought she was going to cry.

I said, 'I see how you feel, Elsie, but it's not you we're thinking of so much as the children. Of course, you can look after yourself. But nobody can be left with three children to bring up and not need anybody's help. After all, that's what one's friends are for, to help when . . .'

She was sitting there with her hands in her lap listening politely to all this stuff, when suddenly, before I realised what was happening, she had jumped up like lightning and turned to the window. I hadn't heard a car coming, but a moment later it swished by. It was Lewis the baker's van. As it passed, I saw her shoulders droop and her whole body relax. She turned back slowly to the room and said awkwardly, 'I'm sorry, Mr Manning, I . . .' She broke off and came back to her chair, dabbed at her hair and then looked at me, all polite and uninterested attention again.

Jill was leaning forward in her chair. I saw that she had gone rather white. She said quietly, 'Why did you do that, Elsie?'

Elsie hesitated. She gestured towards the window and said, 'You mean – *that*, madam?'

'Yes. Why did you go and look out?'

Elsie looked down at her huge hands and said, 'To – to see it go by.'

'The van?'

'Yes.' Elsie suddenly looked up and said very simply, 'If I didn't look, it might go by again – that car might – and then I shouldn't see it.'

I said, 'You mean the car that – that hit Joe?'

'Yes, sir.'

Jill had turned her head away and was staring at a corner of the room. I said, 'But you know, Elsie, that car probably won't ever come by here again. There's no reason why it should.' She shook her head and said quietly but with absolute conviction. 'It will, sir. One day. Eddie reckons it was someone about here. He says you said it was.'

'I told him I thought it might be.'

'Yes, sir. Well, he says go on watching.'

Jill said in a low voice. 'Do you very much want them to – to be caught, Elsie?'

She looked surprised and said, 'Who, madam? Them that did it?'

'Yes.'

'Yes, madam. 'Course.'

Jill said almost querulously, 'But it won't *help* you. It won't feed the children or ... or ...'

Elsie was squinting at her in a puzzled way. 'I don't see what you mean, madam,' she said. 'They ought to be caught and punished proper, oughtn't they? Eddie says find the car and you'll find them.'

I didn't like the look on Jill's face. I said quickly, 'They may not even know it happened, Elsie. Sometimes these things are pure accidents.'

She said with a sort of fierceness, 'Eddie reckons they must have known.'

'But he can't be sure of that.'

Elsie hesitated for a moment, and then the fire suddenly died. She looked down at her big hands in her lap and said sullenly, 'No. 'Course he can't be sure. But he says go on watching.'

'Anyhow, I'm sure Eddie and Sergeant Groves will look after that side of it. Meanwhile there's this question of you and the children.'

'Yes, sir,' she said wearily.

In the end we got her to agree to accept another two pounds a week. More than that she wouldn't hear of taking. 'You and madam's always been very good, Mr Manning. It isn't right for you to give me money. It's them that did it that ought to pay.'

We drove in silence for a while after we left her. Eventually I said, 'That was very unpleasant. But I think she will be all right, you know. She's very tired at the moment, but she's a tough number is Elsie. And the more she can feel that she's doing it herself, the better.'

'And cheaper,' said Jill bitterly. 'Two pounds a week. About what we spend on cigarettes. You couldn't call it dear.'

I pulled the car up on the ridge overlooking the village and said, 'Look, honey – I want to say something to you . . .'

'Yes?' said Jill resignedly.

'We're in this mess now. We've chosen a certain way of tackling it. The only thing to do is to go on and tackle it that way, and to try not to let it get us down. Otherwise life won't be worth living. I know as well as you do that it looks pretty cheap and nasty to be salving our consciences for two pounds a week. But it's better than doing nothing.'

Jill said shakily, 'I don't think I can take it.'

'What exactly can't you take?'

'That place,' she said jerkily. 'And that damned ugly woman looking like that. And the kids. And the going to the window every time a car goes by. She doesn't care about our money. She hardly cares what happens to the kids. Couldn't you see she was bored stiff when you were talking about it? There's only one thing that interests her. I should feel the same in her place. But, God, if she wants her revenge as much as that, don't you see I'd rather she had it, and be damned to what happens to me? I *can't* go on being all smiles and having her saying how good and kind I am, when if she knew, she'd hate my guts and like to see me dead.'

I said, 'Yes, yes. I dare say. But the argument was that nothing we could do would bring Joe to life again, and that going to the police would only hurt you without helping her. I accepted that. Now it's accepted, we must stick to it.'

'But *she* doesn't see it like that. And you don't really believe it. You never have. You only agreed to it because – because it was me and I was your wife, and you had to protect me and so on. Bill believes it all right. That's the way he lives. But it isn't right for you, and you know it.' She suddenly turned and faced me. 'Look – for God's sake let me go to the police and clear the whole thing up.'

That was the last moment that I ever hesitated on that issue. Then I said, 'We talked that out and decided that it wasn't on. If it wasn't on then, it certainly isn't on now.'

She banged her clenched fist on her knee and said, 'But, Jim – don't you see – it's a much bigger mess than you think – I haven't got anybody. Don't you see . . . ?'

I looked at her for a moment, and did see. But I couldn't be absolutely sure. I said slowly, 'Haven't you got me?'

'No – of course I haven't. I'm not on the level with you or Elsie or – or the police – or even Bill. I'm just wangling all round, and terrified that somebody's going to find out some of the dirt.'

I said, 'Are you trying to tell me that – you *are* Bule's mistress?'

She threw back her head and closed her eyes and said, 'Of course, of course, of *course!*'

After a while I said, 'That hadn't occurred to me.'

'Of course it hadn't. You asked me and I said "No" so of course you believed me. Surely you know by now that I *always* lie to get myself out of a jam?' She turned her head away and I saw the tears in her eyes. I loved her and said, 'My poor Jilly . . .' and went to put my arm round her. But she pulled away and sat back facing me and said fiercely, 'Don't be nice about it. For God's sake, don't be nice about it.'

I took my arm away and said, 'All right, darling. I won't.' I thought for a bit and said, 'How long?'

'About three months. No. Four.'

'Pretty nearly ever since we've known him?'

'Yes.'

'Are you in love with him, Jill?'

'No, of course I'm not. It – it was the purest nonsense. Just making a fool of myself because I was bored and – and cross with you.'

'Why were you cross with me?'

'For not seeing I was bored, I suppose. Or not doing anything about it.'

I said, 'I never knew you were as bored as that.'

'But you went away all day. I'm just a useless, idle woman. Everything in the house is done for me. I've got no children. What was there for me to do but make a fool of myself?'

I said, 'Well, you might have done what we agreed you should do when we came here – looked after the gardens. There was plenty to do there, and you just dropped it.'

'Oh, I know – I know. I've let you down about that. And I knew you thought so. But you don't know what it's like to be here all day, with nobody to talk to but the staff and – and then when you came back to find I'd forgotten about the – the bloody peaches or something, and that you were cross with me. There's never been a time for ages when you weren't cross with me, or disapproving inside, or disappointed and thinking I ought to do better.'

This was a bit near home. I said gently, 'But why didn't you tell me this, Jilly?'

'How could I? I ...'

'But I asked you lots of times if everything was all right. I was always asking you. You knew I wanted you to be happy. Why didn't you just tell me you weren't?'

She said helplessly, 'I was afraid you'd be hurt and – and hate me. I knew you liked it here and – and I thought I ought to be able to make it work for you.'

I said, 'Well, kicking up your heels with Bill Bule wasn't likely to make it work for me much, was it?'

'Of course not. But I never meant that to happen.'

I said, 'Then why did it? Can you tell me about it?'

Jill looked down and pulled at her fingers. 'Well – I liked him. And it was fun to be with him and – and just talk nonsense and – and laugh and not be disapproved of, or to worry. It was just – childishness. I think it was because he never worries ...'

'He hadn't a lot to worry about in this, had he, darling?'

'How d'you mean?'

'Well, he was getting all the fun and none of the responsibility. Is he in love with you?'

'I shouldn't think so.'

'If I divorced you, would he marry you?'

'I don't think he'd marry anybody. Anyhow, it doesn't arise, because I wouldn't marry him.'

'Then that's exactly what I mean. It's easy enough to be pretty good company if you're just a temporary lover – just the amusing side of life. It's a bit different if you're married.'

'I suppose so,' she said in a flat voice. There was a long silence. Then Jill said, 'Are you going to throw me out for this?' Somehow I had never even thought of that. I grinned at her and said, 'I shouldn't think so. I don't throw people out much. I feel more inclined to smack your bottom.'

'You're welcome, if that'd do any good.' She threw her head restlessly from side to side. 'But you see, Jim, I've made such an *utter* mess now. You'll never trust me any more, and why should you? And now there's this thing about Joe Pearce and that puts me in wrong with you too and – and—'

I said, 'Yes. It's a pity that happened. It makes it all rather complicated—' A thought struck me and I said suddenly, 'You don't by chance *want* to be thrown out, do you?'

She looked at me in surprise and said, 'Of course not. What d'you mean?'

'Well, you might. Even if you don't want to marry Bule. From what you say, you've been very unhappy. It might be that you were trying to say you were through with me.'

'No, no – it isn't like that at all. I love you. I haven't got anything else real in the world. It's just that I'm afraid you'll never want me any more after – after all this dirt.'

I took her hand and said, 'Look, Jilly – maybe if I were a proper man with proper pride, I should chuck you out and divorce you. I suppose plenty of people would. But it so happens that I love you and don't *want* to chuck you out. I think you've behaved abominably – not so much because you've been unfaithful to me, but because it's meant ganging up with a person like Bule against me. But hell – we all behave abominably at times, and I think I see how it

84

happened. So stop being a mask of woe, and let's start picking up the pieces.'

Jill said, 'I think you're the most generous person in the world.'

I suppose that was what I wanted her to say. Anyhow, it helped the process of seeing it all as a nonsense. I said, 'Well, well – the point is what are we going to do about it?'

'I'll do whatever you say. Of course I will.'

I thought for a bit and said, 'I think I'd better see Bule and tell him I know. That's the cleanest way.'

Jill said, 'I'd just like to say that – that the whole thing was much more my fault than his.'

'I dare say it was, awful. Anyhow I'm not proposing to call on him with a horsewhip if that's what you're worrying about. But obviously he's got to know you've spilt the beans – another lot of beans.'

Jill said suddenly, 'Would you frightfully mind if – if I told him myself?'

'I'd rather you didn't have anything more whatever to do with him.'

'Yes, but, Jim – I got myself into this mess. I'd much rather get myself out of it.' She looked at me with earnest, wide-open eyes. 'You see, if you tell him, it might look as though – well, as though it were you *making* me finish it. I want him to know that it's my own choice, and that I'm through with it because I want to be.'

I said, 'In that case let's have him over and both tell him.'

'No. That's awkward . . .'

She hesitated and then said, 'I've no right to ask you this, but – but let me do it my own way. I know it's right for us. I *know* it is.'

'All right. If you feel like that about it. But mind you, he's got to be left in no doubt . . .'

'He will be. Don't you worry. I shall simply tell him that

I've been an utter fool, and that I've told you and that – that it's finished.' She frowned. 'The only awkward thing is that we're mixed up with him in this Pearce business. It makes it more difficult to make a clean cut.'

'Why should it?'

'Well, you might have to see him about that if – if anything cropped up, and that'd be awkward for both of you.'

'I don't see that anything much *can* crop up now. Anyhow, if I did have to meet him, my position would be a bit stronger than it's really been in the last few months, wouldn't it, darling?'

Jill said, 'Don't. That's the thing I really feel bitchiest about.'

As we were driving home Jill said, 'One minor thing that I hate about this – that's having made it impossible for you to go on knowing the Honbill. I know you've enjoyed talking to him, and there aren't many amusing people round here.'

I just smiled to myself and said, 'Oh, I'll manage, darling.' But I thought it was an odd thing to say.

We were both anxious to get on and get the Bule business cleared up. Jill was for going over to see him, but somehow I felt that it was better to make him come over. I was going out to some meeting in the village that evening, and we agreed that she should ring him up, and get it over while I was out. I thought I should be a couple of hours, but in fact I was only away an hour, and I wondered if he would still be there when I got back. But Jill came out to the garage, and as I got out of the car she said, 'Well, that's that.' I remember she was wearing a dark green frock, and smiling and looking very pretty. I kissed her and she hugged me hard. I said, 'How did he take it?'

'Oh – all right. He's a queer person. He just said that of course I was right from my point of view, but that he never tried to look after other people, and he would have gone on taking what he could get for as long as he could get it.'

I said, 'The Honbill's apparent frankness about himself is one of his best acts.'

'He also sent you any kind regards that you were willing to accept, and any apologies you would believe.'

'Nicely put. The main thing is – does he realise that as far as we're concerned he's *out*?'

'Yes. He does.'

'Good. Then that's that, darling. Now let's forget it.'

6

It is always very awkward when you don't feel as strongly about something as you should. I knew a man who suddenly realised that he was bored at his mother's funeral, and never really liked himself much afterwards. I wasn't bored by the fact that Jill had been unfaithful to me, but neither was I properly hurt and angry and humiliated. I have never quite seen why, but in fact I was merely irritated. My main feeling was that it was just the sort of damned silly thing Jill *would* do, and that it was about time she grew up. Anyhow, it was partly my own fault for leaving her in the country and not noticing that she didn't like it. It would be characteristic of Jill not to tell me something I might find unpleasant, because it might worry me and hurt my feelings; and meanwhile to go and do something absolutely idiotic and hurtful behind my back, in order to put things right for herself.

So I never took what she had told me about Bule very seriously, and when she said it was finished, I accepted that without difficulty or hesitation. I suppose, God help me, I could never really believe that any woman, who was married to and loved by a paragon like me, could really care much about any other man – and certainly not about a mere amusing poseur like the Honbill. I talked to her several times about finding her some more interesting things to do, and I think I arranged for her to come up to London more often and more regularly than she had been doing, to break the monotony of being at Crossways. More than this I didn't do. More than this I didn't think needed to be done.

It was about a week later that Eddie came to see me, and I think it was when I saw him coming up the drive on his motor-cycle that I first realised what the whole Pearce affair had done to me and to Jill. We were outside the house, pottering about with one of the wall roses, when we heard the sound of Eddie's machine. We both turned round and I said, 'Hallo – here's Eddie.' Then it hit me. I glanced at Jill and saw that she was standing rigid and staring at Eddie, and I realised that she was afraid because a village policeman was coming, and that so was I. She didn't look at me and we said nothing. I went forward and made myself smile at Eddie and said, 'Hallo, Eddie, what have we been up to this time?'

He pulled his bike on to its stand and said, 'Afternoon, Mr Manning. I wonder if you could spare me a minute for something I want to ask you about?'

I said, 'Sure. Come in,' and led him into my study; and as we went in I was telling myself that he couldn't have got on to it – that there was no way in which he could have.

Eddie sat down, and I noticed that his rather queer light blue eyes were slightly bloodshot. It was probably because he had been riding fast without goggles, but it made his eyes look angrier than ever. I smiled again and gave him a cigarette and said, 'Right now, Eddie – what's the trouble?'

He said, 'Well, Mr Manning, it's like this – we've never found a trace of that car – the one that killed Joe – and the way we're going on I reckon we never shall, and we all know it.'

'Nobody's ever come forward?'

'No. Nobody has. Neither the driver or nobody that saw any such car. It's a dead end.'

I said, 'Well, it was always a pretty forlorn hope, wasn't it, Eddie? After all—'

'Maybe it was, Mr Manning. But I told you I was going to find that car, and I'm going to, if it takes me the rest of my life. And if the sergeant and everybody is for letting it go, I'm not.'

He was staring at me with the angry eyes and the chin with its deep scar pushed out aggressively. As I looked at him I had to say to myself, 'Don't be a fool – that murderous anger isn't with you. It's with X. Some person unknown. You are a friend and an ally.'

I said, 'But *how*, Eddie? After all, that car may be anywhere in England – and it may belong to somebody who doesn't even know ...'

'No, sir,' said Eddie quietly. 'There isn't anybody who doesn't know if he travelled past there that night, even if he didn't know he killed somebody. With all the broadcasting and appealing that's been done, he'll know he's been asked to come forward. It's what I always reckoned. Whoever did it *knows* he did it, and he's lying low.'

'All right. Supposing we accept that. If he goes on lying low, what can you do about it?'

Eddie sucked at his cigarette, which was only half-lit. 'I've thought about this and thought about it, Mr Manning,' he said slowly. 'And I keep coming back to something you said right at the start, that seems to me 'bout the only bit of sense that's been spoken about it. What was a big car doing down there at all? It's not the best through way from anywhere to anywhere else.'

'Might have been somebody who didn't know the district and had taken a wrong turning.'

'It could be that, sir, I'll agree. And I'll agree that if it is, that's difficult. But what you said was that it seemed to you most likely it was a local car, to be down there, and I'm going to start by saying, "Suppose it was?"'

He was still staring at me, and I looked away and started fumbling in one of the drawers of my desk for more cigarettes. When I looked up Eddie had taken some folded sheets of paper from his pocket.

'So first of all, sir, I thought I'd get a little check-up like to see who *did* come along Tarrant's Lane, and here it is. In three solid days, sir, apart from trade vans, there was only four cars come along there. And all local. There was Mr Frances' Morris going to Mr Margetson's. There was Mrs Margetson going back that way to their place with a little Ford. There was Mr Lindsay's Packard going down to Boyd Farm and' – Eddie looked up and grinned for the first time – 'and there was you and Mrs Manning going to see Elsie in your Daimler.'

I said, 'So you were making your check that Sunday? I didn't see you.'

'No, sir. You wouldn't have.'

'Lurking behind the hedge in a false beard, eh?'

'Well, anyway, sir, the main thing was that no car that *wasn't* local came by there. So that seemed to say you were right. *And* it was a week-end when the traffic was pretty heavy on main roads.'

Eddie slowly folded up one of his sheets of paper, put it away and turned to another. His hands were huge, like his sister's, and the backs of them were covered with freckles and thick red hair.

'Then the next thing I did was to have a look and see what places a car was *likely* to be going to down there – saying that it was a local car going home or going to call . . .' He spread out a rough sketch map. 'Well, there's Margetson's. There's Boyd Farm. You could get to Fould's that way. You could get to Seward's. You could get to

Colonel Lewis's. There's half a dozen cottages, but it doesn't seem anybody'd be likely to go to them in a big car. Apart from that there's the back of Glover's orchard, and the back of yours, and a cart track down to Pyle's farm. But anybody coming to any of them in a car'd come the other way, to the front. You'd never use that gate into your orchard, sir, would you? Not coming in a car?'

I said, 'I don't think I've ever used it in my life – in a car or not.'

'No. And I don't reckon Mr Glover ever uses his either.' Eddie stared for a moment at his sketch map. 'Well, I just told you all that, sir, to show you what I'd been doing. What I really came to ask you was – will you help me going on from there? I know you feel like I do about this, and you want to get to the bottom of it. And I know what you done for Elsie, and I'd like you to know I'm grateful. I wouldn't care for you to think I wasn't doing nothing.'

I said, 'I don't quite see what you mean, Eddie, about helping you. D'you mean have I got any idea about what to do next?'

'Not exactly, sir. It's like this . . .' He hesitated. 'You see what I've done here was to narrow it down to the most likely places that car might've been going. And – well, it's not very pleasant, but on a thing like this I reckon you've got to suspect everybody, whoever they are, who it might've been. Now you take Colonel France. I'd lay ten pounds Colonel France was never anything to do with a thing like this. But you *could* go to his place down there, and so I want to know where his car was that night and so on, so that I can cross him off. See?'

I nodded. 'That seems sound enough. The best way is for you to go and see all these people, and find out where their cars were, and whether they had any visitors who came in cars.'

'You reckon it'd be all right, sir? To do that?' Eddie hesitated. 'Only you see, Sergeant Groves – I think he reckons it's a waste of time. And being local people he doesn't much like it. So I thought you being a magistrate, and knowing how you felt, I'd ask you . . .'

I said, 'I don't see why you shouldn't do it. I must say it seems a pretty long shot, but at least it'll eliminate something.' It was quite all right now. I could look at him and not mind. I said, 'Start with me, say . . .'

Eddie smiled deprecatingly and said, 'Well . . .'

'After all, my orchard backs on to that road. Well, I can tell you straight away. I've got a Daimler, as you know. At that time it was sitting in the garage with a flat battery, and that's confirmed by the fact that it couldn't even come to the station to meet me later in the evening. I didn't get down from London till after this happened, so I and my car are out. Visitors – we had a lot rather later on in the evening, because my wife gave a party. But they didn't come till quite a bit later, and of course they all came to the front.' I sat back and lit another cigarette. 'There you are, Eddie. I think that's the sort of thing you want. And I don't see why anybody should mind giving it to you.'

Eddie said, 'No, sir,' rather dispiritedly and there was a long pause. Then he suddenly raised his head and I saw the scar on his chin again. He just said quietly, 'Right, sir. Then I'll try that next.'

After he had gone I felt oddly cold and shivery and realised that my vest and shirt were wet through with sweat; which was strange, because for the whole of the last part of it I had not only not minded, but had almost been enjoying myself.

I think this again was at a week-end. In the middle of the following week Jill came up to town and stayed the night, and we went out to dinner and the theatre. I remember it, because it was a very good show, and for the first time since the Pearce affair she seemed to be really happy and enjoying herself. She went home on a morning train that would get her down just before lunch, and I was to follow on my usual train in the evening. At least, that was the idea; and it has a wryly amusing side that the only reason why it didn't work out, was that I was trying to spend every minute of time I could with her. I happened to hear at lunch that Garland, one of our directors, was driving down to Rye for a long week-end's golf, and he offered to take me home and drop me on his way. It meant leaving about half-past four, and I hesitated before accepting. But I hadn't anything to do that couldn't be put off, so in the end I decided to be lazy, and went.

The rest is almost pathetically simple. The London road runs past the entrance to Bule's place. There is a long straight past his gates and we were travelling fast. When we were only about a couple of hundred yards away from the entrance, a car shot out of it much too fast, and turned the way we were going. Garland lifted his foot and slowed and said, 'If he'd done that a few seconds later he'd have had it.'

I said, 'It isn't a he. It's a she.' I had recognised the Daimler as soon as it appeared. I could almost have recognised Jill's driving anyway. I don't know why she didn't see me in the driving mirror. We were only about thirty yards behind by that time. Garland said, 'It would be. Bloody women drivers.' I said, 'They are a nuisance.' I thought fast and then said, 'Don't pass, Billy. There's a rather notable pub just here, and I think we need a drink.'

I know we stopped at the Chasen Arms, because I remember seeing the Daimler vanishing in the distance as we pulled up outside it. But I never have been able to remember going in, or having a drink, or what Garland said, or anything else about the rest of the drive until we were at home and Jill had appeared, and I was saying, 'Darling, you know Billy Garland, don't you?' and seeing that quick warm smile, and those lovely, gentle, mud-coloured eyes as she shook hands with him. I turned aside quickly and made a fuss of Claude. We hadn't been long in the pub, and Jill can't have been in more than a quarter of an hour or so. But she never turned a hair.

Billy Garland was a nice enough chap, but he was a bore, and if he had stayed on long I don't think I could have seen it through. We had to ask him to dinner, but luckily he wanted to get on down to Rye, and after a couple of drinks he went. I came straight in from seeing him off and said to Jill, 'Look – I know you've been to Bule's.' She looked straight back at me and said slowly, 'When have I?'

'This afternoon. Now. We nearly ran into you as you came out of the drive. It's a fair cop, my dear.'

Jill said, 'Oh. I see.' She went on looking at me for what seemed a long time in silence, and then slowly turned her head away and said almost in a whisper, 'I'm sorry, Jim.'

I said, 'So am I. Very sorry. But it looks as though that's that, doesn't it?'

'You mean – you're through with me?'

'What d'you think I am? You've played complete dirt and been caught and that's the end of it.'

She said drearily, 'I suppose so. If – if that's how you want it. I've no excuse. I think I should probably have told you anyway.'

I said, 'Oh, come off it, Jill,' and turned away.

'No. I think I should. You see I've known for days that – that I was in it far deeper than I realised and that – it wouldn't do.'

'You mean you're in love with Bule?'

95

'Not exactly in love with him. But – oh, I don't know. I can't explain.'

I said, 'Why bother? We won't quarrel over definitions. You're enough in love with him and so little in love with me that you'll do me this sort of dirt. That's enough for me.'

Jill said without hope, 'You're wrong. I love you more than anybody in the world. But I can see you – you must think that.'

'Tell me what else I could think?'

'I know. I can see . . .'

There was a long silence. Then she said in a low voice, 'Do you want me to go?'

God knows what I wanted. I didn't. I think even then I could have taken her in my arms and said, 'No. You shan't go. I love you whatever you've done, and I'm going to keep you.' But I was hurt this time and I said, 'Yes, I do. I don't see what else there is for it.'

Jill said, 'Well, I'm in your hands, Jim. I haven't a leg to stand on whatever you do, so . . .'

I didn't say anything, and after a moment or two she added, 'It isn't really a bit like you think. I'm sure it isn't. But I don't expect I can make you believe it, and I don't really see why you should.'

It was cooling as I looked at her. I was afraid of what would happen if I let it cool. I said, 'What I think is that you were unfaithful to me; that you lied about it; that you promised that it was all over; and that within a few days you've sneaked back to your lover when you thought I wasn't looking. Is that true or not?'

'Of course it is,' she said wearily. 'You know that wasn't what I meant.'

'Then what did you mean?'

'Only that . . .' She stopped and shook her head. 'No – it's no good. Forget it.'

I said, 'I've had enough of this for the moment,' and went out into the garden and left her sitting there.

I was afraid Jill might follow me and want to go on talking, but she didn't. Claude did, and when I sat down in the orchard he sat down too and registered woe. People always think that dogs are sympathising when they do that, but in fact I think they are usually apologising. Being very self-centred, they assume that if you are angry and sit and glower, you are glowering at them. All Claude was doing was being embarrassed and deprecating and trying to curry favour.

In fact within ten minutes I wasn't being woebegone, but rather disgustingly and surprisingly practical. It's all very well to throw out a dramatic hand and point to the door and tell your wife to pack up and go. That is what I would have liked to do, in some ways. But to get Jill and her possessions out of the place wouldn't be a matter of half an hour and a moderate-sized suitcase, but of a week and a Pickford van. Of course, I could just pack a bag and go myself. But if I wasn't there the place would be in chaos in a week. I mention this, because up till that time I had always assumed, like most people who have never tried it, that to break up a marriage is deplorable, but quite easy. I dare say it is, if you can do it in a temper. But if you try to do it more or less cold, as I was doing by then, you dig up every sort of nonsensical difficulty, down to who's going to feed the cat.

Looking back, I can see what I was finding so utterly confusing. I had had my face slapped and it had hurt. But the really important thing about having one's face slapped is not the pain, but the attitude implied by the slap – the contempt and the desire to hurt and humiliate. I don't think I believed that that attitude was there, or that Jill had any idea of the size of the thing she was doing. I had told her I wanted her to go, and that was true enough, in the sense that I was angry and disgusted with her. But to be finished with her – to have no more to do with her – perhaps never see her again – soon began to seem quite another thing. If a man slaps your face you may knock him down for it, but few people pull out a gun and shoot him – or themselves.

But amidst all this painful refusal to accept things at their face value – this desire to find reasons why the whole business was much less serious than it looked – I always stuck on one point – that I clearly knew far less about Jill than I had imagined. I had always thought of Jill and myself as 'we,' and the whole of the rest of the world as 'they,' and I had assumed that she felt the same. But in this relationship with Bule, however casual and shallow most of it might have been, there must have been times when Jill had seen me just as 'he' – just another person quite detached from herself. I must have been 'he' when she decided to go to Bule's that afternoon. I must have been 'he' when I came in with Billy Garland. I must be 'he' to her and Bule – a person on the other side of the fence, as I had vaguely felt myself to be sometimes, before I knew anything about their affair, but felt that she was ganging up with Bule against me.

Yet she could still look at me as she had always done. It still looked as though there was fundamental truth and good-will in her eyes. And if that was no longer the truth that I thought I could see, had it ever been? Or had I always been 'he?'

I still think that in this whole business one of the nastiest moments was when she stepped forward to greet Billy

Garland and I saw everything that I had ever loved, and knew it was false, and knew that I should never have spotted that it was false if I had not known. I don't think anything was ever the same after that; and that is why I turned away from it and patted Claude.

I don't know what the end of all my puzzling would have been. I still hadn't got anything clear when I went into the house. But as I was in the cloakroom, getting my coat, Jill came in looking like Lady Macbeth in one of her calmer moments. She said, 'Are you going out?'

I said, 'Yes. I thought I'd go down to the Golf Club for dinner if you don't mind.'

Jill said, 'I see. All right.'

I put on my raincoat and walked past her into my study to get cigarettes. She followed me and stood there while I was filling my case. After a while she said, 'Do you mind if I tell you something before you go?'

I said, 'Sure,' and went on filling my case.

She said slowly, 'I only want to say that I know I've been an awful fool and quite a bit of a knave as well. I don't know why. I don't understand it myself. But I also know that I love you and that I haven't really got anything else in the world.'

I looked up at her and I knew that whether it was true or not, she believed it. I said, 'It's a bit late in the day to think of that, darling.'

'Oh, I know. You're perfectly justified in throwing me out and finishing with me if you want to. But – but just be sure that you must, Jim – that you really want to be through with me. Because I so much – don't want you to be.'

I knew I wasn't through with her; but I knew I ought to be, and to gain time I said, 'What's the good of trying to go on with this sort of thing happening? If you find Bule so damned attractive that you'd do this to me, you'd do it again.'

'We could go away. Would you go away with me?'

'My dear, I don't want a wife who has to be torn away from the irresistible attractions of other gentlemen. You can't deal with a thing like this just by running away from it.'

She suddenly said in a low voice, 'Take me away, Jim. For God's sake, take me away. Don't you see that I'm in a mess here all round? It isn't only Bill, it's the Pearce business and – and everything. I can't even *think* about it, unless I can get away somewhere with you and – and get some sense into things.'

I think if she had cried it would have been easier. But she just stood there dry-eyed, and I realised that she looked very tired and almost haggard, like a weary middle-aged woman. I took her hand and squeezed it and said, 'Come on – cheer up. I expect it'll all come wrong in the end, like things always do.'

I knew that taking her hand would make her cry. I think I probably meant it to. She clung to me and sobbed out, 'I can't bear it, I can't bear it. I've done this to you and I never meant to.'

I patted her shoulder and said, 'All right, you old ass. I know.' We stood there for a while in silence. I knew that this was all a bit too easy and that it wouldn't do, but I was sunk now. I turned her round so that I could look at her and said, 'But mark you, young woman, if we do this, there's a hell of a job of reconstruction to be done. Some mighty funny business must have been going on inside you, for this to have happened; and if we're going to get anywhere there'll have to be a lot of plain speaking. See?'

She looked at me with her eyes still full of tears and said,

'All right. Fair enough.' I smiled at her and kissed the end of her nose and she smiled back rather shyly.

None of this makes the slightest sense unless you remember that I had been married to Jill for eleven years, and she had never let me down before in anything that mattered.

7

We went to Paris. It wasn't very imaginative of us, but we went there because it was a place where we had always been happy and very much together. There must be a lot of people who still go to Paris, just as they used to go to Vienna, not because of what it is, but because of what it was when they were younger. Indeed, I can imagine that if you take your happiness with you, Paris would still be a very nice place to sit and enjoy it, just as any field is a delightful place for lunch – as long as you have remembered to bring the lunch. But it is no good just going to a field and expecting it to provide the lunch for you; and it is no good going to Paris nowadays, if it ever was, and expecting to be able to order happiness at a café. You can still nearly do that in Italy. You can nearly do it in some other parts of France. But you can't do it in Paris.

I knew this before we ever started. No place ever solved any of my problems. They always look exactly the same in the Via Tritona as they do in Piccadilly or Ruckby-under-Edge. But there are plenty of people whose answer to any insoluble problem is to buy a ticket to somewhere else; and for some of them it even seems to work, up to a point. Jill has always been a confirmed buyer-of-tickets-to-some-where-else. She loves travelling for its own sake. I think I hoped in some vague way, that taking her even as far as Paris might make her happy, and that if she could be happy, it would bring things into perspective. I still thought they *had* a perspective.

I must say that on the journey it looked as though it

might work. It was nice to be sitting in the Golden Arrow Pullman, and we were much helped by a very aristocratic woman in mink and diamonds who had come to see some people off, and was hopelessly tight. She came and sat in the Pullman with them and drank some more, and the whole thing became a race against time. Would the train start while she was still capable of getting off? And if not, would they carry her off and drop her on the platform, or would she just come with us? I bet Jill six to four that she'd make it by herself. She struck me as the sort who has made it in one long stagger a good many times before. But it took three attendants to help her off, and Jill wouldn't pay, on the grounds that that was at least partially being carried. After she had gone, the woman of the pair she had been seeing off said, 'Poor Polly,' and the man said, 'Yes'; and they both picked up shiny weeklies and never said another word until we got to Folkestone.

What with this, and a dead calm crossing, and seeing the little man who works the lift at the Fontenoy again, and re-opening relations with various bars, and having dinner at Fouquet, the expedition could hardly have started better. I know I never gave a thought to the Honbill or our problems until the following morning, and I doubt if Jill did. Even then, I probably shouldn't have remembered it all, but for the fact that I happened to lean back in my chair outside one of the big cafés in the Champs Elysées and grin at Jill and say, 'Well, madam . . . ?' All I meant was that I was at peace with all the world, and that I wanted to know if she was. But though she smiled back, it was a slightly tentative smile, and I suddenly realised that she had thought I was going to start talking about us. It was a lovely spring morning, and I looked up the sunny stretch of the Champs Elysées, to the Arc de Triomphe against the blue sky, and I have never wanted to talk about anything less in my life. But I knew from that tentative smile that it had got to be done – that there would never be any real peace again until it was tidied up and done with.

'I don't blame you much for the first part. I wish it hadn't happened, but I think I can see why it did, and it was probably at least as much my fault as yours. Anyhow it's a waste of time to talk about things like this being anybody's "fault." But the thing that puzzled me about it, when you first told me, was that you should have been as bored and unhappy as that without telling me that you were . . . And then of course this last business of slipping off to see him again lands slap on the same spot. Only the night before, we were very happy together – at least I was, and I thought you were. I could understand it if you were in love with the Honbill and didn't love me any more, and wanted to go and be married to him. I should hate it, and I shouldn't see quite what I'd done; but it's the sort of thing that *does* happen to people all the time, and I suppose it might happen to us. But you say you're not in love with him – that you don't want to marry him – that you love me and want to stay married to me. And yet you could do that. It doesn't add up. And it leaves me not knowing where the hell I am . . .'

I never know what to drink casually in bars in France. I don't like Vermouth or most of the syrups that the French drink. There are the sort of places where one always drinks Alexanders and the sort of places where one always drinks Porto Flips; but I defy anybody to go on drinking either of them for very long. It's usually quicker and less disastrous in the end to start drinking Pernod from the outset.

'Yes, darling, that's all very well. But if this had just been kicking up your heels with a casual lover – you surely wouldn't have gone back to it like that, as soon as you were out of my sight? My guess is that you're a good deal more in love with the Honbill and a good deal less in love with me than you're admitting – even to yourself. If so, let's face it and tackle it, instead of telling ourselves that it can't be true.'

'It isn't like that.'

The difference between the best French and the best English cooking is that in England the best meal you can buy can always be eaten without noticing it. In France there are nearly always things in any good meal that take the floor, so to speak. You can't ignore them or talk them down. They demand silence, and you have to give it to them.

'Oh, Jim darling, you want everything so clear-cut and tidy. Don't you see that it can't all be black and white like that – at least not for me? There's no simple answer. If I say I suppose I do love him in a way, you'll think I mean something much more serious than I do. And if I say no, I don't love him at all, you won't believe me. I . . . I don't know what you want from me— Yes, but the truth isn't just one thing. It's a – a sort of *jumble* of things.'

The very small Fiat suddenly stopped dead in the Avenue de l'Opéra. A bus close behind braked hard, a car following the bus bumped gently into the back of it. A lot of people started to wave their arms and shout. The bus driver got out, and so did eight car drivers. The passengers poured happily off the platform of the bus and formed a crowd. Two policemen appeared. One line of traffic formed a solid block from the Place de l'Opéra onwards. Everybody sounded his horn. Meanwhile the little Fiat had got going again, and before anybody could stop it, it had gone bunking guiltily on down the Avenue, and out of sight round the corner towards the Louvre, like a small boy who has broken somebody's window.

'Yes, I think that's true enough. I haven't always been frank with you. I don't *like* being frank when it means – saying horrid things and hurting people. It doesn't seem to me to do any good . . . Darling, it's not a question of living in a fool's paradise. It's just a question of not having one's nose rubbed in something unpleasant.'

'But, Jill, don't you see that you get your nose rubbed in it in the end, if it's there? If I'd realised before how you were feeling . . .'

They say that if you sit outside the Café de la Paix for long enough, you will see everyone you know. It is possible to sit outside the Café de la Paix and see someone you thought you knew become a stranger.

'Ever since you came back from the war, in a way. I desperately wanted you back. It was the one thing I'd been living for— Oh, Lord, no – don't be silly, darling. It wasn't anything to do with you. You were marvellous. It was just that I was expecting more than – than *anybody* could have given me. I ought to have gone on and done a job, of course, instead of sitting round expecting you to arrange life for me— No, I don't think Paul dying was anything to do with it. I felt I'd let you down over that. I still do. But I don't think that – messed it up.'

'But it would have helped if you'd had another baby?'

'It might have— Look, Jim – is all this really doing any good? Because it doesn't feel to me as though it is.'

'I must know now.'

It is a very nice bar, though a bit too Americaine. There are the proprietor and the barman and mademoiselle, and they are all mixed up together, and one has never known whether mademoiselle is the proprietor's mistress and the barman's daughter or the barman's mistress and the proprietor's daughter. Mademoiselle is still very pretty but she is older than last time, when she looked about eighteen. The place is always empty. I have never seen more than two other people in it. I don't know what it keeps going on, but it certainly isn't by selling drinks. When we first went there, and just wanted drinks, there was a faint air of surprise and embarrassment. But they know us now, and everybody shakes hands. It is either a brothel, or a black-market place, or something political. I favour black market, but the barman is a very political-looking man.

'Well, darling, that's a thing that I *can* set your mind at rest about. He's certainly not a better lover than you, if as good. You know I haven't a lot of experience of gentlemen, but as far as I'm concerned the Honbill's got nothing on you there.'

'Then where has he?'

'Nowhere, really . . .'

'Oh God, Jilly – try to stop defending and be helpful. I'm trying to find out what this is all about.'

'Well – it's completely silly – but I'm not frightened of him and I am of you. See?'

'*Frightened?* Of *me?*'

'Of course. And always have been . . . look, if you'll buy me another drink I'll try to tell you something.'

One of the extraordinary things about Pernod is that after even a little of it, it starts to change the human race. You can go into a bar full of the most ordinary people, and by the time you have drunk two Pernods they will all have gone, and the most remarkable raree show will have started to appear. Notably very *small* people. If anybody doubts this he can try it for himself. Sit in a bar. Drink two Pernods; and before you are through the second, at least three people under five feet in height will come in. I don't know why. It just is so. And it's nothing whatever to do with being drunk. People who know about this accept it as a matter of course and say to one another, 'Ah – they're beginning to come in small now.'

'You see there's a sort of pattern which I think of as having run all through our married life. It's of having been awful or inadequate in some way – having spent too much or forgotten something or what have you. And knowing that I have. And probably lying about it. And of your finding out and lecturing me about it – very gently, but a bit disappointed with me. And saying that I was sorry. And your being very nice about it, but saying I must make an effort. It was always that I must make an effort. And you were always right, and I knew I ought to. But, darling, I'm a bad thing and lazy and shiftless, and I *hate* making efforts, and I always said I would and knew I shouldn't . . . I can remember now what a triumphant feeling it was sometimes when you decided that it was *you* who ought to make an effort. But it wasn't really any good, because I knew that if you decided that, you *would* – you'd really do it. And I knew that I shouldn't.'

'But, Jilly darling – what a ghastly prig you make me sound. Why on earth didn't you just tell me to go to hell?'

'Because you were *right*, don't you see? You weren't asking me for anything that wasn't perfectly reasonable. It was just that you didn't know that I was no good and a bad person . . . so instead of telling you, I just agreed and – and fought you about it inside.'

There are things about food that one never learns and doesn't want to learn. I still always order truffles, and never like them much. I think it is that I resent not liking truffles, just as I resent not really liking Schumann or Wordsworth, and hate to face the fact that I don't.

The rich French are very hard to bear. The rich anywhere can be pretty trying, but the rich French one dislikes at sight. I am frequently greedy in France, but I never *feel* greedy except when I am in a restaurant with the rich French.

'And it's been like that ever since we were married?'

'Ever since the end of the war anyhow. Darling – I hope I haven't made it sound horrid. I know it's completely my fault. But you did ask me, and . . .'

'Well, I said we had quite a job of reconstruction to do, and my God, it seems we have . . . Look, Jilly, as one working girl to another, do you like me at *all*? And if so why?'

'I think you're the straightest and kindest and most generous person in the world.'

(But you don't love me, madam. You love your ivory carving who giggles with you and doesn't nag you, and doesn't leave you sitting with your thumbs clutched into the palms of your hands and every muscle tense . . .)

'Well I can't help feeling, from what you've been saying, that the only real asset I've got, from the point of view of being married, isn't an asset at all to you, but a hell of a liability.'

'What d'you mean, darling?'

'To me, the only point of being married at all is to be dealing with somebody who you trust completely – who you know loves you, faults and all, so that you can just relax and be yourself.'

'I agree.'

'But you can't possibly have that without completely straight shooting. At least I can't. I can't feel like that about anybody, unless I can be sure that we tell one another the truth. And that's just what you don't like. The only thing you can be sure of with me is that if I feel critical, I shall criticise – that there won't be any private resentments that you don't know about. But if you happen not to like that arrangement, then you can't very well like me.'

'It's not so much being critical, Jim, as – as wanting people to change. People are like they are and they *can't* change themselves.'

'Oh, come, darling. That's pure Honbill. People change themselves in small ways all the time – if they want to. A person who says, "Here am I, complete and unchangeable. Take it or leave it," is just saying that their marriage isn't worth the effort of changing.'

('Effort' again that sullen face that would say 'Prig!' if it dared. One sees the pattern of it now. Is there any other pattern that it could take, after all this?)

The English belief that Paris taxi-drivers are dangerous probably arises because they drive on the wrong side of the road. But crossing the Place de la Concorde at night can be rather like Dodgem cars. The Lapin d'Or is so exactly like about half a dozen other Montparnasse night clubs that I am never really sure if it is the Lapin d'Or I mean: or, if it is, whether I am in it or not, until I see the twin negresses. If they are there it must be the Lapin d'Or. Always assuming that it *is* the Lapin d'Or that has the twin negresses. Anyhow it is not important. It is very hot and there is a very noisy band and a very small floor, and champagne is no longer avoidable, so everything is in order.

The pathetic thing is that though there is really nothing left to say, we keep on saying it. I have to keep biting on the groggy tooth and Jill has to keep saying that it is quite sound. Sometimes we can keep off it for half an hour. But what else is there to talk about? We talk as though we knew one another well. But since we only met a few hours ago, it makes no sense. Dancing makes no sense either. We dance as though we were in love, and we aren't in love. At least, not with one another.

'. . . My dear Jill, it isn't a question of giving you another chance. What I want to give you is a chance to be happy, and I don't think you're ever likely to be happy with me, from the sound of it . . . Well – simply because I've done my best, and the result has been to make you miserable. The only unfortunate thing is that you happen to have married me. You could have found scores of people who could have run life your way.'

When the cabaret starts they come and move the tables back about eighteen inches, and then you're comparatively safe – except from the Slav dancers, who nearly always kick things off the table or tread on your toes. I knew a man once who had lost an eye in the Great War, and always wore a black patch. Everybody always assumed that he lost the eye in action, but somebody who didn't like him told me that he got it put out with some sort of prong, carried by the Devil in a scene in a night-club cabaret. I always think of that when I go to the Lapin d'Or – and I always wonder if he drew a disability pension. 'Lost, owing to the exigencies of military service . . .'

'Yes, yes, yes, darling – but what are we to start again *from?* Don't you see that I haven't the faintest idea what sort of person you really are, now? You talk about getting together, but on what basis? I'm certainly not going to lecture you any more or try to change you, now I know how you feel about it. And frankly I'm damned if I want you if we're just going to coo at each other and not mean it. So what?'

'I think I could try more now, Jim. I think I've seen something – seen what happens if you won't try. That it just makes a mess for everybody—' (Lady, you're a liar. You haven't seen anything. You never will, because you don't want to. And why should you, as long as there's a handsome and witty gentleman to tell you you're always right?)

When you go downstairs to the lavatory at the Lapin one of the twin negresses gets up too and follows you down. I suppose they take it in turns. When you come out of the lavatory, she is always standing talking to the attendant, so that you have to squeeze by her, and she grins whitely and says, 'Pardon . . .' I have never been sure quite what the idea is. Presumably one might pick her up and go back to her table. But they do it even if you are with a woman or a party. Once one of them half-opened the door of the men's lavatory as I came out, and then gave a little squeal of horror, and looked at the notice on the door, and went through a terrific comic performance of having made an awful mistake. I smiled and gave her a slap on the rump as I passed, and she seemed perfectly happy and satisfied. But this was unusual. Normally they just stand there, where they are in the way, and grin and say, 'Pardon . . .'

Perhaps Pernod. Perhaps champagne. Perhaps Pernod followed by champagne. Perhaps just Jill's face looking as though you could trust it with your life, and knowing you can't trust it as far as you can throw it. Anyhow, here it comes.

'Maybe I hadn't got much to give, but I gave you all I had. I've never refused you anything that I knew you wanted – in fact, the thing I've enjoyed most, has been finding things I thought you wanted and giving them to you. You say I've neglected you, because I was away during the day doing a job. If that's being neglected, ninety-nine per cent of the women in this country are neglected. You say I've criticised you. Perhaps I have, and if so I'm sorry. But at least I've never criticised you to anybody else. I've never kept anything from you. I've been faithful to you. I made a contract with you, and according to my lights I've kept it . . .'

Lord, I thank Thee that I am not as other men are, or even as this publican.

Sometimes you can hear and feel it coming out of you, and hate it. But you can't stop it. Exactly like being sick.

'You've compared that with what you can get from your boy friend, and it makes me seem pretty pompous and dull. Let's face it. By his standards I am. He's never done a day's work in his life, and nor have you. He's never taken an inch of responsibility for anything, and nor have you. He's a spoilt child, and so are you. You're an admirable pair, and I wish you joy of one another. But I warn you of this – Bule wouldn't lift his little finger to keep you off the streets. He isn't interested in anything in the world but the Honour-able William Bule, and if you think he is, you're kidding yourself. He likes you fine – and why shouldn't he? You're a good free mistress who can even pay for her share of the drinks.'

'I have no illusions about the Honbill.'

'No? Well just look at him over this. He came to my house as my guest. He posed as a friend of mine. Under cover of this, he seduces my wife, who he's bright enough to see is an empty-headed little fool. He knows that I've forgiven you and that we're trying to get together. Yet he'll join you in doing me dirt again three days later. Nice guy.'

'I've told you it was my fault.'

'Oh bunkum! No man has to do that just because some fool of a woman wants him to ...'

'Jim, I'm sorry, but this has gone so far that – that in justice to Bill, I must tell you something. I never *did* finish it up with him. When I saw him, I mean, and told you I had.'

'Have you *ever* told me the truth about anything, darling? Think hard. Because I'm really interested.'

'Yes. I've told you I loved you, and that was true. It still is.'

'I think we'll go home after that, if you don't mind.'

Crossing the Seine, with all the lights of all the bridges shimmering in the water, and the taste of stale tobacco and stale champagne and stale anger in my mouth, I remember thinking, 'Up until to-night I was all right. Up until to-night there wasn't much to be proud of, but it passes, and I won't have it back. But the hairy heel has popped out now.'

We had always slept in one bed, and there had never been anything that that wouldn't put right, up to a point at least.

We always asked for a double bed in hotels, and there was a double bed here. We didn't say anything, and there was nothing of reconciliation or solution in it. But we were cold and tired out with it all, and we went to sleep in a heap to warm each other, as a man might curl up with his dog to warm and comfort him. Jill said, 'Good night, darling,' and I said, 'Good night.' My last waking thought was that I should have said, 'Good night, Jill.' It worried me that I had said 'good night' with childish coldness. But it didn't keep me awake.

8

And yet the following day neither of us would face it. That was like Jill; and anyhow she may have felt that she had all to gain and nothing to lose by going on trying to patch. But I cannot for the life of me understand why I was still in any doubt. I think it was mainly because she *looked* the same. It was a long time before I finally realised that this physical appearance, and the little tricks of voice and gesture, could belong to somebody who wasn't the Jill I had thought I knew.

Anyhow, after a certain amount of rather shy and sheepish giggling about the previous night, we decided firmly that we had been rather drunk, and that what people said when they were drunk was not evidence. Pernod Fils might reasonably have felt that, as they'd made us tell something like the truth for the first time in our married life, this was rather unfair.

Nevertheless, we had enough sense to realise that there was no point in staying in Paris. In fact we hung on for another day, but it was a cold-blooded business; and in the end we suddenly made up our minds at three o'clock in the afternoon to fly back, happened just to catch a flight, and were at Heathrow by seven. As we drove into London, Jill said, 'I'm not quite sure where we go from here. Are we heading for home right away?'

I said, 'No. Not until we've decided what we're going to do when we get there. This expedition hasn't settled much, God knows. But at least it's made it pretty clear that if there is any solution to this, there's no quick and easy one.'

Jill said, 'You know, the maddening part of it is that I'm nearly there. I've got the tantalising feeling that if we could only just get through the next few weeks, I should be a far better thing for you than I've ever been.'

'Then what's stopping you, honey?'

'Well – you won't have me at the moment, will you?'

'Not as long as you're in any doubt whether you wouldn't rather be with the Honbill. I don't want you about yearning for somebody else.'

'It's not a question of yearning and you know it. It's simply that – well, I can't see it all as quite so horrid and despicable as you can, because it didn't *feel* like that. I can see that it was a piece of utter folly and that it's got to stop; but if I pretended that I hated the whole thing and hated him, it would be kidding you, which is just what you say I usually do. . . . . There you are, you see. Now I've made you angry by being frank.'

'Never mind making me angry, my dear. Maybe for you to be frank and me to be angry is about the best thing that could happen. Anyhow, it's a change.'

We stayed in London a couple of days, and it was always like that. If I could ever get her guard down, out it came. She was in love with Bule – head over heels in love with him. And whenever it did come out, it still surprised me. Of course, most of the time her guard was up, and it was all over – a piece of nonsense from the past. And then I would look at her and say to myself, 'Liar, liar, liar!'

It must have been a jolly two days for her. To do her justice, I think she was trying, in her queer way, to play straight with me. Something had broken that night in Paris, and even if what had broken was our whole relationship, I think it was a relief to her that she no longer had to pretend all the time. But she still seemed to feel, or to talk as though she felt, that it could all be put right in some simple way – and still spoke as though she wanted it to be.

It was in a place in Soho that I finally made up my mind. We hadn't been talking about it for once, and I happened to say, 'By the way, did I tell you that old Rogers is dead? Died in his chair at the Club, just before we went away.'

Jill said, 'How on earth did they know?'

'Know what?'

'That he was dead? The people at the Club?'

This was so completely uncharacteristic of Jill that I very nearly answered it perfectly seriously. Jill hardly ever made jokes, and she had rather liked old Rogers. Then I suddenly realised that this was to all intents and purposes a quotation – the very accent of Isaiah.

I laid down my knife and fork and said, 'Jill dear – let's face it. You're hopelessly in love with Bill Bule. How about starting from there? It's so much quicker.'

She was genuinely surprised. She looked at me in a puzzled way and said, 'Why on earth did you suddenly say that?'

'Because what you've just said about old Rogers is purest Honbill. I've noticed it time and again in the last few days. You talk like him, and you think like him. It's like a fourteen-year-old with a pash, imitating the gym mistress.'

She said, 'Nonsense!' very crossly.

'Of course it's nonsense. But it's a fact. He's right in your system, my dear, and as long as that's so, all this talk about our getting together is a waste of time, and you know it. So let's agree to put our cards on the table, and try to work it out in a civilised and friendly way.'

There was a long pause, and then she said almost sullenly, 'All right . . .' She turned to me suddenly and said half angrily and half giggling, 'Why the devil did you have to drive down with that fool of a man, Garland, and see me coming out that day? If you hadn't, I should have had the whole thing fixed and over in a fortnight, and you'd never have known and – and everything would have been quite all right.'

I said, 'Everything would have been very fine and dandy indeed – particularly for me. *What* a pity.'

Later that evening I went out and walked about by myself in the Park, and by the time I came back I knew what I was prepared to do.

'I can't do anything with you in this state, when the whole business of Bule is still striking you as a lovely game that's meanly been taken away from you. After everything that's happened, we could never go back to our old relationship. It's dead. All we could do would be to build a new and better one. But we can't do that with you looking back regretfully over your shoulder. You're quite right about the next few weeks. They *are* vital. Because during them, this thing you've got about Bule will either work itself out or get worse.'

'I'm pretty sure it will work itself out.'

'It may or it may not. But one thing's certain. It won't if you just hang around with me and yearn about it. Because apart from anything else, I shall get so angry that I shall say the sort of thing I said in the Lapin d'Or, and then you'll be more and more certain that you'd rather be with him. My bet is that half the attraction of the Honbill for you is that you've only had him in very small doses – and those with a nice dash of naughtiness in them to give the whole thing a relish. I can see he could be a grand chap to spend an illicit two hours with, but I should think he'd be pretty average hell to live with. I may be wrong, but if I am there's nothing to be done about it anyway, so I must take a chance.'

'What sort of chance?'

'I suggest that you should leave me – which is what you'd like to do anyway; and that you should both find out just what this grand passion amounts to. In the meantime, I would neither start divorcing you nor promise to have you back afterwards. It would simply be a chance to find out what you really want. If, after a month – or a couple of months – you still wanted him, then we'd give it up as a bad job and I'd divorce you. If you decided you'd had enough of it and wanted to come back to me, then I would be prepared to talk that over. I know it isn't a pretty idea, but the alternatives are to divorce you right away, which I don't want to do; or to have you back half-hearted, which I won't. What d'you say?'

There was a long silence. Then Jill said slowly, 'Well . . . of course – from my point of view it gives me just what I want – a chance to get it out of my system and – and finished properly and neatly. But how about you? Could you – take it?'

'I don't know. I can try. Anyhow I'm not just offering you a nice holiday with a guaranteed open-armed welcome at the end of it. I might find being without you such a relief that even if you wanted to come back I wouldn't have you. That's the chance you'd be taking.'

'He's going to Spain in about ten days' time. The obvious thing would be for me to go too – if we were going to do this.'

'That's up to you. I don't even want to know where you go or what you're going to do. As far as I'm concerned you'd simply have left me. I should take no action for two months. After that, unless we'd arranged something that we both wholeheartedly wanted, I should just divorce you, and that would be that. The only thing I'm offering you is the chance, if this *did* happen to be just a nonsense, to avoid mucking up both our lives over it. That's the most I can do for you now, my dear.'

We went down to Crossways the next day. It had been agreed that Jill should see Bule at once and tell him the position. She went off in the car the following morning without our saying another word about it, and I assumed that that was where she had gone. I had taken a fortnight off from the office for our Paris trip, and we had only used five days of it, so I decided not to go back until things were a bit clearer. While she was out, I pottered round the glass houses.

Jill came back about midday. As she got out of the car I saw that she looked worried, and my first thought was that Bule was probably fighting shy of the sort of show-down that I was suggesting. The Honbill never liked being inconvenienced.

Jill came into the lounge. I said, 'Well – how did it go?'

She chucked her gloves down and said, 'Rather bloody.'

'You don't mean to say that the love of your life doesn't *want* to take you to Spain?'

She looked surprised and said, 'Oh that? Oh no – that's all right. But there's still some mess going on about the Pearce business.'

I had almost forgotten about that and I was startled.

I said, 'What sort of mess?'

'Well, apparently Eddie's been nosing round and checking up on people locally, and there's some question of what Lee's saying.'

'Who's Lee?'

'Bill's chauffeur.'

'How does he come into it?'

'I don't know. Bill was rather maddening about it, and wouldn't tell me properly. But he says he thinks he ought to see you.'

I said, 'That's a trifle awkward in the circumstances.'

'I know. I said so, but he seemed to be pretty worried about it. Anyhow, I was to ask if you'd ring him. He'll come here, or you can go there, just as you like.'

I thought for a bit and said, 'All right. But before I do, I'd better just know how we stand about our own affairs. Is he taking you to Spain?'

'Yes. If you think that's a good thing to do.'

'I don't. I think it's a very bad thing to do. But I don't see what else there is for it. What did he say?'

'Oh, you know what he is.' Jill sounded rather tired and disillusioned. 'You can never really pin him down or – or find out what he really thinks about anything important. He just skates about on the surface.'

'Yes.'

'He says it'd be lovely and so on. But I don't think he sees what's involved for me.'

'Or doesn't choose to.'

She shrugged. 'Maybe. Anyhow he says he'll take me.' She hesitated. 'I nearly told him to go to hell at one point.'

'Why didn't you quite?'

'I don't know,' she said moodily. She got up and picked up her gloves and bag. 'But then I don't know any bloody thing at the moment. I'm a complete mess. Anyhow, will you ring him?'

I rang up Bule and arranged to go out to his place that evening. When I got there he was standing on the steps with his hands in his pockets looking longer and more gracefully boneless than ever. It struck me that he had come out like that because he thought it would be easier and less embarrassing than having me shown in in the usual way. But if he was embarrassed, nobody would have noticed it.

When we got inside I said, 'What's all this about the Pearce business?'

He said, 'You'd rather talk about that first?'

'I understood it was what you wanted to see me about.'

'Yes.' He lit a cigarette and looked at it thoughtfully. 'Well, James – we appear to be in a slight spot. In your Sherlock Holmes period, you followed the normal practice of the Master by throwing out a hint to the local Lestrade – to wit Eddie – that he might check up on the movements of local cars on the night that Pearce was knocked down. Yes?'

'Yes.'

'Well, Eddie has been doing just that, and while you were away he came to me. Now you remember we agreed that my movements with my car should be – left pub just after six, returned here, changed, received telephone call from you just before six-thirty and later went to your place just after seven. In other words, at the time when Pearce was hit, I was here, and the car was in the garage.'

'Yes.'

'So I told Eddie that, and he went away perfectly satisfied – and indeed, as far as I know remains so. But now comes the snag. I have a chauffeur – one Lee. Lee is not only a bad chauffeur but a very bloody man, and he's under notice. Lee saw that scratch on the car – in fact he patched it up. It also happens that he was in the car with me in the village when I told Eddie the story of my movements.' Bule took the cigarette out of his mouth and looked at it thoughtfully. 'Later,' he said gently, 'Lee comes to me and in the politest way in the world informs me that I seemed to be making a slight mistake about the

123

times . . .' He raised his eyebrows at his cigarette, '. . . because it happens that he, Lee, came up here at half-past six and the car wasn't here then. He seems to think that this is an important piece of information, and he wishes to make it not only important but valuable.'

'You mean he's trying to blackmail you?'

'Oh, nothing like *that*, James – nothing like that. Lee's obviously an old hand at the game. He just thinks, very politely, that I've made a slight mistake, and perhaps Eddie would like it corrected, and don't I feel that perhaps I – or even he – had better correct it?'

'What did you say?'

'I told him to buy himself a watch that kept better time. But as he persisted, I eventually told him that I would check on my movements to make sure I was right. Apart from everything else, I wanted time to think about it. It was rather a facer when he brought it out. God knows what he was doing here at half-past six anyhow. A bit of petty thieving I should guess. He steals like a jackdaw, anyhow.'

'Are you sure of that?'

'That he steals? Lord, yes. That's one of the reasons for firing him. But I can't actually prove it.'

'How much do you think he really knows?'

'My guess is that he knows nothing whatever except about the scratch, and that the car wasn't here; isn't sure whether he's on to something or not; and is simply trying it on. As far as that goes, the thing is to ignore him. But if he goes to Eddie, it must make Eddie interested in my car, which I don't want, for obvious reasons. So what I think we've got to do is to stop him from going to Eddie. That's where you come in.'

'You mean the telephone call business?'

'Yes. And more than that. He's a vicious little rat, and he

hates me. If he can make mischief he will, even if it's ineffective mischief. If I tell him about the telephone call he may realise that his story's no good, but he'll still tell it, just for fun, and that might lead to complications. What we've got to do is to frighten him out of it.'

'How?'

'Well, there's no doubt that he'd like to try a bit of blackmail, given the slightest encouragement. If we could get him to pop *that* question in the hearing of a respectable magistrate like you, we should have him cold. At least he'd think so. He's very stupid, luckily.'

'But he'd never do it before a witness.'

'Of course he wouldn't. You'd have to be behind the arras. In fact I thought you'd better be in there.' He waved an ivory hand towards a curtained alcove, and grinned at me. 'Oh, come, James – don't look like that. I thought *everybody* had always wanted to hide behind something, listen to the villain talking and then appear dramatically? The Unseen Witness and so on?'

I said, 'I'm afraid I'm hardly in the mood for that sort of thing just at the moment.'

Bule raised his eyebrows and said, 'Well, well – that's a bit unfortunate, isn't it?'

I was so far away from the whole story, after the last few days, that it was on the tip of my tongue to say, 'Why the devil should I go through a lot of nonsense like that to get you out of a mess?' Then I suddenly remembered. I think he saw what was going through my mind, because he said, 'After all, I'm not exactly asking you to do this for *me*, James. I thought we had a mutual interest in avoiding trouble over this affair. If yours has disappeared because of anything that's happened, just say so.'

'What d'you mean?'

'If you're no longer interested in keeping Jill out of

trouble, then I must do my best by myself. I should quite understand. And I expect she would, too.'

I said, 'Look – do you realise what you're doing to that girl?'

'I'm just trying to keep her out of a nasty mess.'

'I don't mean over that. I mean what you're doing over – over her whole life?'

He spread out his hands. 'I'm not doing anything. I'm merely trying to be accommodating. That's my lazy, good-tempered nature. My difficulty is that I can't find out what anybody wants for ten minutes together.'

'You know perfectly well that you're letting her muck up her whole life for – for a piece of nonsense.'

'What d'you mean – "letting" her? How can I stop her? After all, James, Jill isn't fifteen. Presumably she knows what she wants.'

'She hasn't any idea.'

'Well, then, surely it's up to you to tell her, if you know? Personally, I don't go in for arranging other people's lives for them. I have enough trouble arranging my own. Anyhow, I gather that this proposition that was put to me this morning about going to Spain was your own idea? Well, what do you expect me to do about it? Say I won't take her? Why should I, when I can't imagine anything pleasanter?'

'And the fact that it'll be pleasant for you is all that matters? You don't care what it does to her?'

Bule got up and fumbled in the cigarette-box. 'But I don't *know* what it'll do to her, my dear man. It isn't my business. I probably shouldn't have proposed it myself, since I gathered that you'd gone to Paris to get together and that I was a thing of the past. But if people offer me something I want, it's no use for them to expect me to say

"No." I'm not like that and don't profess to be. I have none of your pleasure in hurting myself – or other people.'

He was standing there in his slack-muscled way looking down at me. Then I had jumped up and hit him. It is the only time in my life that I have hit anybody so instinctively that it seemed to happen without my volition. It was as though my fist had hit him without orders from the higher command. I have always known since what murderers mean when they say that they killed somebody without meaning to. If I had had a revolver or a chopper in my hand I should probably have shot him or split his head open in the same blank, mindless way. Even so, something must have made me avoid the carved ivory face, because I hit him very hard in the chest, and he staggered back so that the arm of his chair caught behind his knees, and he sat down with a crash in the chair sideways, with his long legs dangling over the arm.

He sat there for a moment looking startled and shaken. Then slowly he smiled up at me and said, 'Yes, James. Yes. I see your point. But what are we going to do about Lee?'

Bule was away about twenty minutes. Then he came back and said, 'Lee now awaits us in my study. I've told him that since the business about these times still seems to be on his mind, he'd better tell his story to a magistrate – to wit you. He seems a bit put out. I suppose he's beginning to realise that there's no money in it.'

I said, 'All right. I'm ready.'

'No hurry. We must give him time to arrange Act II for us. A gold match-case is in the top drawer of my desk, which is slightly open. I don't think he can miss it, and once it's in his pocket we've got him. But we must give him a minute or two.'

'Supposing he doesn't take it? It's a damned risky thing to do.'

'He'll take it all right. I tell you, the man's a complete jackdaw. If anybody yawned in front of Lee, he'd have a grab for their false teeth.' Bule lit a cigarette. 'This is a much better idea than the blackmail thing, James. I can't imagine why I didn't think of it before. If we'd caught him trying to blackmail, we could have scared him, but he still might have thought he's got something on me. As it is, he'll both see that his story's no good *and* want to get out of the district good and quick.'

I got up and said, 'Well, come on – let's get on with it.'

Bule sighed and said, 'I wish you had a greater capacity for enjoying yourself, James. All right. I should think he'd have pinched it by now.'

Lee looked more like a musician out of a cheap dance hall than a chauffeur. He was a small, rather dapper man with a thin, sallow, rather Latin face, a hooked nose, and shiny black hair worn with sideboards that came about two inches down his cheeks. He looked remarkably nasty, and that somehow made it all easier.

Bule introduced him to me and went and sat down at his desk. He didn't look at me, but I saw his eyelids droop slightly and I knew the match-box had gone all right. Bule stubbed his cigarette out and said, 'Well, now – what I've brought you here for, James, is this – I made a statement to the police the other day about my movements on the night that Joe Pearce was killed. In that statement I said that I got home before half-past six. Lee seems to feel that that statement was incorrect.' He cocked an eyebrow at Lee.

Lee said. 'Well, I don't see how that could be right, Mr Bule, because . . .' He spoke very quickly in a Cockney accent mixed with something else. I think perhaps he wasn't English. Bule held up a hand. 'Wait a minute . . . I've tried to explain to him, James, that I am quite sure of my times, but it still seemed to be worrying him, so I thought he'd better talk to you, both as a magistrate, and as a person who can confirm what I say.' He nodded to Lee. 'Now fire away.'

The little man said in his queer ugly gabble, 'Well, you understand Mr Bule, I don't want to make no trouble but I'll swear the car wasn't here when I left near on twenty to seven.'

'Then you must have got the time wrong.'

'No, sir. I don't see how that can be.'

'Why not? We all do it at times?'

'Ah, but I'd put my watch right by the six o'clock news an' I happened to look at it as I went out and it was near on twenty to seven an' there was no car here then, not when I looked at my watch.'

Bule said rather irritably, 'But, my dear man, this house is full of electric clocks. They keep excellent time. I myself was watching the time because I was going out, and Mr Manning confirms that he spoke to me here just before half-past six. So the only possible answer is that if you looked at your watch and it said twenty to seven, your watch must have been wrong.'

'But I put it right by the six o'clock news, Mr Bule.'

'Then what d'you suggest happened?'

'Well, if I might suggest it, Mr Bule, perhaps you made a mistake.'

'And Mr Manning?'

'Well, perhaps he didn't know to ten minutes when he phoned you, Mr Bule.'

Bule said, 'What time was it when you spoke to me, James?'

I said, 'Nearly twenty-five past.'

'There could be no mistake about that?'

'No. I had a train to catch at six-thirty, so I had to be watching the time.'

Bule raised his eyebrows at Lee and said, 'You see?'

There was a pause. Then the little man said sullenly, 'Well, I don't know I'm sure, Mr Bule, but that car wasn't here because I looked . . .'

'In fact everybody's making a mistake but you?'

'That's right, sir.'

Bule looked at me and spread out his hands in a helpless gesture.

I said, 'Have you got your watch on you now, Lee?'

'Yes, sir.'

'Mind if I see it?'

He pulled it out of his waistcoat pocket. It was a very old cheap affair, with a luminous face. I said, 'It keeps good time, does it?' 'Yes sir.' 'Never gains?' 'Never, sir.' I glanced at the watch and at my wrist and said, 'Well, it's eight minutes fast now.'

Bule smiled. The little man said anxiously, 'Ah, but I'd put it right by the news, sir.'

'That evening?'

'Yes, sir. Just before.'

'You'd been listening to the radio?'

'Yes, sir. An' then the news started . . .'

Bule said, 'What programme had you been listening to?' Lee hesitated. Poor little devil, he only had to say he didn't know. He probably *had* put his watch right by the radio. But he was the sort that has to lie to improve his story, even if there's no point in it. He said firmly, 'Some jazz music or other.'

Bule's eyebrows went up. He said, 'You're sure of that?'

'Yes, sir.'

Bule got up and went over to a corner. He said, 'Well, here are all the programmes for the last six weeks . . . let's see – what date was . . . ?' He opened a copy of the *Radio Times*. 'Ah, – here we are – Phil Lucy's Band with Kay Harrington in Dance Hall Memories. That it?'

'Yes, sir,' with pathetic eagerness.

'You're absolutely sure that's the programme you heard and that after it you set your watch by the six o'clock news?'

'Yes, sir.'

Bule said, 'Well, that programme took place two days later, just before the seven o'clock news on the Light Programme.' He tossed the *Radio Times* on the desk and looked at me with a shrug.

Lee said feebly, 'It was something like that I'd swear . . .'

Bule said, 'My dear man, I suggest to you that you're simply thinking of some other evening, and happen to have got it mixed up with this one. Wouldn't you think so, James?'

I said, 'It certainly looks like it.'

Lee shook his head and muttered something about, 'Well, Mr Bule, I could swear . . .'

Bule said, 'But you *mustn't* swear to these things when you're not really sure. Anyhow, don't let's waste any more time on it. Satisfied, James?'

I said, 'Oh, yes. Lee's obviously made a genuine mistake.'

'Of course he has. Satisfied, Lee?' Then, as the chauffeur hesitated '. . . because if you're not I'm afraid there's no more I can do about it.'

'No, sir,' said Lee sullenly. He hesitated again for a moment and then said shortly, 'That'll be all you want me for then?' The tone was half insolent, and I saw Bule's eyes open a little wider. He smiled very sweetly and said gently, 'Well, no, Lee. There is just one other thing – I'd like my gold match-case back.'

He held out his hand.

There was a moment's pause and then Lee said, 'What match-box, Mr Bule?'

'The one you've got in your pocket that you pinched out of this drawer while I was out of the room.'

I saw the little man's Adam's apple move convulsively. He said rather breathlessly, 'You want to be careful, Mr Bule, making charges of stealing against somebody who never . . .'

'You say you didn't take it?'

'I haven't taken nothing. I'm not a thief, Mr Bule, and you'll get yourself into trouble accusing me . . .'

Bule shrugged his shoulders. 'All right . . .' He turned to me. 'James, you're a magistrate. How does one handle these things? There was a gold match-case in this drawer when I went to fetch you. When I came back it had disappeared. This man was here alone, and I want to charge him with stealing it. What do I do?'

I said, 'You're quite sure it disappeared while you were out of the room?'

'Oh, yes.'

'I see. Well, if Lee says he hasn't taken it, you can suggest that he turns out his pockets and lets himself be searched.'

'Fair enough. What about it, Lee?'

Lee's face had gone a queer colour that reminded me of yellow oilskin. He said more quickly than ever, 'You got no right to search me; you touch me that's an assault; you'll get yourself into trouble . . .'

I said, 'You mustn't search him by force, of course. If he won't let you do it voluntarily, and you feel sure he's got it, the only thing to do is to send for the police and charge him.'

Lee stood there just looking from one of us to the other and gulping. I suddenly felt uncommonly sorry for the poor little rat. I said curtly, 'If you *have* got Mr Bule's match-case, Lee, I should advise you to give it up at once.'

He said, 'I ain't got it,' almost inaudibly. Bule shrugged and said, 'All right, Lee. As you like.' He went across and lifted the telephone. As he did so, Lee took a quick step forward and put the match-case down on the desk as though it was red hot. I never actually saw him put his hand in his pocket to get it. It was a rather unpleasant engine-turned gold affair with Bule's monogram on it. Bule said, 'Ah – thank you,' and picked it up. He stood for a moment tossing it from one hand to the other and looking at Lee. The chauffeur was breathing heavily and staring up at him with his head slightly on one side, looking curiously animal.

Bule said, 'I suppose I ought to charge him, James?'

'I think you must. A lot of these people who go round getting jobs and stealing have got records a yard long . . .' It was a pure shot in the dark, but if you saw Lee and heard him, you felt it couldn't miss. It didn't. The little man started to talk very fast in a very low voice, so that I only heard about one word in ten. But from the way he looked and the bits I did catch, I gathered that this was his standard give-me-another-chance patter. From the pace he went through it, I should guess he'd used it a good many times before.

Bule said wearily, 'Yes, yes. Three wives and seventeen children.' He went to the telephone and said to me, 'Who shall I get on to? Eddie or Sergeant Groves?'

'I should think Groves.'

Lee took a step towards him. He was still talking in the rapid mutter. I caught, 'never regret it and God bless you when a man's down . . .' There were some bits that we hadn't done yet, but the whole thing was making me feel sick so I made a cut and said, 'Just a minute . . .' Bule turned with the telephone in his hand. I said, 'It's your affair, but is it worth the trouble?'

'How d'you mean?'

'Well, of course, he's a little rat, and you ought really to give him in charge. But as it happens you've got the thing back...'

Lee had stopped talking as soon as he understood me. He looked from one of us to the other in the moment's silence.

Bule said in surprise, 'You mean – let him get away with it?'

'Well, it's all wrong, of course, but...'

Bule stood and looked thoughtfully at the little man for several seconds. Then he sighed, and slowly replaced the telephone. Walking across, he took out his wallet, counted out ten pounds, and put the wallet back in his pocket. 'You are due to leave,' he said very grimly, 'in just under a fortnight's time. Here is ten pounds in lieu of that fortnight's wages. I will give you exactly an hour to get out, and if you're anywhere where I can get at you after that, I'll give you in charge. And you can thank Mr Manning for getting you this chance. Now get out – and quick.'

Lee took the notes and looked at them stupidly, almost as though he was afraid of them. Then he started the rapid mutter again, and again I heard, 'Never regret it.' Bule put a hand on his arm, led him to the door and opened it. The little man flinched as though he thought he was going to be kicked. But Bule just led him into the hall and let him go, making a vague gesture after him like a man driving cows.

Bule came back into the room and turned to me with a wide grin and those boyish eyes. He said, 'Admirable, James. Mr Manning, as the magistrate, gave a most polished performance. I particularly liked the mixture of contempt and compassion in the last bit. I don't fancy he'll be calling on the police for a bit.'

I said, 'Poor little devil.'

'Yes, yes, I know. And what makes it more pathetic is that over that business of the time he was telling the truth, poor sweetie, which is a thing he hardly ever does. Still, he's got ten pounds without doing any work for it, and I suspect he's picked up a good few trifles from about the place, so he hasn't done too badly. Now I think we've earned a drink.'

I said shortly, 'Not for me, thanks. I must be off.'

He smiled gently. 'All right, James. As you like. And thank you for your help.'

Bule had a positive genius for putting one in the wrong.

9

I didn't see Bule again before he and Jill went to Spain about a week later. I did my best not to see Jill either. Being back at the office kept me away all day, and I spent most nights in town. Whenever we were together, Jill talked as though she was very unhappy about going away with Bule. She didn't want to go – it was absurd – she didn't like leaving me alone and so on.

Oddly enough, I fancy that the only part of all this that had any sincerity behind it was not liking to leave me alone. Jill herself has a horror of loneliness, and however little she might have loved me, she would not have wished me that. For the rest, the prospect of going to Spain with a maiden aunt, let alone with Bule, would have been a big attraction. All the apparent resistance of the idea was simply the old game of getting me to take responsibility for the decision.

I suppose they saw one another quite a lot during that week. I never asked, and Jill didn't mention it. From the time we got back from Paris, I acted as though we had already parted for all practical purposes, and that what she did was no concern of mine. Not wanting her to be dependent on Bule, I paid some money into her account. Apart from that, I washed my hands of the whole business.

I have often wondered since about this decision to let her go away with Bule. But looking back, I still don't see anything else I could have done – at least, anything that would have been any use to me. If I seem to have acted oddly, it must be remembered that even now, I did not and could not think of Bule as being serious competition for my own wife – in any permanent sense. He was not a man who liked or wanted permanency. Sooner or later, even Jill must see that though he might give her some things that I couldn't, he didn't even *want* to give her most of what she expected from me. I had decided that this was an affair in which Bule was practically bound to win all the battles, but I was bound to win the war, if only because he wasn't really fighting seriously.

It was some time in the first half of May when Jill went off. They had arranged to go to London separately, meet there, go to Paris, and fly more or less straight on to Madrid. I drove Jill to the station. She was looking very pretty, and I couldn't help thinking that she didn't look a day older than she had done when we went on our honeymoon. This seemed only fair, since she certainly didn't appear to be much older in any other respect.

We didn't say very much in the car. By that time there wasn't much worth saying. I only knew that for my part, the sooner she was gone the better. She turned her head and looked at me several times as we drove. But I kept my eyes on the road, and when she put a palm upwards on my knee, which she had often done before when we were driving, I took it in my left hand for a few moments, and then put my hand back on the wheel when we came to a corner. I knew the protestations were coming sooner or later. All I wanted was to make it as short as possible. As long as the train wasn't late, it could only be a few minutes.

As we stopped in the station yard Jill said, 'Jim – are you sure you know what we're doing?' I said, 'No, darling, but I must find out.'

'Then why do we have to do it?'

'We don't. But what's the alternative?'

'Why not let's . . . why don't you come with me – now – and we'll go somewhere – anywhere . . . ?'

I said, 'Paris, for example?'

She gave what sounded like a little groan and slumped back in her seat. Then after a moment she said, 'Yes. You're quite right. Sorry. I always do that. Pure panic.'

I said, 'Get on with you, you old crook. You know perfectly well that you're going to enjoy this a lot, so don't try to kid yourself or me that you're not. Come on or you'll miss your train.'

I had timed it nicely. By the time we were across the bridge the train was in sight. As it drew up she said, 'Good-bye, darling . . .' and clung to me as I kissed her. I said, 'I don't know whether I ought to say "Have a good time." Perhaps it had better be "Come back quite well" as though you were going to a spa for your gout.'

Jill said in a low voice, 'Wait for me. Try to wait for me.' Her eyes were very bright but she didn't cry.

I said, 'Articles are left at owner's risk.'

She had a lot of baggage and the train was pretty full, but we packed her in eventually, and she even had her passport, her tickets and her money, which was almost without precedent.

There is something very odd about looking at the rear of a train as it takes somebody away from you. I am never sure whether the feeling is surprisingly emotional or surprisingly unemotional, but it has a strong and very characteristic flavour.

I am going to find it very difficult to write about the next month or so. It is one of the bits in this whole affair that have faded. I can remember the incidents – and more particularly, the lack of incidents. But nothing I can really remember justifies how I felt at the time. There was certainly nothing very complicated about it superficially. I was lonely; which I had expected; which I had been before in my life often enough; which I am now. But I know that the loneliness that I felt then was not just the loneliness that I had expected, or known before or since; not just a negative blankness, but a positive pain, which was as near being in hell as I ever want to be.

For the first week or so it was all right. I was still going up and down between home and London, and of course it was a bit dull in the evenings, and particularly at the week-end. But I played golf, and went out a good deal, and it was perfectly endurable. There were even some things about it, like getting off in the morning, that I positively liked better without Jill. I disliked sleeping without her. I always do. But I slept well enough; and if during this first week I wasn't exactly happy, I certainly wasn't very unhappy either. I got a cable from Jill, as we had arranged, just saying that they had arrived safely in Madrid. A few days later I got a very short air-mail letter giving me an address in Madrid but saying they were going south almost at once. It was the most ordinary of lovely-weather-we-stay-here-till-Wednesday holiday letters, which said nothing what-ever of interest. Certainly when that arrived, things were still all right.

And then it hit me. I have no recollection of any intermediate stage, though there probably was one. I simply remember it as though I was slightly bored but quite all right one day, and half crazy the next. At the office it wasn't so bad. The mere fact of a known routine, involving other people, and of the work that *had* to be done, kept me going. Yet although I knew what was waiting for me at home, something made me catch my usual train evening after evening, and go back and take it.

The form that it took at first was an awful mixture of

restlessness and lethargy. There were plenty of things to do about the place – all the things that I usually spent my spare time on, and enjoyed doing. But I seemed to be quite incapable of doing them. I wandered about from the glass-houses to the fruit, and from the fruit to my workshop, and from my workshop to the rose garden; and in each I saw half a dozen things that needed to be done. But I could never muster the energy to start doing any of them. Usually, if I see anything that ought to be done about the place – a fruit tree that needs spraying, or a rose that needs briar taken off it, or a gate that needs a screw put in it – I am not happy until I have done it. In fact, Jill had often said that I never had time to enjoy the place, because I was always worrying about the little jobs that I ought to be doing. Yet all this simply disappeared. I remember seeing that one of the outdoor peaches had the usual slight attack of leaf-curl. I knew quite well that half an hour's work would deal with it in that stage. I knew if it wasn't tackled then it would spread. I had plenty of time, and desperately wanted something to do. Yet I remember standing and looking at that tree, and in the end turning away and leaving it untouched, to go and look for something to do.

It was the same over reading. I had thought that with Jill away, I should have time for that vague reading that we are all going to do one of these days and somehow never do. Instead of browsing about for the thousandth time through Montaigne and Aubrey, I would settle down to those authors whom I should have read properly, and never had. I would really *read* 'Humphrey Clinker' and 'Sartor Resartus.' I would read Johnson himself, instead of just reading Boswell. I would avoid reading Shakespeare and Marlowe and really *read* Marston. That was the theory. In practice I don't think I read anything but the daily paper during the whole of that month, and I didn't read that very carefully.

Going out for dinner or a casual drink was the only thing that kept me sane. But even that had its snags. Nobody knew what had happened to Jill and me. Amongst our friends we were always regarded as completely devoted to each other. To be asked about Jill – to have to lie about where she was – these things were not helpful. Yet there was nobody I could possibly tell the truth. For when Jill came back, the whole chance of our being able to go on living in that district depended upon no one ever knowing what had happened.

Of course, it is easy to see now what I should have done. I should have stayed in town. And when I was at home, I should have filled the house with people. I should have arranged for every minute of my time to be taken up with this and that. It would have been easy enough. But I had never thought it would be necessary, and by the time I realised that it was, I couldn't do it.

And so, through my own idiocy, I was thrown back on the one fatal occupation – thinking about it all; and writing interminable letters to Jill, practically none of which was ever sent, or even finished. I have some of them still, and they make rather terrifying reading. Sometimes they are loving. Sometimes they are shockingly bitter. Most often they start off with a tremendous effort to be fair and objective, and deteriorate into a welter of pity for myself and criticism of her. If any fragment of my sense of humour had been working, I should have seen the absurdity of it – should have known that I was making a contemptible fool of myself, and that seldom can any man have made such a fuss about the simple fact of his wife preferring another man. Had I been able to talk to anyone, they might have pointed this out to me. But I couldn't see it myself, and there was no one to show me.

All I can say in excuse for these letters is that they never satisfied me, and that that was why they remained unfinished and unposted. Always, whatever I said or thought, I came up against something that disgusted me. If I blamed her, I disliked the case-making and the self-pity. If I blamed myself, the smug humbleness and general air of I'll-bear-the-sins-of-the-world turned me sick. I had told her in Paris that to talk about the 'blame' for a thing of this kind was a waste of time and beside the point. But to stick to any attitude as sane and adult as that was beyond me. Like Ma when the lion ate Albert, I seem to have been determined that '*Someone* had got to be summonsed,' and all this was an effort to decide whether it was she or I. I am thankful to say that at least it was hardly ever Bule. Either I had enough sense to see that he was only a symbol, or else for my pride's sake, preferred to think so.

I can only remember one thing in the whole of this period that really made me laugh – and that was in slightly the wrong way. One week-end I had decided that it simply wouldn't do, and that I must work or go crazy, and went out into the workshop and started to saw a big plank in half, just for the sake of sawing. While I was doing it, Doc Frewen dropped in, in the casual way he often did. I told him that we hadn't got any cases of diphtheria or broken legs about the place, and that as business we were a dead loss; but instead of going away, he came and sat on the bench and watched me sweating at this plank, and talked.

Of course, the first thing he did was to ask after Jill. I trotted out the usual cover story about her nursing a friend who was ill, and that set him off. He was very fond of her, and he proceeded to tell me how marvellous she was, and how lucky I was to be married to her.

'Jim my boy, you've a wife in a thousand.'

I went on sawing and said, 'I *haven't* got her at the moment.'

'Maybe not, but she's one in a thousand all the same.'

I said, 'I hope so, Doc. I can't believe there are many like that about.'

Doc Frewen shook his head. He was sitting on the bench with the edge of it squashing his fat thighs out even fatter, and he was looking very solemn and pompous. He said, 'No. And I'll tell you another thing, Jim – in the end you love that girl more for going and buckling in and looking after a friend like that than as though she just stayed here and fussed over you. It's right in character, isn't it?'

That did stop me sawing. I looked at him for a moment and then said, 'That's it, Doc. Right in character. Practically type-casting.'

When he had gone I threw the saw across the shed and leant against the bench and laughed until my eyes were full of tears.

I can't say that the letters I had from Jill in this period helped much. There were only two of them. In fairness, it must be remembered that she was in the middle of a holiday with her lover, and neither lonely nor depressed; and it isn't easy for people who are in heaven to understand quite what is going on in hell. They were entirely friendly and affectionate letters, and most of them were taken up by descriptions of where they had been and what their plans were. But they nearly always contained a bit that was difficult to take in my position and mood.

The first, written about a fortnight after they left, contains some observations on Seville, a joke of Bule's, and some instructions to Mrs Lewis about the laundry, and then goes on: 'Isn't it a bit dull at Crossways by yourself?

Why don't you go away somewhere amusing? Regarding us, I would rather talk to you about it than write. But frankly I do feel more and more that we have let our lives become very dull and colourless, and that this will have to be put right if we are ever going to get anywhere. I think we've taken too little trouble over finding amusing people, and things that we really *like* to do ... The same is true about money. After all, compared with most people, we are very well off, and it seems silly that we've spent so much time worrying about whether we could afford quite small things ... I feel I've got a lot of this clearer now than I have ever had it – and what is more I don't think I shall ever be afraid again to tell you what I really think ...'

Probably rather unfairly, I read this to mean that Jill (presumably from Bule) had now learnt how life should be lived, and proposed to explain it to me. I also couldn't help reflecting that at no time in my recollection had Jill ever kept within a very generous allowance; nor had we ever kept within our income.

I don't know how I replied; probably rather crossly. Jill's other letter, which is dated twelve days later, is mildly apologetic without being very reassuring.

'I'm sorry if I made you angry. Of course, I didn't mean that you'd made life dull for me. You've been marvellously kind and generous. But I think you were right when you said in Paris that I had never really told you what I wanted. I can see now that this wasn't fair, and at least I won't do that again. All I meant was that I do feel you sometimes seem to make things difficult and unpleasant and boring for yourself *on purpose*, and quite unnecessarily ...' ('Jim likes being bored' – she obviously didn't recognise the near-quotation.) 'After all, we're both still quite young and there are so many things to do and places to see ...'

In neither of these letters was there a word to suggest

that Jill felt she had acted badly, or had any regrets. In both it was assumed as a matter of course that we should continue to be married – and on her terms. In my reply to the second one I seem to have used the word 'impudence' – at least, Jill always maintained afterwards that I said her letters were impudent. If I did, it was a pompous thing to say, but in the circumstances in which I read them, they probably did strike me like that.

Oddly enough, it was neither the bland confidence of Jill's letter nor my own desperate loneliness and depression that finished my effort to hang on alone at Crossways, but a small chance incident. I went one day to a sitting of the local bench, and it happened that one of the cases before us was a man charged with driving a car when drunk, and knocking down and injuring an elderly woman. There was no question of our trying the case in full, or sentencing the man. Our job was the purely formal one of deciding whether there was a *prima facie* case against him, and whether he should be committed for trial. His version of the story was not put before us at that stage, but from the formal police evidence it was a thoroughly bad case in which there was unlikely to be any very effective defence. I had nothing to do in the matter, except to agree with the rest of the bench that there was obviously a case to go for trial. But even so, it brought back to me like a slap in the face, the whole miserable business of Joe Pearce – the wretched shoddy lying – the bluffing and bullying of Bule's poor little rat of a chauffeur, and all the rest of it. I had known well enough when I first agreed to keep it quiet, that I was putting myself in an utterly false position. But so many other things had happened that I had managed not to look at it too closely. I looked at it now – and smelt it.

And my reaction was not one of self-contempt so much as one of anger – anger with Jill. I told myself that having put me in a position where I had been forced to sacrifice everything I believed in to save her from the results of her own silliness, she had repaid me by doing me dirt with a bounder, and writing conceited letters telling me that I didn't understand the technique of life. There was a great deal of it like that – a sort of orgy of self-pity, with myself as the noble and high-principled figure, drawn down to ruin by my great love for an unworthy, etc., etc. It was about my bottom point in many ways, but it had at least two salutary results. The first was that I went straight home and got drunk. The second was that next day I arranged to move into my club.

That was just about a month after Jill left, and on the whole I think it was a good thing to do; because the next week was certainly better, even if it wasn't exactly filled with joy and singing. There were at least people to talk to, and what was even more important, people to drink with. The only snag was that I found, as I had done in Paris and since, that if I drank much, I got very angry about it all, and wanted to tell somebody. Mercifully, I never did. But I can remember going up to my room one night and realising that I wasn't completely steady on my feet, and sitting down on the side of the bed and telling myself that Jill was turning me into a drunk.

At the week-end when the club was empty, it was pretty grim, and I don't think I should have stuck it for long, if Morgan Weir and Loo hadn't turned up. As it was, I was sitting in the Café Royal having a drink and wondering how the hell to get rid of a Saturday evening, when somebody bit my ear from behind. I turned round, but in fact if I'd had five seconds to think I could have said, 'Why, hullo, Loo – hullo, Morgan,' without even looking, and without even knowing she was in England; because Loo is the only person I know who's likely to bite my ear in the Café Royal. Anyhow, there she was, looking more like the cover off a pulp magazine than ever, and roaring with laughter about having bitten my ear, and there was Morgan looking like a picture of American manhood, in clothes that didn't fit much and a hand-painted tie. They seemed glad to see me, which was pleasant, because nobody had seemed very glad to see me for some time; and for my part, as I kissed Loo it struck me that they were just exactly what I wanted at the moment.

I had first met Morgan during the war, when he was an American major with a quiet voice and a nice grin who worked in Intelligence. Then he went back to the United States and turned up again after the war having married Loo, which seemed on the face of it to be a piece of folly, if understandable in some ways. But after a time, people get reconciled about Loo, because even if she is impossible, and will look and act like a tart, she goes on doggedly enjoying herself all the time, and bullies everybody else into doing the same. Jill and I had long decided that small doses of Loo – say about one evening a year – were quite fun. And certainly this was the moment for a dose.

I said, 'I didn't know you were over. Why haven't you rung up?'

Morgan said, 'We only got in at noon, and pretty near all we've done is ring you up at places that said you were out.'

Loo said, 'Is Jilly in London?'

'Jill's in Spain.'

'She's in Spain and you're *here*?' Loo laid a hand on Morgan's arm. 'Listen to what he says, honey,' she said breathlessly. 'That guy – the one I've always wanted – and his wife's in *Spain* . . . !' She turned the huge blue doll's eyes on me, and said in a hushed voice, 'You wouldn't be feeling *lonely*, Jimmy?'

The sensible reply to this sort of question from Loo is to say, 'No. Not at all,' very firmly. But I wasn't feeling sensible, so I said, 'Yes. Very lonely.' Whereupon she flung her arms round my neck and kissed me and said to Morgan, 'And then you asked me what I wanted to come for.' She patted my hand. 'Don't worry, Jimmy darling. The Weirs have landed. Everything'll be all right now.' She then wriggled and made a loud noise that sounded like 'Eek!' and which indicated pleasure. I said, 'Loo, dear – I come to this place quite often, and I may have to come here again. So . . .'

'Why shouldn't you come here? It's a nice place. But it could be brighter. D'you think if I was to get out in the aisle there and tap a little routine, the customers'd like it?'

'The customers probably would, but the management wouldn't.'

'O.K. Whatever you say. Then can they make champagne cocktails?'

'Yes.'

'Then what are we waiting for?' She sat back and gazed at me while Morgan waved for a waiter. 'Morgan,' she said softly, 'his wife's in Spain. After all these years of waiting and longing. What d'you know?'

They were going to stay in London about a week and then go on to Venice. I said, 'It seems to me you two take about four holidays of three months each a year.'

'Holiday?' said Morgan. 'What's a holiday? I'm selling agricultural machinery.'

I said, 'Do you know Venice?'

'Not a thing. Never been there. Why?'

'Because you can't go round selling agricultural machinery there. You'll have to sell fishing nets. Or perhaps water softeners.'

Morgan said, 'O.K. Make it water softeners. I'm not proud what I do.'

'How long are you going to stay there?'

'Depends on how many water softeners I can sell. Maybe a month.'

We ordered another drink and Loo said, 'You remember my gold net pants – the ones you liked?'

I said rather indignantly, 'I don't remember anything of the sort. You're thinking of someone else.'

'Maybe you're right. Only I was going to say if it had been you who liked them I've got some now that would roll you in the aisles. Wait while I show you . . .'

I said, '*No*, Loo,' very quickly and Morgan said, 'Honey, you got this place wrong.' He turned to me and said apologetically, 'She read somewhere that Oscar Wilde used to come here.' I said, 'So he did. But that's all the less reason for her to behave like that. If you don't pull yourself together, Luella, I shan't take you out to dinner.'

Loo was one of those small American girls who look as though bits of them have been inflated with a bicycle pump to an exactly pre-determined pressure. She was wearing what Jill always called one of her brothel-smocks, which fitted everywhere it touched her as though they had put it on and then pumped her up in it. It wasn't that she didn't know any better. It was just that she liked to look like that; and what was much odder, Morgan didn't seem to mind. At dinner, she ate about as much as Morgan and I put together; and though she had come straight from America, and the Soho place where I took them wasn't in very good form, she kept saying the food was wonderful.

Morgan and I had been drinking coffee for about a

quarter of an hour, and Loo was just topping off with a large plate of raspberries and ice-cream, when she got on to the subject of Jill again.

'What's that Jill think she's doing, going off to Spain and leaving the old man alone? Why didn't you go?'

I said, 'I didn't want to.'

'Why not? Hell – everybody wants to go to Spain.'

'Not me.'

'Why not? You'd look fine in those clothes and one of those hats. Why you still about, Jimmy?'

'I couldn't get away.'

'The Jill girl gone by herself?'

'No. With friends.'

'I wouldn't let that girl go anywhere with friends if she belonged to me. Looking like that and Spaniards around in those hats. You ought to keep her on a lead, like Morgan does me.'

'You may be right.'

'And you sitting around in the what's-its-name on a Saturday night with a small gin, looking like . . .'

Morgan frowned slightly and said, 'Push it along, honey.'

She looked at him in surprise and said, 'O.K., O.K., I was only thinking . . .'

'Well, don't. Eat up your nice ice. Anyway if he'd gone to Spain we shouldn't have seen him, should we?'

Loo said, 'No. That's so,' rather soberly. She was looking from one to the other of us, slightly worried. Morgan very seldom snubbed her, and she couldn't see what she had done. It was all too difficult, and anyhow they were birds of passage and it didn't matter if they knew. I said, 'It's all right, Loo. Jilly and I have been having a bit of trouble, that's all.'

'You mean she . . . ?'

'She's pushed off to Spain for a bit – just – just to get it out of her system.'

'With – with somebody?'

'Yes.'

There was a moment's silence. Then Loo said softly, 'Oh, gosh ... My big, big mouth ...' I suddenly realised that the ridiculous great doll's eyes were full of tears.

I grinned at her and said, 'It's all right. Don't look like that about it.'

She suddenly turned to Morgan and said in a vicious voice, 'Kick my ankle. Hard.' To my surprise he moved his foot as though he was doing it. She winced and then said, 'Thanks, honey.'

Morgan said gently, 'I'm very sorry, Jim. 'Course we'd no idea ...'

'How could you have? Anyhow, seeing you two is the nicest thing that's happened to me for weeks, so don't let's waste time talking about it. How about a liqueur? Loo, darling?'

She still had tears in her eyes but she grinned back at me and said, 'Can they fix me an advocaat and cherry brandy?'

'What – together?'

'Sure. You float the cherry brandy on the advocaat.'

I said, 'I do not. I assure you I do not. But I suppose there's no reason why you shouldn't if you want to. Brandy, Morgan?'

'If you please, sir. And just a spot of Benedictine in it.' I had forgotten that Americans were like that about liqueurs.

They were staying at Claridge's, and they insisted on dropping me first at the Club. We all sat on the back seat of the cab with Loo between Morgan and me. As we got in she said, 'I'm useful for three on a seat. I squash.'

Just before we got to the Club she put her arms round me and kissed me. Morgan was looking out of the window.

Loo whispered, 'She'll come back. Of course she will. She loves you. Hell, I've been there. She won't go off with anybody else – not for long.'

I had cabled Jill that I was moving to the Club. I don't know exactly why, except that we had promised to let one another know where we were, and I didn't like her not to be able to get hold of me quickly if she wanted to. On the Monday I had a letter from her. This time it didn't tell me that I was a dull stick whom she proposed to brighten up. It was mainly a long worry about what sort of time I was having.

'It just wouldn't be true to say that I'm not enjoying this, in a way. But whenever I think about you it seems completely fantastic that I should be here while you are by yourself and hating it. I was always afraid you *would* hate it, and that's why I kept asking you if you were sure it was right. I'm so afraid now that you'll feel that I went away and left you, and never be able to forgive me. Must you stay in London? Couldn't you go and stay with somebody or go abroad or something? London's probably better than Crossways, because at least you have the Club and so on. But London can be pretty bloody I know ... Don't *not* go away because of work. Treat this as an emergency and do something that you'd like. Because apart from anything else, then you won't hate me so much ...' She didn't say much about us except, 'I'm learning a lot of things, and when this is over I think I might be a lot more worth having than I've ever been. If you can wait for me.'

She didn't say anything about when they were coming back.

I saw Morgan and Loo practically every day. They were rushing round seeing a lot of people, but we usually arranged to meet, if only for a drink, and I went to a couple of shows with them. It made a big difference – in fact, so much difference that I wondered sometimes what would happen when they went off to Italy. They were due to go at the week-end.

On the Thursday, Loo went down to the country, and I had Morgan to dinner at the Club. It was odd to have him without her. When she was there she made so much noise that I tended to forget how much I liked Morgan.

I said, 'It's a sort of cathedral hush without Loo.'

Morgan said, 'She's only fifty miles away. If we listened quietly we could probably hear her.'

'She doesn't seem to be a bit a better girl than when I saw her last.'

Morgan smiled his slow smile and said, 'Loo likes to act it out.'

'Do you ever get anybody who – who misunderstands it? I mean . . .'

He chuckled and said, 'Sure. All the time. Loo meets some guy on a train and does her stuff, and five minutes later you see him start putting his tie straight and shooting his cuffs and his line.'

'You don't mind?'

'It makes me laugh. The guys are always so pleased.'

I said thoughtfully, 'If Jilly'd acted it out a bit more, I don't think we should have had this mess.'

He said, 'No,' rather uncomfortably; then, after a pause he said defensively, 'But that's not her way. Jill's not like Loo. She's quiet.'

Later on when we were sitting over a pint of beer, I happened to say, 'By the way, just what *is* your job now? I've never really known.'

Morgan slowly took out a cigarette and lit it. 'Well, Jimmy, I told you I was selling agricultural machinery. But you say I can't be selling agricultural machinery in Italy . . .'

'You can in Italy. But I don't see how you can in Venice.'

'O.K. Not in Venice. You said I better sell water softeners. So water softeners it is.'

'Meaning what?'

'Hell, meaning I sell water softeners. Don't you understand plain American?'

It was only then that I thought of what his job had been in the war.

I said, 'Oh – I see. Sorry.'

'Come to that I don't need to be selling anything. Can't a man go on a holiday? I only put the agricultural machinery in because I thought you'd like it.'

'Anything amusing? Don't say if you'd rather not.'

He stretched himself out at great length. 'No. Not anything really. Just looking up two or three people that the boys back home want looked up.'

'D'you speak Italian?'

'Not a word. They wouldn't have sent me if I did. See, if you're an American, the best thing to-day is to go around looking like an American and talking American – and talking it pretty loud. Then you're just another American – and in most places there's plenty of those about. See?'

'You'll find plenty in Venice.'

'So they tell me.' Morgan took a pull at his beer. 'You know Venice? Know your way about there?'

'Depends on what you mean. Nobody *really* knows his way about in Venice unless he lives there, and often not then. It isn't that sort of place. I couldn't tell you all the turnings to get from the Accademia to the Colleoni statue. But I could take you there.'

'You speak Wop?'

'Just enough to get about.'

'Read it?'

'After a fashion.'

Morgan nodded slowly and drank the rest of his beer. 'Wouldn't care to come with Loo and me?' he said casually.

I was slightly startled. I said, 'What for?' rather foolishly.

'Holiday. Show us round. Be nice to have somebody who could read the menu.'

I said without conviction, 'I don't think I could get away.'

'That's up to you, Jimmy. I just thought maybe it'd fit. Jilly being away . . .'

'But you see, we have all these damned currency regulations. We're only allowed to take . . .'

'That can be fixed,' said Morgan calmly. 'My firm sells a lot of water softeners in Italy.'

'You mean you can get lira and I could pay you back in pounds?'

'I doubt you could. I don't see who you'd pay. But I can get lira.'

There was a long silence and then I realised that I must go. I said weakly, 'It's damned good of you, Morgan, but I wouldn't think of upsetting your party. After all it's Loo's holiday and . . .'

Morgan smiled and said, 'We can fix her.'

I didn't travel with them. Morgan had some things to do in Milan, and wasn't reckoning to be in Venice until the latter part of the week, so it was agreed that I should stay and clear up while they flew to Milan, and follow by train. I hate flying at the best of times, but more particularly I hate flying to Italy. Anybody can have that view of the Alps from the air, if I can have the sight of the Simplon Orient Express waiting at Calais; if I can get into it and smell the peculiar smell of it; if I can settle down in one of those peculiarly shaped, peculiarly decorated sleepers, and realise that I shan't have to move my stuff out of it until I get to Venice; if I can have that glimpse of Paris, while they get the train from the Gare du Nord to the Gare de Lyons; if I can wake up in the night during that hurtling run down to the Swiss border, and lie in my bunk feeling that the train is only touching the rails about once in a hundred yards; if I can wake up in the morning and realise that I am in Switzerland, and God helping me, that I shan't be in it long; and above all, if I can get out when the train is through the Simplon Tunnel and stops at Domodossola, and go to the station buffet and drink a cup of Italian coffee, and see people smiling and laughing as they talk, and realise that Italy still exists, and that in a queer way I still exist too.

It was odd to be making that journey without Jill – to have no one to grin at excitedly, and to remind of all those things, and to remind one of them. And when we got to Domodossola it was cold and wet as it often is. Yet the station buffet worked as it has always done; and for the first time since Jill went away, I was filled with a sense, not of happiness, but of power and confidence – almost of triumph. I knew then that I was not defeated, and that it would take more than Jill or anything she could do to defeat me.

After that the journey down to Milan, and the messing about there, and the long dull slog east across the Lombardy plains, was an anti-climax. It always is. One is tired of the train, and the last hours in the dark seem like weeks. But I got out at last, and sent my luggage on by a porter, and came up the Grand Canal by water-bus; and one still came on the Rialto Bridge as the water-bus rounded the bend, and the dim lights in the water were as they had always been.

I had not suggested that we should stay in the small hotel that I like. The first time you go to a town you don't want to be dragged off to somebody's 'little place.' Anyhow they wouldn't have liked it. So we had booked at one of the grand places at the mouth of the Grand Canal, and had rooms that looked out at Santa Maria della Salute, all proper. We had arranged to meet in the lounge at nine, but they didn't turn up until half an hour later, having gone out and lost themselves within ten minutes of arriving. I had been looking forward to meeting in that lounge, but somehow I had half forgotten whom I was to meet; and when they came in, and I saw Loo, and heard her voice bubbling greetings at me, and kissed her, it was one of the coldest and loneliest moments of my life.

10

I have never been sure whether Mr Phillips Oppenheim got his ideas of how Intelligence people behave from watching them, or if they got their ideas of how to behave from reading him; but I've never yet seen any Intelligence job, however serious, in which there wasn't a lot of colourful flim-flam that was pure Oppenheim. One of the bravest men I ever knew in the business carried a sword-stick and wore a cloak when he was off duty. I suppose that sort of thing is a perquisite of the job.

Morgan wasn't at all like that. I never knew, and don't know to this day, what he was doing. I never asked him, and he didn't talk about it, except to ask me occasionally how to get to such and such a place. But even so, there had to be a few odd things about the whole business, just to make it all nice and mysterious. There was, for example, the question of money. Instead of having a straightforward credit at a bank or a travel agency, as any ordinary tourist would have done, Morgan always had to get his money, in cash, from some improbable person who lived in a place which was hell to find, and who usually wasn't there anyhow.

I know about this part of it, because two days after we got to Venice, he asked me if I would go and get us some money. He said he wanted me to go because he didn't know how to get to the place, and because the man was an Italian who might not speak English; but I guessed that the real reason was that he didn't want to chance being seen going there. So I went by myself. The place was right down by the old Ghetto, and it turned out to be a shoddy one-room office that professed to belong to an Italian film company I had never heard of. There was only one man in it, and he seemed to be a sort of commissionaire. He was wearing a shabby uniform and badly needed a shave. But he insisted that he was the man I was looking for. Surprisingly, for an Italian living in Venice, he spoke neither English nor French; and as I didn't want to order him a meal, or tell him he had pretty legs, the limitations of my Italian were mercilessly exposed. I was very dubious when I saw him, because Morgan had given me a letter which just politely asked that the bearer should be given any money he wanted. Morgan had told me to get a million lira, and it didn't look the sort of place that could produce the price of a cup of coffee. But it was nothing to do with me, so I handed over the letter, whereupon the commissionaire nearly rolled on the floor with politeness, put his hand in his pocket, pulled out a huge wad of 10,000 lira notes, and counted out a hundred of them without turning a hair. It seemed to be rather less than half the bundle, so I suppose it was chicken feed to him. He didn't ask me to identify myself, or sign for it; so if Morgan had happened to lose that letter, and somebody had picked it up, I don't see what there would have been to prevent him from going in and asking for the total reserve of the Bank of Italy, and taking it away with him.

I found Morgan and Loo sitting in the sun in the Piazza San Marco drinking coffee. I was never sure quite how far Loo was supposed to know about Morgan's job. I noticed that he never said anything about it in front of her. So I asked her if she had had her photograph taken with the pigeons, and told her the nice passage in the old editions of Baedeker about 'Those whose ambitions lean in this direction' being able to be photographed covered in pigeons. I thought this would be too much for Loo, and sure enough she said her ambitions leant in that direction until they were nearly falling on their faces, and went off and was photographed for a long time.

When she had gone I told Morgan about the commissionaire who needed a shave.

He said, 'Fine. Well, look, Jimmy, supposing you keep a hundred thousand for drinks and so on, and I'll take the rest.'

I said, 'All right. Then that'll be roughly sixty pounds I owe you.'

'We'll worry about that later on.' He seemed to be expecting me to hand him the money. I said, 'It's a lot of paper. Hadn't we better wait till we get back to the hotel?'

He looked surprised and said, 'Why?'

'Well, damn it, this is about the most public place in Venice.'

Morgan smiled his lazy smile and said, 'Don't think that matters, does it, Jimmy? It's just money.'

So there it was. After all that fuss, I handed over nine hundred thousand lira to him, sitting outside a café with half Venice wandering about round us. Morgan looked at it and said, 'How the heck do Italians carry all this paper?'

I said, 'Not many of them have to worry much about carrying a million.' I was rather irritated about the whole thing. Loo came back trying to wipe a pigeon mess off her sleeve and said, 'My ambitions went and leant too darn far.'

It was pleasant showing them round Venice. Loo particularly liked the Colleoni memorial, and the cat in the Taverna that comes and sits up to the table with you and eats a plate of shrimps, picking them up one at a time in its paw, very delicately. When we were looking at the inside of San Marco I tried my favourite theory on them – that the whole of Venice, and the inside of San Marco in particular, is really very American indeed in spirit, only slightly earlier in date; and that when there is a mist so that you can't see the top of the Campanile, it's really very like the times when there is a mist in Manhattan and you can't see the top of the Empire State Building. But they didn't get it. I have tried this theory on Americans before, and they always think you are being sarcastic.

On the third day we had a flood tide in the morning. I had hoped we should get one, because they are always fun. Nobody does any work, and everybody who's got anything that floats gets it out, and people put duck boards across the Piazza San Marco and fall off them into the water, and large numbers of young men roll up their trousers so as to show as much very brown leg as possible, and wheel people through the water in wheel-barrows or carry them in their arms. We saw a man sitting in a flooded café with his feet up on another chair, soberly drinking coffee, with the water just about two inches below his behind. Loo had the time of her life with the young men with brown legs. Jill had always been shy of letting them carry her, because she said she was too big and it would be so shaming if they found they couldn't manage it. But Loo, being small and blonde and curved and uninhibited, was a great joy to them, and there was a lot of squabbling over who should carry her. In the end Morgan and I got tired of it and went and sat in Florian's and drank coffee while they carted her about. The water was all gone by midday and Loo turned up and asked me anxiously whether that would happen again the next day. She said that it was a mistake not to put anything about the young men with brown legs in the guide books, because it would be a great attraction to tourists.

There was a cable from Jill that evening. It said, 'Darling, delighted Venice marvellous idea love Morgan Loo and Ciros.'

It was all very well. In fact sometimes, when it was sunny and we were sitting down in the corner by the Rialto Bridge, and drinking the sort of Italian white wine that has nails in it, it was very well indeed. But there were times when I couldn't help feeling rather a drag on the party. After all, they were still very much in love; and though no two people could have been kinder, I was undeniably playing gooseberry. It didn't matter so much during the day, when I was showing them things, and taking them to restaurants, and telling them what to eat. But in the evenings, I sometimes felt that they must wish they were alone – particularly as I wasn't very bright company. Loo talks so much that anybody can be pretty silent when she is there. But it must have been pretty hard work, even for her. I tried several times to get them to go off for an evening without me, but they never would, and after a while I began to get really worried about it. Then one day we saw Lila in a bar, and I saw how to do it.

Lila was an old Venice acquaintance of Jill's and mine. We first met her just after the war. She was a blonde then, but this time her hair was quite black. I hardly recognised her, but I thought she looked better with black hair. She is always about in the bars and dance places, and Jill and I often had a drink with her. She was shy of drinking with Jill there at first, but soon got used to it. Lila is a very well-mannered girl and a great gambler. When the Casino at the Lido is open, she spends a lot of time there, and if she wins, always wants to stand you drinks. I introduced her to Morgan and Loo, and they got on very well, except that I don't think Lila really approved of Loo's clothes. I never knew a woman who did. She asked after Jill very respectfully, in very bad English. Her English never seems to get any better, despite all the Americans who come to Venice.

Of course Morgan and Loo were delighted with her. She is an attractive girl and she knows exactly how to be friendly and amusing without being a nuisance. She sat and had one drink with us, and made Loo laugh a great deal with a very nice story in broken English about nearly winning a fortune in a lottery, and then went away quietly and politely, at exactly the right moment.

When she had gone Loo said, 'Now that's a honey. Why didn't you tell us about her before?'

I said, 'I'd completely forgotten she existed.' Which was quite true. But I saw that Lila might be a way out of the gooseberry business.

So the next day I told them I was going to desert them for the evening, because I had a date with Lila. This was quite different from just suggesting that they should go out by themselves, and they seemed very pleased. I think they were mainly pleased because they thought it would be fun for me.

I didn't particularly mean to do it, in fact. I hadn't made a date with Lila. I thought I would just wander round the town and if she showed up we could have a drink together, and if not, it didn't matter. The main thing was to get Morgan and Loo away by themselves and feeling happy about it. I left them about seven, and went to a couple of the obvious places, but Lila wasn't there, so I just sat in them and drank Italian cognac, which is a peculiar drink, but one that you can get used to if you try hard enough.

The trouble was that as soon as I was by myself it all came up at me again as black as thunder. I hadn't thought much about Jill since the moment when I had met Morgan and Loo at the hotel, except at odd moments and when looking at certain things that reminded me of her. Before we came, I had wondered whether the whole thing would be hell in that way. But it hadn't been, and one of the things I had been pleased about had been finding that I still liked Venice, whether Jill was there to like it too or not. But sitting in these bars alone was quite another thing; and by eight o'clock I might have been back at Crossways in one of my worst bits. It got so bad that I decided to go and have dinner and then go home to bed, before I put myself in the lagoon. It was quite an afterthought that as I was on my way back to the hotel I looked in at the International, and found Lila sitting on a high stool talking to the barman, looking very dashing in a flame-coloured frock with a wide black belt and a black stand-up collar. I think she was bored. She seemed very glad to be collected.

The International consists of a bar about eight feet square, with a small dance-hall-cum-night-club behind it. They do their best to overcharge you, but the Italians haven't the proper gift for it like the French, or even the English, and the drinks only cost about half as much again as they do in an ordinary bar. Lila and I went inside. It looked much as usual. There were about a dozen girls, several of whom I remember having seen before. Most of them were dancing with American sailors off the cruiser that was anchored in the lagoon. There is usually an American warship of some kind in the lagoon nowadays, and when there is, a sizeable chunk of the crew is usually in the International. The rest are in the Piero.

Lila wanted champagne. I suppose she is on a percentage there. I ordered it for her, but stuck to cognac and soda myself. 'Champagne' in the International means Asti Spumanti and, though there are circumstances in which I will drink champagne, there are no circumstances in which I will drink Asti Spumanti unless they use force.

Lila said, 'The American lady with you is good.' She meant 'nice,' and even so she said it with a question mark. I don't think she could quite place Loo and you couldn't blame her. I said, 'You don't have to worry about Loo. She's rather crazy but quite harmless.'

Lila nodded and said 'American' as though that explained everything. 'They two are married?'

'Yes.'

'And the lady? Where is she? Not here, eh?' She always called Jill 'the lady' and addressed her as 'lady.' I said, 'No. She's in Spain.' I could see that Lila was a bit puzzled. Having started by finding it odd to have a drink with me with Jill there, she was now finding it odd to be having a drink with me without Jill. I grinned at her and said, 'We're quarrelling.'

Lila looked deeply concerned and said, 'You and the lady are quarrelling? Oh, *no*?'

'Yes, we are. That's why she's in Spain and I'm here. Silly, isn't it?'

She shrugged her shoulders and gazed into the distance rather sadly for a moment. I think she had thought better of Jill and me. Then she turned and picked up her glass and smiled at me over it and said, 'Ah, well. Never mind.'

At the next table there was a very young American sailor with a middle-aged woman whom I knew by sight. She was one of the regular International girls. He was a very fair Scandinavian-looking boy of about twenty, and pretty drunk, and he was trying to tell her about his home. I don't suppose she knew more than half a dozen words of English and she was barely pretending to listen. Every now and again she said, 'Yais, darling,' without ever taking her eyes off the people dancing. He was a Californian, and he was telling her about his home just outside Los Angeles, and how Pop worked in an aeroplane factory there. And he'd worked there too, before he joined the Navy, and he had two sisters, and one was married and had a baby girl. He had some photographs, and he took them out and showed them to her. She said, 'Yais, darling,' and barely glanced at them and gave them back to him. But he looked at them for a long time himself, and then he put them away and stared down at the tablecloth and went on talking about California. I thought he was crying, but she suddenly turned and whispered something in his ear, and he nodded and said, 'Sure, sure,' and they got up and danced. He wasn't very steady on his feet and his eyes were half closed, but he could still manage. It was only about ten o'clock then. I told Lila what he'd been saying and she said, 'The poor young ones. Often they wish their mothers.'

I said, 'Well, perhaps that is his mother he's with. She easily could be.' Lila looked puzzled. Her English wasn't quite good enough for that sort of thing. When I had explained, she told me about the Californian's partner, who was not, it appeared, a good sort of woman.

We danced once or twice, and Lila told me about some more fortunes that she had nearly won, and about how she had been in Rome during the war when the Germans were there.

But it was rather heavy going, and I don't think either of us was really enjoying it much. When she had finished the Asti Spumanti Lila just said firmly, 'Now we go somewhere else. This place is no good,' and we went off to the Piero, which is a good deal bigger than the International. As we came away the Californian was still stumbling unsteadily around with the matronly looking woman, his eyes half closed, and a sad far-away look on his face. I suppose he got back to his ship somehow. They usually seem to, though Heavens only knows how.

Things were a good deal brighter at the Piero. Lila

wanted more champagne, so I bought her another bottle of Asti Spumanti and told her that if she drank it she would have earned my undying respect and admiration, but that her blood was on her own head. She had stopped being quite so distressingly ladylike now, and she showed me some photographs of herself that somebody had taken. He had taken them, she explained, because he thought he could even get her work in films. Or perhaps it was as a model, I can't remember. I shouldn't think they would have got anybody work as anything. They were very large, glossy, heavily retouched prints, that made her look much plainer and coarser than she really was. Most of them were in the small-town-photographer style with Lila against a bit of ancient scenery, with a piece of tulle round her shoulders and a flower in her hand. In the only one that was at all like her, she was sitting on the arm of a chair, showing a lot of leg. She was a bit doubtful about that one, which she felt was a little common. But she was very proud of the others.

About twelve-thirty, and about half-way through the second bottle of Asti Spumanti Lila began to be very cheerful and friendly. I think she had finally forgotten about Jill and ceased to worry about the etiquette of the thing. She began to sing softly as we danced; and to squeeze my hand and to ask me to tell the band to play this and that; and when we got back to our table after one dance she asked me for a pencil and wrote something on the menu and passed it to me triumphantly. It said, 'I lov you.' I happened to say that if she drank the rest of the Asti Spumanti she would be very drunk and she said, 'Then to-morrow I will not be dronc.' I said, 'Like our song,' and hummed 'We were drunk last night, we were drunk the night before...' Lila was charmed with the words, and made me repeat them several times, till she could sing them herself. Then she insisted that she must have a note of them. I offered to write them down for her but she refused and tapped her ear and said, 'Like this,' and wrote the words out for herself. I remember that the first line ran 'Iwas dronc lasnit.'

About half-past one she had finished the Asti Spumanti and was sitting quietly for considerable periods with her eyes shut, while the band played the things she had asked for. I said, 'Listen, Lila – where do you live?'

She opened her eyes and whispered very conspiratorially, 'You see presently.' I said, 'Yes. But I don't think it would be a bad idea if you told me now.' I had a pretty clear idea of the end of this evening.

To my surprise she gave me the name of quite a sizeable hotel and then shut her eyes again. She had given up practising her English on the back of the menu by that time. I looked round the room and decided that I didn't want any more of it. I was cold sober and very wide awake, and the Piero is not a place in which to be feeling like that at one-thirty. I said, 'You know, I think the place for you is bed.' She got up without a word. She could still walk surprisingly well, though I think she was practically asleep.

It wasn't far to the hotel. That is one of the advantages of Venice – it's seldom very far to anywhere. The only thing that Lila said on the way there was, 'You have to give your passport.' I didn't see what she meant until we got to the hotel, but sure enough the night porter wouldn't let me go upstairs until I handed over my passport.

Luckily Lila's room was on the first floor. I don't think she could have done another flight of stairs. But she knew which door it was, and went and leant against it with her eyes shut, and held out her bag to me. I found the key after a while and let us in. I have no recollection of the room, except that it was big. Lila sat down on the bed, still with her eyes shut, and said, 'Darling I . . . lov . . . you,' with considerable difficulty.

I said, 'Fine. And now you're going to sleep, which will be nice.'

I had a bit of a job undressing her, because by this time, if I got her on to her feet, her knees gave way. It is very difficult to undress a person who can't stand up. Anyhow I managed it in the end, and shoved her into bed somehow, and covered her up. I think she had been asleep some time by then. There wasn't anywhere obvious to hang her frock, so I laid it across a chair. It occurred to me that it would be a charity to give her some aspirin or an Alka Seltzer or something. But I hadn't any on me, and I couldn't be bothered to go rooting about to see if she had, and anyhow she was asleep. So I just put a couple of thousand lira under some thing on the table beside her bed, and put the light out and came away. The night porter gave me back my passport in a morose way. He was a morose man.

It was beautifully cool outside, and a bright starlight night. I knew it was no good going to bed, so I walked through the Piazza San Marco and out by the pillars. The chairs were still out in front of a café there, so I sat down and looked at the lagoon and the lights on the American cruiser that was anchored down below Danielli's. It was about two o'clock by then. I don't remember what I was thinking about, but I can guess.

I must have been there about half an hour when I heard something happening over on the cruiser. A launch put off from it and came up to one of the landing-stages, and seemed to put someone ashore and then go back. A man came up from the stage. He was only about thirty yards away, and I knew his walk. I said, 'What-ho, Morgan.' Apart from the water lapping, and the distant chug of the launch going back, it was very quiet and I didn't have to raise my voice. He came over and said, 'Oh – it's you.'

I said, 'Come and sit down. It's nice here.'

'Where's your girl?'

'Out cold.'

'Drunk?'

'Very.'

'Are you drunk?'

I said, 'No. Worse luck.'

He lit a cigarette and said, 'Well – did you have a nice evening?'

'We had a wonderful time. We danced. We sang. And I didn't drink Asti Spumanti. I always have a wonderful time not drinking Asti Spumanti.'

'Why did what's-her-name get so drunk?'

'She did drink Asti Spumanti. Two bottles. All by herself.'

'Does she always do that?'

'I should think so. Why don't you sit down? It's nice here.'

Morgan said, 'No. Me for bed. It's late. How about coming home, Jimmy?'

I said, 'No. I don't think this is a bed night. And it's nice here.'

He hesitated for a moment and then said, 'O.K. Well – I'll be seeing you,' and went off. I heard his footsteps going right along the Piazza. I could have heard them farther but for the lapping of the water. I went on sitting there until dawn, watched the Ducal Palace getting pink, and then went home. I was sleepy by that time, and slept very well. I only saw Lila once again while we were there. She seemed rather ashamed of herself, and tried very hard to give me my two thousand lira back. She was a nice girl, but she hadn't the right approach to her job if she was going to make a success of it. I don't know what can have happened to her after that.

I had a letter from Jill the next day. It said again that she was very glad that I had gone to Venice, and that the thing to do was to take down my hair and enjoy myself. It also said, 'I've had several talks with Bill about us. He's always very nice and reasonable about it, but he says that he doesn't really feel there's much he can say. It's entirely a matter between us. Naturally, he doesn't want to do anything that will break us up . . .' ('Naturally' struck me as rather good.) The letter ended with a lot of affection. There was still nothing about when they were coming back. But there was a P.S. 'I suppose you didn't hear anything more about the Pearce business before you left?'

In the afternoon I got out her last three letters, and it didn't seem to me that they were getting us anywhere in particular – and certainly not together. I thought it was time to say so, so I wrote, 'When you went away it was to give you a chance to decide whether you wanted to go on being married to me or not. Judging from your letters, the answer so far is that you do, on condition that I do this and that and realise this and that. Fair enough. I realise that I've done some damned silly things, and I should try not to do them again. But I don't see any sign that you're offering anything in exchange, or feel that *you've* learnt anything. And that's hopeless. After all, you made this bust in our marriage, and you must do some putting together again if you want it. I'll help you all I can, but I can't do it by myself. The one thing I do ask you – and I've a right to ask this – is *don't* come back unless you're genuinely through with Bule, and see the whole thing for what it is. Because by definition, as long as you've got any use for him, you can't have any for me, and vice versa.'

That was when we had been in Venice about a week.

11

The next day Morgan said to me, 'How far away's Padua?'
'I don't know exactly. Not far. It's the next sizeable station up the line.'

'Well, I've got to go there. What sort of place is it?'
'Nice place. You must go and see the Giottos.'
'Sure.'
'There's a chapel that's solid with them. And a Donatello equestrian statue of a chap whose name I always forget. Have a look at that and compare it with the Colleoni. It's earlier of course. Early Quattrocento instead of late. See how much Verrochio learnt from Donatello.'

'I'll do that. I got to go to-morrow and I shall be away a night.'
'Want me to come with you?'
'No. You stay here and keep Loo out of mischief.'
I said, 'That's a tough assignment, Morgan.'
'O.K. Then she can keep you out of mischief. Got enough dough? I shall be back Wednesday.'

We were out late that night, and Morgan went off the following morning before anyone else was up. About ten I went and had a bath, and then went and knocked on Loo's door and said, 'Are you awake or up or anything?'

Loo said, 'Sure, Jimmy,' very sleepily.

I said, 'Well, I'm going across to Florian's. See you there when you're ready. No hurry.'

It was a beautiful sunny morning, and I sat for a long time drinking coffee and looking out at San Marco, and thought again that from the outside it always looks as though it might take off and float in the air. It's only when you get inside that you realise why it doesn't. What with x pounds of solid gold in the altar and all that marble, nothing could lift it. The only other people in my bit of Florian's were two English women. They were talking about local government. One said, 'So the council's hands are completely tied. We're supposed to pass these things, but in practice it doesn't make the slightest difference whether we do or not. Nobody in the district wants the scheme. It's simply imposed from Whitehall. We're a rubber stamp.'

The other said, 'My dear, it would be just the same in both Egham and Staines.'

I rather liked this, and started to try to make up a ballade with 'It'd be just the same in both Egham and Staines' as its ending line, but all I could get was the envoi:

'Princess, your clumsy and cretinous daughter
Appears to possess neither beauty nor brains?
Don't blame this effect on Virginia Water,
It would be just the same in both Egham and Staines.'

Before I could get any further I saw Loo coming across the Piazza. She was looking particularly fruity, in light blue slacks that weren't at all slack anywhere much above her knees. I said, 'Where do you *get* some of the things you wear?'

'What sort of things, Jimmy?'

'Those trousers, for example?'

'Oh, I've got a place that makes a lot of things for me.'

'But what do you say to them, Loo? How do you explain that . . .'

'Darling, I just go in and say "I want so-and-so, as improper as possible." They get it fast enough.'

I said, 'You're incorrigible, Loo.'

'Well, then they know where they are, honey. I think people like to know where they are.'

I said, 'Well, I've been told to keep you out of mischief to-day.'

She looked at me with wide-open indignant eyes. 'Me? I like that! That wolf goes off to Padua, and leaves me looking at cathedrals and thumbing a guide book and . . .'

'This afternoon we'll go and look at the collection of illuminated manuscripts up above here. They're magnificent, and most of the best ones are English.'

Loo took my hand. 'Sure,' she said cordially. 'We'll do that. That'll show him.'

We spent a surprisingly pleasant day. I had never had Loo to myself for more than ten minutes before, and I found that by herself she was much less exhausting than one would have expected. Perhaps she was playing it quietly for my benefit. Apart from clamouring to buy a large fish in the market because it had a friendly face, and striking up a violent flirtation with a handsome young non-English-speaking man of uncertain nationality in the Accademia, she was quite restrained; and after lunch we sat in the sun for nearly an hour, hardly speaking a word. In almost any other country in the world I shouldn't have cared to take her about in that get-up. There would have been too much risk of having to hit somebody. But in Italy, even the loungers have a certain sort of good manners, and though Loo's trousers provoked a lot of flattering interest, it never became vocal. All the same, I was relieved when she went back to the hotel and changed after tea.

In the evening she wanted to go and eat a dish of shrimps with the cat, so we did that, and what with one thing and another, the day went by, and it was nine o'clock before I even noticed it. We were sitting in a bar and I was drinking cognac and Loo was working her way through various flavours of Aurum when she said, 'You never told me how you went with your girl the other night.'

I told her. She listened, looking rather solemn, and when I had finished she said, 'Sounds like a lot of fun.'

'It was all right. It was nice sitting by the lagoon.'

Loo nodded. 'Sure.' She puckered up her face into a curious expression, so that for a moment I thought she was in pain. Then I realised that she was only thinking. Probably she didn't do it very often, and it called for real effort. After a while she said, 'Listen. Jimmy – you don't have to, but you've never told me anything about it – about you and Jill. And I don't get it.'

'What don't you get, my dear?'

'How come. What's it all about. You don't have to say if you'd rather not. But . . .'

I said, 'You ask me questions and I'll try and tell you the answers.'

'She's gone off with this guy?'

'Yes.'

'What sort of guy?'

'Very charming. Good company.'

'Good looker?'

'Yes. Very tall. Pale. What are usually called well-cut features.'

'Got money?'

'Plenty. Much more than I have.'

'Hell, the girl's crazy. What's he do?'

'Nothing. He doesn't have to. He collects coins.'

'And women?'

'I should think so.'

'Does she think she's in love with him?'

'In a way.'

'I guess I know which way. Why does she think that?'

'I think she's bored with me. She thinks I'm dull.'

Loo looked at me for a few seconds with the big china-blue doll's eyes. 'I can imagine that,' she said frankly.

'Thank you, my dear.'

'You're not, but you might make a girl think you were. See what I mean?'

'Yes. I think probably I *am* dull anyhow. She also thinks I want to improve her.'

Loo shook her head. 'That's bad. Do you?'

'Yes.'

She hesitated and then said, 'Well, hell – it doesn't matter. Morgan wants to improve me if it comes to that.'

'No he doesn't. He likes you like you are, poor sap.'

'Don't you like Jilly like she is?'

'Not like she is at present.'

'But before this? You liked her fine.'

'Yes. But there was a lot going on inside that I didn't know about. And I don't like that.'

'You expect a hell of a lot, don't you, mister?'

'Yes.'

I bought some more drinks. Loo said, 'How did all this break?'

I told her. Not the Pearce stuff, but everything else. I tried to keep it fair, and it wasn't too bad, though there was an edge on it at times. When I had finished Loo said, 'Well, well, well . . .' and had a pain again for a while. Then she said, 'It's no business of mine, and everybody knows I'm the dumbest thing on the Eastern seaboard. But why did you have to send her off like that? Why didn't you just put her across your knee?'

I said, 'I only put people across my knee for amusement.'

'I'll get that down in my memo book. But wouldn't it have been the best thing?'

'I don't want a wife who'd rather be with somebody else.'

'You certainly want a *lot*, mister. So she's to be married to you for fifty years and never look at another man?'

'Not at all. I tell you – I didn't care at first. I wasn't even jealous. It was doing me dirt after I'd tried to be nice about it that got me.'

Loo sighed. 'Darling,' she said, 'let's face it. You played this hand with your left foot.'

'Yes?'

'Yes and yes. First of all, what right had you not to be jealous? Hell, a girl's got a right to a husband who's jealous.'

'I thought of that. But I just wasn't.'

'But honey, you could have broken the crocks and raised a shout. There's nothing in it. Anybody can do it.'

'I dare say I could have. But I wasn't jealous, so why should I?'

Loo sighed again and said, 'O.K. Push it along. Then take this doing you dirt stuff. You got that all wrong. There's the boy and she likes him and he's given her a good time. Of course she'll pop back for more when you aren't looking. Who wouldn't?'

'After she'd been very sweet and loving to me the night before?'

'Well, for Pete's sake – what d'you expect she'd do? Spit in your eye? You're her meal-ticket, aren't you? Anyhow, I expect she liked you fine that night. I bet she likes you fine right now. But the other guy was her fun just then.'

'And her fun was as important as that?'

'Honey,' said Loo patiently, 'get this into your head – women are women. See? Not men. See?'

'Granted.'

'Granted, hell. You don't grant a darn thing in the way I

mean.' She leant forward. 'Listen – when you talk about "honour" and "doing you dirt" and so on in a thing like this, you're talking about something no woman understands.'

'Oh, come, Loo . . .'

'Let me finish. I don't say she hasn't got *her* sort of honour and *her* sort of dirt, but it's different from yours. You men all talk to us girls about honour and the way you look at it, and we say, "Yes, honey" and "Sure" and "How right." But we know it doesn't mean a thing to us.'

I said rather sarcastically, 'This is fascinating. Tell me about your sort of honour. Does it include double-crossing your husband, and playing penitent, and then going and doing it again as soon as his back's turned?'

'It could.'

'Very convenient sort of honour.'

'Not always. Because it can also mean not doing a hell of a lot of things that you could get away with all right.' Loo put on her agonised face. 'See, Jimmy darling, you start off and you say, "This is right and that's wrong," about things before they ever happen. And then when they do happen you sort of look it up in the gag-book and you find it under "Right" or "Wrong," so you do it or don't do it. But a woman doesn't *have* a gag-book. She just ad-libs as she goes along.' She shook her head thoughtfully. 'There's practically nothing you could ask me that I could tell you was right or wrong just – just by *itself*. But you put me where it was all happening, and I'd tell you fast enough whether it was right or wrong from the *feel* of it.'

'Circumstances alter cases, in fact?'

'Sure. And the people. And the time. And how you happen to feel. And what clothes you're wearing. And if the help's in a bad temper.'

'It's a nice flexible morality, my dear.'

'Why not? You can't have it all in the book, because the book's not big enough.'

I took a drink and thought about it. I said, 'Well then, according to you, Jill's acted entirely rightly, properly and honourably throughout, because it felt right to her; and I'm just a poor stooge of a male that doesn't understand. Fine. So what do I do about it? Stand around saying "Bless you, my children"?'

Loo said, 'Now wait a minute. I never said she'd done right. But let's look at the facts. There are plenty of women about who'll two-time anybody. But Jilly's not a bitch. You know it. I know it. Everybody knows it. Right?'

'I don't think she's a bitch. But I think she's a fool.'

'Could be. But what I'm getting at is – if she's done this and we know she isn't a bitch, it must be because there's been a mistake somewhere.'

'I don't know how you work these things out.'

'I'm as surprised as you. Well, what was the mistake? Clear enough. It was ever getting into bed with this guy in the first place.'

I said sarcastically, 'I expect it "felt right."'

'No, it won't have done, because doing that for the first time never does – quite. But there was something made her do that, and *after* that it all follows. See, honey, you got it just the wrong way round. A man's got a right to be mad with his wife if she gets into bed with another man, because that may be starting something big, and there oughtn't to be any need for it anyway. But once it's all started, it's no good being mad at her because she promises not to do it again and then does. Because once she's started and found it's fun, she'll promise anybody Brooklyn Bridge for a Christmas present if it'll give her a chance to go on. I would myself. Because by that time it *does* feel right.'

'You mean that if I was going to make a fuss I ought to have made it before?'

'Sure. A good loud fuss, pulling her round by the hair. Then she might have remembered that you're her man. But if you stand around being all reasonable and civilised and appealing to her honour and decency and so on, you're nothing but her husband. And what's a husband but a meal-ticket?'

I said, 'You make marriage a bit commercial, don't you?'

'Well, snakes alive, honey, isn't it? Unless you're a career wife, which isn't any sort of wife at all, you're hired to be around when your husband wants you. You sell exclusive rights in you, including film, radio, and shop show-cards. In return you're fed and clothed and so on. If that isn't a commercial deal, what is? If you happen to love him and he happens to love you – fine. But you can do that without being married. There's nothing commercial about love. But there's a hell of a lot that's commercial about marriage.'

'What you're saying is that I acted like a husband instead of like a lover?'

'Correct.'

'And it's fair to cheat your husband, but not your lover?'

'Not *fair*. But you might do it. Whereas you wouldn't ever do the other thing.' Loo frowned effortfully. 'Don't you think that because I say marriage is commercial, I mean everybody has to cheat. You're in business and you don't cheat. Why not? Because you know it's a mug's game. Because you know you can do better by playing it straight. But if you get in a mess, you might pull a fast one in business, that you wouldn't on a friend.'

'But why did Jill get her business in a mess?'

'I don't know, honey. But maybe she'd been trying to play it *too* straight.'

'How?'

'Well, has Jilly ever looked at another man before this?'

'Not as far as I know. She's always been absolutely loyal.'

'Sure. Well, perhaps if she'd noticed whether any man she met had two eyes, or whether he was tall or short, or was a nice guy or a heel, this wouldn't have happened. But she didn't. We all noticed that she didn't. There was only Jimmy in all the world. And it was such a shock to her to find there *was* another man but you, that it knocked her all endways.'

I said, 'You might be right there. I said something rather like that to Morgan the other day.'

'To Morgan? He ought to know, poor old sap. Honey, can't you imagine what they say about me – the women? "That poor nice guy, Morgan, married to that fast little so-and-so. What a pity he hasn't got a decent woman!" But Morgan isn't worrying. He knows about most of the women that talk that way. And so do I. Maybe I do act it out like Morgan says. But once it's acted out, it's *out*. There's no more inside to blow up suddenly and make a mess. If I went to bed with a guy, at least I'd know what I was doing. I wouldn't wake up in the morning and wonder how it all happened. Which is about what this girl Jill's done.'

'And Morgan wouldn't mind?'

'I don't know, honey,' she said simply. 'See, we've only been married three years. So far I've managed with the old sap. He's quite a lot for anybody my weight. If I got anything to spare, I take it out on guys like that one in the picture gallery.'

I shook my head. 'It's all very well, Loo. But men have got a nasty name for the likes of you.'

'I know. I've been called it. But if you're a woman, you got to realise that you don't owe something just because people send you in a bill. I never take more from any man than I'm prepared to give him back. Hell – good little Luella. Nice girl. I talk too much. Let's have another drink.'

I said, 'Let's go and have it somewhere else.'

There was a man playing the piano in Ciro's. He wasn't the one who had been there in the autumn, but he played very well, looking down at his hands all the time, as though he found them interesting and surprising. He didn't beam round the room, or grin at you, or act as though he thought you ought to notice him. He just played and looked at his hands.

Loo said, 'About what I was saying – you understand I know it all. Being twenty-seven, and having been married three years, and with my head-piece, I should, shouldn't I?'

I said, 'Don't worry. You're doing quite well. But what you *haven't* told me is what I do about it now?'

Loo agonised. 'You want her back, Jimmy?'

'Yes.'

'What d'you want back? Jill, or just your wife?'

'I can't be sure. Sometimes I don't see why I want her back at all. But it's just – well, she's my person. And I think I see how to do it better now. And . . .'

'O.K. Anyway you want her back. Why did you let her go away with this Bule?'

'The idea was to get it out of her system. When she sees what he is . . .'

Loo shook her head irritably. 'Jimmy – forget it. It doesn't matter if he's the biggest heel from here to there, and she knows it, it won't help you, if he's got his claws well in. She won't get anything out of her system that way. She'll just get a hell of a lot more in.'

'You think I was wrong to try to do it that way?'

'I think you were plumb crazy.'

'Why?'

'Because of what I said to you about it feeling right. If Jilly's living with you, she may be playing hookey with him, but that's just fun and games at odd times, and all the rest of life's still there and proper. But if she goes off with him, and they live together, then all the little things start coming into line. The way he acts at breakfast. The way he lights a cigarette. The way he orders her a drink. You can go on going to bed with a guy for long enough, and it means no more than what it does mean. But you start getting used to the faces he makes shaving, and how he likes his coffee, and how he acts with waiters, and that's serious.'

'And supposing you find that he's bone selfish and simply out for what he can get? That he's just saying "Damn you, Jack. I'm all right?" '

'I tell you, honey, it doesn't make any difference.'

I said, 'You're seriously telling me that a woman doesn't care how she's treated?'

''Course she does. She cares a lot. She cares whether she's brought flowers, and smiled at at the right time, and whether her new hair-do's noticed. But she doesn't care so much whether a guy takes out an insurance policy to give her a pension when she's sixty, because she isn't sixty yet, so what the hell?'

'Your women are a pretty superficial lot, my dear.'

'They're not *my* women, Jimmy – thanks be. But they're a superficial lot by your reckoning. Until they have kids. Then maybe it's different, that being what they're for, apart from being pets.'

'Are you and Morgan going to have any kids?'

'We're building the factory and getting the jigs made right now. Next year we go into production.'

The man at the piano started to play *Plaisir d'Amour*. I said, 'Well, if everything you've said about women were true, I don't think I should want any part in them.'

'That's up to you, honey. If what they've got for you isn't worth what it costs, stay out of the market. I wouldn't blame you, for one. Or come right in and try and get what you want at cut prices. But don't buy and then squeal because what you've got is itself, and not something different. That just makes trouble.'

I listened to the chap playing for a while and then said rather moodily, 'So you think I ought to get her back?'

'Right away.'

'And then what?'

'Take her off some place.'

'And have her pining for comrade Bule? What fun.'

'Well, you got to fight for what you want, Jimmy. If it's not worth fighting for, it's not worth having.'

I suddenly said violently, 'I'll be damned if I'll fight for my own wife with any bounder who likes to flatter her. If I haven't done enough to have her without that, I won't have her at all.'

Loo grinned at me and said gently, 'Listen, mister, that's Jilly you're talking about. Not just your wife.' She looked at me for a moment and then stretched herself and yawned and said, 'How about taking me home, Jimmy? My ma doesn't like me being out late.'

It was only about half-past eleven. I took her back to the hotel. She held my arm but we didn't say anything. When we got there I said, 'I won't come up, Loo. I don't sleep if I go to bed too early. I shall go for a walk.'

She said, 'O.K., honey. 'Night, and thank you for a lovely day,' and kissed me. Being kissed by Loo was always rather like going into a florist's shop on a warm day.

*

I went out again, but I couldn't decide what to do. I tried my place by the lagoon, but it was cold, so I went back to the International. There was nobody in the bar. I looked round the partition at the dance hall, but I couldn't face it, so I just had a cognac and came away.

It must have been about half-past twelve when I got to bed. Usually I lie on my left side first, and then when I get sleepy I turn over on my right side and go to sleep. That is, if it's going to work. If it isn't, I have to turn on my back, and then I know I'm sunk, and that it's going to be a long job. I lay on my back for a long time with my eyes open, just looking into the darkness. I thought, 'If I could cry, that would help.'

It was quite easy. I just said to myself, 'I'm lonely. I'm lonely,' and that did it. A lump came in my throat that really hurt, and I could feel the pillow wet where the tears had gone.

I hadn't locked my door and Loo came straight in. I saw her in the light from the corridor. She was wearing a long dressing-gown affair. She shut the door behind her and it was very dark.

She came over to the bed and said, 'Move over, mister.'

I said, 'Here – wait a minute, Loo . . .'

She said, 'It's all right, honey. Hold your horses,' and lay down on the bed beside me and put her arms round me. She didn't get into the bed. I gave a sort of giggle and said, 'I suppose this *feels* right, eh?'

She said, 'This feels fine. Now you go to sleep before I put you out with a blackjack. You've had plenty of to-day.'

The thing she was wearing was made of satin. She still smelt like a florist's shop but it was a different florist. She stroked my hair and said, 'You wouldn't be a sap, would you, Jimmy?'

I said, 'Me? No. I'm a great big he-man who just happens to be acting like a kid of eight.'

She said, 'Fine. Well, now, go to sleep and forget it.'

I knew I couldn't go to sleep. In fact the last thing I can remember thinking was that I certainly shouldn't be able to. I did half wake up when she went out of the door. I didn't see her, but I saw it closing behind her, and heard the click of the latch. But it was only half-waking, and after that I slept till half-past ten the next morning.

12

Morgan came back just before lunch the next day. I asked him if he had liked the Giottos and he said yes, they were dandy, but I don't think he'd been near them. He asked me if Loo had been good, and I said she'd been just about as usual. He said he was sorry about that, and he'd take it out of her some time.

We went on doing nothing in the usual way for a few more days, but I knew it wouldn't do for much longer. I never like being in Venice for more than about a fortnight at a time. After that it begins to give me claustrophobia. I suppose it is the narrowness of the streets. After a while I begin to feel that the buildings are shutting down on me, and long for a good wide street with a chance of being killed by a bus.

Besides, I wanted to get on now. When I had left London, my one thought had been to get away and stop thinking about everything. But somehow my day with Loo had finished all that. I had a feeling that I had got all I could out of the expedition now, and that I must start and shift for myself again.

Loo wasn't bored with Venice. She was never bored with anything. If all else failed she just used to go out and get lost, and enjoy herself asking the way back. But I think Morgan was getting tired of it.

I did suggest tentatively that we should go across to Florence, but I gathered it might be several weeks before he could get away. He offered to fix the money if I wanted to go.

I wasn't very keen to go to Florence. I wasn't keen to go anywhere. I simply wanted to get away from Venice. But on the following Monday I had a letter from Jill that settled it for me. She said, 'I don't know what your plans are, and for goodness' sake don't change them if you're having a good time. But we're reckoning to get back to Paris next Saturday, the third, and I did wonder whether you'd have cared to meet me there, rather than wait till we both got home. We've got a lot to talk about, and there might be something to be said for doing it on neutral ground. Bill will be about, which may put it out of court for you. But of course you needn't see him unless you want to, and I should be available just exactly when you wanted me. Alternatively, if there's anything you want to say to both of us, he's quite willing.'

She didn't say anything else, except that she loved me, and it didn't sound so very promising. I had always hoped, in a vague way, that by the time I saw her again she would have finished with Bule for good. But it wasn't a bad idea to meet on neutral ground, even if Paris hadn't been very successful last time. I wrote back saying I would meet her on the Saturday night, and, air mail from Italy being what it is, I sent a telegram as well. In my letter I said I didn't mind about Bule being in Paris, and that I might like to see them both at some point; but that of course I wanted to see her alone first.

Morgan and Loo came to see me off. I wanted to say something to Loo, but it wasn't easy to get into words. On the morning that I was going, I went out and bought her a handbag from a shop in Merceria. She had been admiring it ever since we got there, and when I gave it to her she squealed like a stuck pig. It was only when I was in the train that I realised that I had bought it with Morgan's money – or with Morgan's water-softener company's money. Apart from that, I just squeezed her and said, 'Good-bye, awful. And thank you.' As the train went out they stood on the platform and waved to me with their arms round each other. Loo only came to his shoulder. I think they must have gone straight home from Italy, because I've never seen them since, and, very rudely, never wrote to them. I have absolutely no recollection of the journey back to Paris, except buying a flask of Ruffino through the window at Verona, and putting it in the bottle-holder in my sleeper. For some reason I never opened it, and when we were pulling into Paris I gave it to the steward.

I got to Paris in the morning, and their plane wasn't due till the late afternoon. I had arranged to meet Jill at the bar where they are surprised if you want drinks, at about six, so I had the day to put in. I spent most of it wandering about Paris and drinking coffee, and getting used to the traffic. It is always extraordinarily dangerous to go to any big city straight from Venice, because you forget that you can't just stroll about anywhere, thinking, without any danger of being knocked down. In the afternoon I did go and sit in the Jardin des Tuileries and try to think seriously about what I was going to say to Jill. But it all depended on what Jill was going to say to me; and though I could make several guesses at that, I couldn't be sure.

Their plane was due in at about half-past four. I went to the bar promptly at six, and decided not to have a drink till Jill came. But, as she hadn't come by half-past, I felt I couldn't sit there any longer without drinking anything, so I ordered a Pernod. For the next half-hour I decided that the plane had crashed, and for the life of me I couldn't make up my mind whether that would be a bad thing or a nice clean way out of a nasty mess. But at seven I felt I ought to have another Pernod, and by the time Jill appeared it was quarter to eight and I was on my third. This probably explains a good deal of the rest of that evening.

Jill was full of apologies about being late, but in fact it wasn't anything to do with her at all. They had engine trouble not far out of Toulon, and had to make an emergency landing. They had also flown at about a hundred feet for a long way, making everything very bumpy and everyone very sick. It sounded as though it had been complete hell, but Jill apologised all the same. That is one of the great snags about Jill. She can never see the difference between things that are her fault and things that couldn't possibly be. So she apologises for everything, and feels responsible for nothing.

She had gone a marvellous dark honey colour in Spain, and was looking extremely well and attractive. It was some time later before I realised that we hadn't kissed when we met. It just never occurred to me, and I don't think it did to her.

She badly needed a drink after the aeroplane, and by the time she had told me all about that, and had asked after Morgan and Loo, and been told about Loo and the young men with brown legs, and one thing and another, it was half-past eight and we were both hungry. It was a particularly good dinner, and we had a lot of silly little things to tell one another, and Jill looked very attractive, so that somehow there never seemed to be an appropriate moment to start saying anything serious or important. And then, of course, by about half-past nine I was feeling more cheerful and relaxed than I had done for weeks. I looked at her as we drank our coffee, and told myself that this was all very well but we must start and get down to brass tacks. But I knew I most desperately didn't want to, and suddenly I decided that I darn well wouldn't. It could all wait.

I said, 'You know we ought to talk seriously, young woman?' The smile went off Jill's face and she said, 'I suppose so,' and looked dutifully solemn. I grinned and said, 'Well, don't let's. Let's leave it till to-morrow. I don't feel like being serious to-night.'

Jill looked at me in surprise and then heaved a sigh of relief. She said, 'Oh God, darling, can you really bear it if we don't? I was just thinking that I *couldn't* . . .'

I said, 'All right. Let's just be awful and irresponsible. Just till to-morrow.' We looked at each other and giggled, and Jill took my hand and squeezed it and said 'Darling,' and I ordered two fines, and told her about Morgan and Loo and their curious mixtures.

About eleven o'clock we were sitting in the Dome when Jill looked at her watch and said, 'This is going to make you angry . . . Don't let it, because you haven't been angry and it's so lovely when you're not . . .'

I said, 'What have you done now?' I was feeling extremely happy, and not at all likely to be angry about anything.

'Well, you see, I thought we might dive straight in and – and talk . . . and . . . well, I didn't know what it'd be like, and I thought probably after a bit it would be a good thing to stop. So . . . I told my gentleman friend that I'd sort of – meet up with him after.'

I hadn't been thinking about Bule, but I suddenly saw him now very clearly. He was getting up and greeting her and saying, 'Darling – how did it go? Was he hell . . . ?'

I said, 'So you want to go now?'

She said quickly, 'Of course I don't. It's the last thing I want to do. I've told him that of course I shall be with you exactly when you want me and – and so on. But I was thinking perhaps I'd better just go and – and say I'm not coming, as it were. Because otherwise he'll go on waiting, and he isn't too good after the aeroplane.' She looked at me with a sort of tentative cheeky grin. 'Would you mind frightfully? You can say "impudent" if you like.'

'Where were you meeting him?'

'In the Deux Magots. He was going to get there at half-past ten, and just wait till I came. I wouldn't be a minute, honestly, if – if you'd wait . . . I only want to tell him to go back to bed and not hang on for me.'

I said slowly, 'All right, Jilly. If you must try to have it both ways, you must.'

She looked at me and I suppose she saw that at that moment it was all there for the asking and saw no danger in taking it. She said, 'I suppose you . . . wouldn't come . . . too?'

I said, 'What for?'

'Well . . . then we could all have a drink together. I mean . . .'

There might have been hope in anger. But there was no hope or anger left in me. So I smiled and said, 'Really, Jilly, if this weren't a public place I'd . . .'

He had smiled so she knew, of course, that it was all right. She grinned at me and said, 'Well, you said let's be awful and irresponsible. And it would be fun. And we needn't ever *tell* anybody . . .'

Bule was sitting in a corner of the Deux Magots drinking Armagnac and looking extremely handsome. The sun had turned him a sort of pale brown with a hint of green in it, so that his face and hands looked almost transparent. He waved in greeting when we came in. He didn't seem in the least surprised or disconcerted to see me. His first words to me were, 'Hallo, squire. You look like a man who's been gazing on the scampi when they're brown.'

Jill said, 'You all right now?' and he said, 'I'm fine. Have an Armagnac? It's rather good.' They spoke to each other in a curious abrupt, neutral way, never using one another's name, or with any colour in their voices. I couldn't help noticing the difference between this and the slightly Vox Humana effect that Jill had been using with me. Something made me think of what Loo had said about getting used to a person shaving, and for one moment I wished to God I hadn't come. But it was too late then, and anyhow it was what I had come to see. Then Bule started to tell me how frightened he had been in the aeroplane, and how he'd thought Jill was being extraordinarily and rather shamingly brave, until he realised that it was just that she was feeling too sick to care whether they crashed or not. He reproduced her expression beautifully, and anyhow I wasn't proposing to care about anything now.

And I didn't care. I don't profess to know why not. There are a lot of things about the whole business that I don't know, and that is simply one of them. I can only say that for the rest of the evening I didn't care, and it didn't hurt to see them. It wasn't that I refused to look. On the contrary, I looked, and saw the whole thing a lot more clearly than I ever had before. With him, Jill was a completely different person – a person I had never seen before. She talked more, and better. She was much less tentative. It was only very occasionally, when she was speaking to me, that the note came back into her voice that made everything she said seem to end in a faint question mark. Bule was completely calm and entirely charming. In fact he gave less of an impression of ganging up with her against me than he had done before I knew anything about their affair.

I think the other thing that made it possible was that, frankly, they were something of a relief after Morgan and Loo. It seems an odd and extraordinarily ungrateful thing to say – that I enjoyed being with them better than with two people who had been kindness itself to me. But there it is. I should be grateful to Loo for the rest of my life, and I was very fond of Morgan. But with them there was always a slight sense of being in a nice nursery. With the other two, for that evening at least, I was with children of my own age.

And Heaven knows that wasn't very old, after a while. Bule knew Paris very well, and as far as I could judge he spoke French quite perfectly. (He spoke it well enough for it to be difficult for me to follow him at times when he was speaking to a Frenchman. I never have any difficulty with French as long as it is spoken badly.) We went to two or three places he knew of and one that I did, and the longer we went on the more childishly we behaved. Bule had a line of completely solemn fantastic behaviour that was very funny – at least it seemed funny then. I remember that as we came out of one place he said, 'Ah – a horseless carriage – one moment,' and went up to a cab, and asked the driver to go to the Moulin Rouge. I was surprised, because I shouldn't have thought that we wanted to go to the Moulin Rouge, but Bule had started an argument with the driver about what the fare would be. This went on for a long time, but at last they came to terms, and Bule pulled out his wallet and gave him the fare. The driver started his engine and waited, whereupon Bule said, 'All right – off you go.' The driver looked rather puzzled and said, 'Aren't you coming?' and Bule said in a surprised way. 'What, us? Why should we want to go to that place? Toddle along now.' The driver hesitated for a bit and thought it over, and then shrugged his shoulders and actually started off. I have often wondered since how far he went. I realise that this isn't funny now, but it was funny at the time, with a sort of Bump Supper funniness. I remember laughing a great deal over it. 'The various stages of drunkenness,' as my encyclopaedia says, 'are marked by a progressive decline in self-criticism.'

Bule's idea of an amusing place in Paris tended towards curiously decorated cellars where somebody – usually a man – sang songs which were quite incomprehensible to Jill and me, but apparently very funny to everybody else. But he always came away quite readily when we got bored. Towards the end of the evening my recollections are rather vague, but I remember going right across to Montmartre, and finding that the fair was still working. I think we went on roundabouts, and I remember that Jill wanted to go on those sickening over-and-over swings, and was rather scornful because neither of us would take her. The one thing I am sure about is that Bule and I sang *The Silver Swan* in a café, singing whichever of the parts seemed most essential at various moments. Nobody seemed to mind.

By about four o'clock I was getting very tired, and I think they were too. After all, we had all been travelling, and they had had this business with the aeroplane. But in our various ways we were all afraid of letting it stop. It was an hour later before I finally realised that they were in an awkward position, and that it was up to me to call the halt. I had no doubt what to do. I just said, 'It's high time everybody was in bed. In fact it's been high time for hours,' and piloted them out of the café and into a cab. I saw Jill looking at me, and I smiled at her reassuringly and said in a matter-of-fact way, 'Where are you staying?'

Bule said, 'At the Pierre Franchot, Avenue Kleber.' I said, 'That's fine. Then the best thing will be for you to drop me and go on.' Nobody said anything. I felt very strong and in control of everything, and fatuously pleased with myself. As we drove, Jill squeezed my hand hard and I squeezed it back. When we got to my hotel I said to her, 'About to-morrow. Don't let's make it too early. Everybody'll want some sleep. How about meeting at the Capucines at twelve?' She said, 'All right, darling,' in a low voice.

I got out and said, 'Well, good night. Sleep well.' I saw the outline of Bule's transparent face as I shut the taxi door. The door made a curious echoing bang. I have never forgotten what a curious noise it was. I didn't look back, but as the night porter opened the door to me I heard the taxi grind away.

I slept very well, but not for long, and I was up by ten the next morning. I felt fine, considering the previous evening. It was raining, so I had to go inside the Capucines to wait for Jill. She was almost on time. She said straight away, 'I say – about last night. I can't think why I did that. I hope you didn't have too horrid a time.'

I said, 'Don't be silly. It was rather amusing. Anyhow I needn't have come if I didn't want to.'

'That was what you meant – about going home?'

'Oh yes. That was what I meant.'

Jill said, 'Thank God for that. I thought it was, but I wasn't absolutely sure.'

I ordered coffee. After a minute, Jill said rather helplessly, 'Well, *now* where the hell are we?'

I smiled and said, 'Oh come – it's fairly obvious, isn't it?'

She said, 'You don't think I'm – through – with that do you?'

'No. Do you?'

She didn't say anything for a long while, but just sat staring moodily out of the window. At last she said, 'I was going to tell you I was and – and that I wanted to come back. I do, too. Oh damn it, why didn't we just go on and talk? If the plane hadn't played the fool...'

I said, 'I've only ever asked you for one thing in all this – that you shouldn't lie to me.'

'But it *isn't* lying. Not really. It's just...'

I said, 'Jilly darling, I loved you very much last night, and I still love you this morning. But I don't *want* you – not like this.'

'But why not? I could stop. I could wash it out...'

I said, 'Look – you must know perfectly well that you're quite different with him from what you are with me – from what you've ever been. You're not afraid of him. You're easy. You're happy. I don't know why. I suppose it's something that I've done to you – or not done. But as long as that's so, I can never have you back. It wouldn't be fair to either of us.'

'But I don't *want* it to be like that. You're the only person I rely on – the only person in the world I trust...'

'Maybe. But the sad part is that you don't love me.'

She looked at me for a moment and then said, 'Yes, I do.' It was so dubious that I just laughed.

'But what are we going to *do*? If you won't have me...'

'All right. We'll put it that way if you like. I won't have you.'

'Well – if I won't come, then, or whatever we call it? What happens? Do you want to – to divorce me?'

I said, 'Presumably.'

There was a long silence, and then Jill said, 'The real snag is that you've never given me a chance to say – the – the things I'd *planned* to say.'

'You didn't need to. They said themselves clearly enough.'

Jill went on slowly and carefully, 'I was going to say, "Darling – this has partly worked. I see an awful lot of things that I didn't before I went away ... *But* there's no denying that for the moment I'm – sort of separate from you, and I do find it difficult to get close. And I do like Bill. It's no good saying I don't ..." '

'No good at all.'

'"*Therefore* I'm rather frightened of – of just cutting it out completely because of what it might do to both of us ..." '

'And *therefore* what I want is to have it both ways?'

'You can call it that if you like, but let me finish. Supposing I give you my word that I'll absolutely cut out the – the sexual part of it; and that I'll honestly try to do a better job by you ... could I be left – something? Just for a bit, until we were closer ... ?' She trailed off into silence.

I said, 'I don't quite get it. What exactly are you suggesting? That you go on being a sort of sister to him?'

'No. But just that I could – well – see him occasionally. It'd soon die out—'

I didn't say anything, but I suppose my face did.

After a while Jill said miserably, 'I thought it might be worth saying. It seems to me better than – than the other thing ...'

She suddenly beat her knuckles on the table and said almost desperately, 'You *must* realise that – that people can't switch what they feel on and off like a – an electric light ...'

I said, 'Yes – I see that.'

I left Paris the next day, and didn't see Jill again, but I saw Bule for a few minutes. He rang up and suggested it. He said, 'I gather that you didn't feel you could accept Jill's suggestion. I'm sorry about that.'

I said, 'So am I. But there it is.'

'It's your affair, but, if I may say so, I think you're asking rather a lot of her.'

'Well, let's agree that it's my affair.'

Bule nodded. After a moment he said, 'I just wanted you to know that if you *do* split up I shall be extremely sorry. It's not a thing that I've ever wanted, and I don't believe it's really necessary.'

'What makes you think that?'

'I believe that it'd be perfectly possible to settle the whole thing on a friendly basis, without all this bitterness.'

I said, 'The only suggestion I've had for settling it so far is that you and Jill should be given exactly what you want – at my expense.'

'It didn't feel like that to me. Or, I fancy, to her.' He looked at me with the large blue eyes. They were not friendly. I imagine he'd been having a bad time with Jill and disliked me for making her unhappy. 'All I wanted to say,' he said coldly, 'was that if you *did* consider the suggestion she made, I would give you my word that I should stick to the letter of the arrangement. Of course, if you won't consider it, that doesn't arise.'

I said, 'You mean that if my wife wanted you to make love to her you would repel her advances?'

Bule sighed and said, 'I can't see any good coming out of this now. You must have your hate, and that makes it impossible. I can do no more.'

I said, 'My dear man, you've already done plenty.'

13

As soon as I got to London I went to see Carey Gleave. Carey has the reputation of being one of the most irritable men in London, and one of the best solicitors. I have never seen quite how he manages to combine the two, but he does. He is a most extraordinary shape, with a small head, narrow shoulders, and a sudden very large and seemingly irrelevant stomach. The whole structure sags. There are pouches under his eyes, his cheeks hang down, his shoulders droop and his stomach droops.

He sat there and sagged while I told him my position. Apart from Loo, he was the only person I had ever told; and, as with her, I left the Pearce business out, but told him all the rest. Carey just sat there and looked sulky until I had finished, without saying a word. Then he shifted himself irritably in his chair and snapped, 'Oh God! All right. So what?'

'It looks as though I may have to divorce Jill. So I thought you'd better know the position.'

Carey said, 'And I suppose you think you've acted like a hell of a good, loving husband, and are very proud of yourself?'

'Not particularly.'

'Then you'd better start being. You may as well get something out of it, because it's going to cost you enough.'

'Why?'

Carey sighed. 'James my boy, it's no good saying brightly that you may have to divorce her. You can't. Not unless she lets you.'

'You mean because I've condoned it?'

'Of course. Every damn thing. If she likes to defend, and you tell the story to a judge that you've told me, you may get a dressing down, but you certainly won't get a divorce.'

'Jill wouldn't defend. She'd never do a thing like that.'

'She's done a good many other surprising things, hasn't she?' Carey looked at me with dislike. 'The trouble with chaps like you,' he said viciously, 'is that you get something like this started, and mess about with it until it's in a nice tangle, and then come to me to sort it out.'

'That's what you're for, isn't it?'

'I dare say. But why couldn't you have come to me when you first found out about this Bule chap?'

'I didn't think it was important.'

'Then why is it important now?'

'Well, obviously, Carey, there's a difference between your wife just making an ass of herself in a childish way, and – and being head over heels in love with somebody else.'

'Not in law, my boy.' Carey closed his eyes. 'The law,' he said wearily, 'allows you to divorce your wife if she commits adultery. It doesn't say anything about being in love. The only relevant thing . . .'

I said, 'Oh, come on, Carey – I know all that. Legally speaking, I've made it all very difficult by forgiving my wife before, instead of kicking her out. Fine. Where do we go from there?'

'You say you want to divorce her?'

'I don't want to, but I may have to.'

'There's no question of having to. It's for you to make up your mind. How about doing that for a start?'

I didn't say anything for a moment and this irritated him. He said, 'What the hell's the use of coming to me unless you know what you want? You come here and you tell me all this, making it perfectly clear that you'd give your ears to have the girl back, and at the same time saying somebody or something may make you divorce her.'

'Well, assume that I *do* want to divorce her?'

'Then you'll have to get some evidence.'

'She's been living with him in Spain for weeks, and she's in Paris with him now.'

'With your full permission. Wash-out. She's only got to say . . .'

'But I tell you she won't say anything. If I decide to divorce her, she'd never defend.'

'James my boy, I get three chaps like you a week. They want to be on both sides in the same war. It won't do. The divorce laws aren't there for friendly and loving couples who think they'd like a change. They're there for people who don't like each other one bit. If you go into this, you've got to reckon that you're on one side and she's on the other, and you've got to play for your own hand. Otherwise you'll go *on* making a fool of yourself.'

'But that's bunkum, Carey. Scores of people feel . . .'

'I'm not talking about what anybody feels. I'm talking about how they *act*. You can feel what you like. But I've got to put you before a court as an injured person claiming his legal rights. You've been injured and you've forgiven the injury. Before you've got any standing, you'll have to be injured again.'

'You mean I've got to go through the motions of having her back, and then she's got to go off again?'

'Not necessarily. Not if she isn't going to defend. If you write to her and say, "Come back or else . . ." and she writes to you and says, "I'm not coming. I'm staying with him." And then somebody can prove that on a certain date they took her and Bule morning tea . . .'

'Oh God – all that stuff? After everything that's happened already?'

'Yes, sir. All that stuff. Because everything that's happened already has been washed out. By you.'

I said, 'Moral – if anything goes wrong with your marriage, don't try to save it.'

Carey was staring out of the window with dull, sullen eyes. 'I don't know, James. If people can't take that much trouble, they can't want a divorce very badly.' What he was asking was clear enough. I said, 'You know quite well that I don't want to divorce her if I can help it. That's why I've made all this mess.'

'You're not the first to do that.'

'But what else could I do if – if this goes on?'

'You could do nothing. Just part. Or you could get a legal separation. Or you could try to scare him off.'

'How?'

'Threaten to run him for big damages. The courts don't like rich co-respondents. I'm thinking aloud ... No – it wouldn't do anyhow, because they'd defend and you'd come unstuck on the Spanish business. I wouldn't recommend any of those myself. If you must do something, I'd go for the ordinary decree and make a clean job of it.'

There was a long pause. I said, 'I must think it over, Carey.'

'That's right,' he said witheringly. 'You think it over, and when you've decided what you want, come back and tell me and *then* I'll see if we can get it for you. Until then, I'm handicapped.'

Apart from seeing Carey, I only stopped in London long enough to put Crossways in the hands of the agents. I couldn't afford to give the place away, but I asked the same price as I had given for it, and, as I had spent several thousand pounds on it, I hoped it would go quickly. That was the one thing I wanted now. Yet the same evening I went down there.

I had been away a month, but the change in the garden was extraordinary. The daffodils had been coming out. Now they were over, and the tulips were in full flower. When I went, the roses had only just been pruned. Now some of them would be out soon. It was the same with the fruit. It was the same with everything. I don't know why I was so surprised by it. There isn't anything very startling in a garden changing a lot in one month, in spring. But I had a curious sense of being left behind – of having stood still for those weeks, while it all went on without me, not waiting and not caring, almost contemptuous in its indifference.

Yet inside the house it was just the reverse. Everything was in its usual place, tidy and ready. But nobody had been sitting in the chairs, and there was no ash in the ash-trays, and the morning paper was in the hall unopened, and it was all empty and static, like a stopped clock. I had come out by taxi instead of telling Lewis to come and meet me with the car, and I had to let myself in without ringing, and Claude hadn't appeared, so that I hadn't seen anybody. I knew perfectly well that the house was alive at the kitchen end, and in the Lewises' flat over it. But at this end it was perfectly still and silent, and I stood for quite a while in the lounge, listening to the silence, before I could bring myself to go along the passage and see the Lewises, and let life start again. It wasn't until I was talking to Mrs Lewis that I realised that I should have to tell them now – about selling the house and going. But not just then.

Elsie came through the kitchen while I was there. I said hullo to her, and she answered in her shy way. She looked even uglier and gaunter than ever. When she had gone I said, 'How has Elsie seemed?' Mrs Lewis looked puzzled and said, 'Oh – she's been all right, sir,' and I knew she didn't understand why I had asked.

It didn't take long for the news to go round that I was back, and several people rang up in the evening. Most of them asked after Jill. I hadn't got any story worked out, so I just said I had left her in Paris, and that she was well, and let it go at that. What was more significant was that two people *didn't* ask after her. I was still trying to work out whether there was any likely explanation of this, except the obvious one that they knew something, when the telephone rang again, and I stopped thinking about it. Because the call was Eddie, and he wanted to come and see me.

Eddie didn't say anything on the telephone about bringing Sergeant Groves with him, but Groves came; and as soon as I saw both of them I thought I was in for something awkward. It would have been quite possible for them to have come about something else, but it never entered my head that it was anything but the Pearce thing; and indeed, before they'd even told me what they wanted, I said, 'Well – got any further?'

Groves said, 'You mean about the Pearce job, sir?' and I kicked myself gently and said, 'Yes.'

Groves glanced at Eddie and said, 'Well – that was what we wanted to have a word about, sir ...' He was a big, handsome, dark man, with large, very gentle brown eyes like a cow's. I thought he seemed a bit uncomfortable and hesitant, and I didn't like that. Eddie just sat there glowering down at the floor in his sullen way.

Groves said, 'I'll tell you frankly, sir, I never reckoned we'd find anything on it. But Eddie here's gone on – acting on some tips that I think came from you in the first place ... ?'

'You mean checking up on the movements of cars?'

'That's right, sir. Well, he didn't get far for a while, did you, Eddie . . . ?'

Eddie shook his head silently.

'. . . but some weeks back he got a tip and he's worked on that and . . . well, now he's told me about it and I must say I think perhaps we ought to inquire further.'

I had a quick guess at what had happened and guessed right.

Groves said, 'Just after you went away, Eddie got this . . .' He pulled a letter out of his pocket and handed it to me. The postmark was somewhere in south-east London, and it was addressed simply 'P.C. Eddie Cater, Maidley, Sussex.' The letter was badly written with a scratchy pen on cheap lined paper. It said, 'Have you found out where the "Honourable Bule" was half-past six when Joe Pearce was killed if he says he was home it's a lie he wasn't but somewheres else. "Where." And ask him about a scratch on his car and how it got there and had to be painted out quick. This is true good luck.'

I went on looking at the letter for a while to give myself time to think. It might have been worse, if the little rat had had any brains; but the main thing now was to make them talk.

I looked up and said, 'One of these gallant affairs with no address and no signature, eh?'

'Yes, sir.'

'London postmark.'

'That doesn't mean anything, sir. Anybody can post a letter in London. It must be somebody local, or that *had* been local, or how'd he know about it?'

'Yes. Not a very educated writing, but not disguised, I should say.'

'That's what we thought, Mr Manning. I reckoned a

servant that had been at Motley Court or something like that. Mr Bule's had a fair lot of changes lately. There was a maid and a chauffeur . . .'

I said, 'Oh, yes. Little chap named Lee whom he sacked for stealing.'

'Did he? Well, that's the sort of chap it might be. Wouldn't come to us, but'd do this out of spite.'

'I should say it was probably Lee. Nasty little man with a bad record. Besides, he'd know about the scratch on the car.'

'So he would. Well, the proper place for a letter like that is in the fire – usually. But Eddie felt . . . well . . .'

'That he ought to see if there was anything in it?'

Groves said apologetically, 'Well, we hadn't got anything else to go on, Mr Manning.'

'I don't see what else you could have done – if only in justice to Mr Bule.'

'That's what I thought, sir,' said Eddie grimly. 'If a chap's afraid to sign his name you can't take much notice of what he says. But all the same, I thought I'd better follow it up just to make sure. And so I did. And this is what came out of it . . . '

He fumbled in his pocket and produced the inevitable bit of paper. 'About the scratch – there's no doubt about that. There *was* a scratch and it's been painted out like this chap says. Long scratch on the door. No way of telling how long ago it was done. Then about Mr Bule's movements . . .' Eddie consulted his paper. 'Mr Bule says,' he said slowly, 'that he was over at the Three Lions at Levening; that he left there just after six and drove home, and was home by twenty-five past, and didn't go out again till near on seven when he came here, sir?'

I said, 'Well, he certainly came here because there was a

party that night. And certainly most of the people came about seven.'

'Yes, sir. Well, now, Mr Bule says he was home by six twenty-five and this chap in the letter says he wasn't.'

I said, 'He doesn't tell us how he knows.'

'No, sir,' said Eddie expressionlessly. 'Anyhow, it was in that time Joe was hit.'

It was on the tip of my tongue to say, 'Well, as a matter of fact I can settle it for you,' and to trot out the telephone call story. But I thought I'd just see if we were up against anything else, so I kept quiet.

Eddie said, 'So the next thing I did was to go over to the Three Lions and see if they remembered Mr Bule being there . . .'

Groves said quickly, 'Of course, it wasn't any question of doubting Mr Bule's word, Mr Manning. But after this in the letter . . .'

I said, 'Of course.' I was looking at Eddie and I had a sudden almost terrifying vision of him, with that sullen face and the angry blue eyes with pale lashes, and the scarred chin, ploughing doggedly on in spite of Groves, or commonsense, or hell or high water.

Eddie said, 'Well, they did remember Mr Bule being in because they know him – least, they're pretty sure it was that evening. Mr Bule was there and he was with a lady. They didn't know her, and can't recall what she looked like. And they reckon, as far as they can remember, they did leave about six. Bought two bottles of gin.'

Eddie folded up the paper and put it away. After a moment's silence I said, 'In fact they confirm what Mr Bule said about leaving at six?'

'Yes, sir. They confirmed that, near enough.'

'If he left there at six, he'd certainly be home before half-past.'

'Yes, sir. If he went straight home.'

'Well, there's no reason to suppose he didn't, is there?'

Eddie said gently, 'There's the lady, sir. Mr Bule never said anything about her. Did he bring a lady here?'

'Not as far as I know. But how does she come into it?'

'She could have proved what he said.'

'But surely the people in the pub prove it anyway?'

'Not what time he got home, sir. If she went back with Mr Bule, she could've proved that.'

Like a fool I said, 'But there's no reason to suppose she went home with him. They may just have been having a drink together.'

'That's just it, sir,' Eddie said slowly and sullenly. 'Mr Bule was with a lady. If he went straight home he'd be there by half-past...' He looked up. 'But if he took her somewhere first ... ' He stopped for a moment and then added, '... then he might not have been, like this chap says.'

Groves shifted uneasily in his chair. He shook his head and said, 'I don't know, Eddie. I don't reckon...' They looked at one another for a moment and then Groves turned to me and said in a curious formal voice, 'What d'*you* think, Mr Manning?'

I saw then why they had come to me. Bule had told them about the telephone call, but they had never mentioned it. I said, 'Well, on coming to think of it I can help you here, because I've just remembered that I phoned Mr Bule at his house that evening myself from London just before half-past six...'

A broad smile spread over Groves' face and he sat back in his chair and turned to Eddie. Eddie's face was quite expressionless.

I said, '... and he told me he'd got some gin which he

was taking to the party. I couldn't get down in time for it myself. In fact that's why I phoned him.'

Groves said, 'Well, there you are, Eddie...' He turned to me and said, 'Thank you, sir. That's just what we wanted to hear. See, Mr Bule mentioned this telephone call of yours, and we just wanted to see whether you had any recollection of it. I'm sorry to have troubled you, Mr Manning, but I wanted to satisfy Eddie here that what this chap here said was just spite – somebody who doesn't like Mr Bule and...'

I said, 'It might not even be that. Might be just a dud watch.' I was looking at Eddie. His head was up so that the scar on his chin was showing. I smiled at him and said, 'So I'm afraid that rather disposes of that, Eddie. Sorry.'

'Well, *we*'re not, sir,' said Groves sincerely. 'The last thing we want is to have any suspicions of a gentleman like Mr Bule, do we, Eddie?'

''Course not,' said Eddie quietly. 'But it's like you said, Mr Manning – there hasn't got to be anybody you rule out – till you're sure.'

Groves had risen to his feet. I did the same. Eddie hesitated for a moment and then got up too. He said suddenly, 'You are sure about the time of your call, sir?'

I said, 'Oh yes. I had a train to catch, and had my eye on it.' He nodded slowly and turned to the door without another word.

As we went through the hall, Groves said to me in a low voice, 'I'm sorry about this, Mr Manning, but y'see...'

I said, 'That's quite all right. Glad I could help.'

'... only I know Mr Bule's a friend of yours, and of course I didn't much like...'

'Eddie's worked very hard on this.'

'Yes, sir. Between ourselves, I wish he'd stop bothering his head about it. I never reckoned it was any good, and he's spent time on it that could have been better used. But there it is – it was his brother-in-law, see.'

'It's very natural.'

Eddie had gone ahead of us and was slowly pulling his motor-bike off its stand. Groves said, 'He's very stubborn, Eddie is, when he gets an idea in his head. Very stubborn. But I hope he's satisfied now.'

I said, 'He never will be.'

'Well, not satisfied, sir. None of us are that. But willing to give it up as a bad job.'

I said, 'I hope so.' But I thought of Eddie's face and I had no such hope.

When they had gone I went back and worked it out. I was entirely calm – much calmer than when I had talked to Eddie before. I knew now that Groves was no trouble – that he only wanted to forget the whole thing. But Eddie had got his teeth into something, and instinctively he would never leave it now, even if all reason was against him. But as long as it *was* against him, there was nothing to be afraid of.

I looked at it, and for a while it seemed to me that the one thing that stopped Eddie was the ironical fact that I was a gentleman of honour and a magistrate, who would tell the truth, whilst all he had on the other side was an anonymous letter-writer who would lie. If it ever occurred to him that apparent gentlemen of honour may lie, and that anonymous letters may tell the truth, he was there.

Apart from Lee's story of the time and the scratch, there was the woman who was with Bule. He had seen the significance of that. There was the gin, and the fact that Jill was giving a party. There was the fact that the orchard door could be reached from Tarrant's Lane . . .

And then I realised that it wasn't like that at all – that I was doing what one does in those guessing games, when one knows the answer, and can't see why it isn't quite obvious to the people who are trying to guess it. From Eddie's point of view, even if it ever occurred to him that I would lie, there was no earthly reason why I should. It was only if he knew that the woman with Bule was Jill that my part in it began to make any sense at all. And why should it occur to him? It wouldn't have occurred to me.

I had reckoned that it might be weeks before I could find a buyer for Crossways, even though it was a bargain. But in fact it didn't work out like that at all. Within three days people began to turn up to see the place, and by the time I had been back just over a week, the first three people who had come to see it had all written and offered me the price I was asking.

The old boy I finally agreed to sell to – his name was Forest – was anxious to get into the house as soon as possible, and my first instinct was to tell him that I would go at once. I wanted the place off my hands, and I wanted to get away from the district before the news about my break-up with Jill got round. I had no desire to stay about there as a pathetic deserted husband.

It was only when I was on the point of saying that he could have possession at once that I saw the danger, and for a moment it sent me right back on my heels. If I suddenly packed up and went, without Jill's reappearance, the whole thing would be pretty obvious, and within a week it would be all round the district that she had left me; and in another, that she had run away with Bule. I tried hard to tell myself that Eddie wasn't Sherlock Holmes or Father Brown or Lord Peter Wimsey, but just a village policeman; and that he would never see that this gave him the name of the woman who was with Bule, and where Bule went that night, and why I told the telephone story. But I remembered Eddie's face and it wouldn't do.

So I stalled on the date when I could give Forest possession, and that night I rang up Paris to see if Jill and Bule were still at the Pierre Franchot. They were, but they were coming back three days later, and I arranged to meet them in London.

We went out to dinner, and it was very strained – quite unlike what it had been when we met in Paris. I think perhaps they had begun to feel for the first time that the whole thing was real, and not just an amusing game. Jill was very shy and jumpy, and Bule was cold and seemed angry inside, as he had done in those last minutes in Paris. Incidentally, I thought he looked rather ill. His Spanish tan had faded very quickly and left the queer greenish colour behind.

It suited me that they seemed a bit depressed. I only wanted to talk business, and I didn't want any more charming evenings. I told them about Eddie, and explained why it might possibly be dangerous if their affair got to be common knowledge.

I was rather surprised by their reactions. I had expected Jill to be scared, and Bule to feel that I was worrying about nothing. But it was the other way round. Jill said, 'But after all, Eddie's pretty dumb, and that would take a bit of thinking out,' and Bule said shortly, 'Well, he hasn't done so badly so far, dumb or not.' He thought for a bit and then said to me, 'They can't prove anything as long as you stick to the telephone story . . .' He said it with a trace of a question mark at the end, and I realised that he was wondering again whether I might rat because of what happened over Jill. I smiled and said, 'No.'

'No. It's cast iron. Even if it *did* occur to them that it

might have been Jill in the car, and that I might have taken her back to the orchard gate, and so on. Given that nobody actually saw us there, which they didn't – and given that somebody is prepared to swear that I answered the telephone at six twenty-five, they can suspect their heads off, but they can't prove anything. Still, I agree that it's got to be avoided . . .'

Jill was looking at him in a worried way now. We ate for a bit in silence. Then Bule said, 'In fact the whole thing's in your hands.' He said it sullenly – almost petulantly, without looking up from his plate, and I saw those brown eyes go to his face again for a moment, in exactly the worried way that they used to go to mine when I was cross.

Later on I said, 'What are you going to do about your house? Will you sell it?'

Bule looked surprised and said, 'I don't think so. Why should I?'

'Well, you can't very well take Jill back there with you, can you? To that district?'

He hesitated long enough to make it clear that he'd never thought of that. Then he frowned and said shortly, 'I don't know yet. I shall have to think about it.'

Jill was looking down at her coffee cup. Bule was still frowning. If he had been a child one would have said he was pouting. I laughed inside myself, and it wasn't a kind laugh. She might be prepared to play All for Love, but I couldn't see the Honbill being prepared positively to move house just to make things easier for his mistress. I thought, 'They haven't a clue, either of them. They haven't thought about it, or seen how to make it work. And one of them doesn't care and the other doesn't know.'

I said, 'Well, it's nothing to do with me . . .' and turned to Jill and said, 'Now, about Crossways. If we want to get out of the district without making it all quite obvious, I think you'll have to reappear there for a little while before we go. I'm sorry.'

Jill said, 'All right,' in a low voice, and went on looking at her coffee cup.

'You'd have to collect your stuff. And anyhow I fancy it may help Carey over the divorce. We needn't be there together much, which wouldn't be any fun for anybody. I shall stay in London during the week, and go down at week-ends. There's no reason why you shouldn't come up to town too, whenever you like. But in view of what we've been saying, I think we must show the flag down there a few times.'

'All right.'

'I also think that if you're both down there, you two ought to keep apart.'

They looked at one another for a moment. Bule said curtly, 'I shall probably stay in town anyhow.'

I said, 'That'd be by far the best thing.'

Neither of them said anything. They just went on sitting there, side by side, like sulky kids.

14

So that was how it was finally arranged. I was to tell little Forest that he could have the house in a month's time. Jill was to go back to Crossways, and break the news that we were going, to the staff and the district generally. I was to go down at week-ends. When the time came we were to fade out gracefully, still more or less holding hands until we were in the train, and then we would pack it in. Meanwhile, Bule thought he would stay on in London.

I suppose it was my characteristic insensitiveness, but I never realised, when we made this arrangement, just what being at Crossways with Jill, even occasionally, would be like in these conditions. In fact it was a particular sort of hell. We spent as little time together as we could, and to do her justice, I don't think Jill was consciously being a hypocrite. But after all, Crossways was her home, and she was going to lose it, and I was her husband and she was going to lose me. She was frightened and utterly confused, and though she never once asked me, in so many words, to change my mind and go on with her, every practical and visible step we took towards parting made her miserable. But the thing that made it intolerable was that, despite the tears and general misery, there was never the slightest doubt that she was in love with Bule, and that he was the only thing that really interested her. She telephoned him every day. She wrote to him. She could never keep him out of any discussion, no matter how casual, for five minutes; and whereas when I was there she couldn't wake up in the morning, and seemed always to be dead tired, on the morning that she was going to London to see him, she was up at six and away as bright as a bee on the seven-thirty train. Half a dozen times when she was feeling miserable she had me half-convinced – half ready to believe that even now I had only to hold out my hand and she would be back as I had always known her. But if a spark came in me, there was never any answering spark in her. And if I was sometimes left with the nasty feeling that I was refusing a reconciliation when she wanted it, five minutes later I would hear her having one of those interminable low-voiced conversations on the telephone with Bule. I have never been more relieved in my life than I was to get away after that first week-end.

I think it was somewhere about then that I first realised that in a few weeks' time I should have nowhere to live, and went and found the flat in Clarges Street. It was a deadly place, with that peculiarly impersonal modern furniture that you get in furnished flats – the sort that, when you leave, only has to be dusted to remove all trace that you ever used it, or ever existed. What I was going to do with it – what sort of life I was going to live – I had no idea. But somehow, to have an address and a telephone number of my own – not to be one of the pieces of flotsam and jetsam at the Club – gave it all a feeling of solidity, even though I never spent a moment in the place except to sleep there.

I also think, though I am not sure of this, that it was in the same week that I first met Philippa McArthur. Anyhow it was at a cocktail party, and we argued about Menuhin.

It had been part of the idea that at the week-ends Jill and I should go about together a certain amount, and entertain people. Oddly enough, that wasn't so bad – mainly because

Jill didn't mind, and even seemed to enjoy herself. I think Jill would get quite a lot of pleasure out of putting on her prettiest asbestos frock, and going and drinking flaming paraffin in hell. Our cover story over selling Crossways was that I found going up and down to London too tiring, and Jill came in for a lot of sympathy about it. On one occasion she was registering noble resignation, and pointing out that my work must come first, when I caught her eye. She was sipping her drink at the time, and the drink got mixed up in a giggle and she nearly choked. Several people took me aside and asked me whether I didn't feel it was rather unkind to be uprooting her like that.

I remember one particular evening at the Doc's. Jill was beginning to look very tired and washed out in the morning, but she still had her honey-coloured tan, and looked very good when she was made up. She was talking to somebody, and I was watching from across the room, and it struck me that the new ease and competence that she showed with Bule was carrying through when he wasn't there – that she could do it now with other people. I think that was the first time that I ever fully realised that Bule's Jill might be the real one and mine the fake. I can only assume that I hadn't thought of this before because I didn't want to.

Jill doesn't drink much as a rule, and if she does it makes very little difference to her. I have an idea that she decided to get drunk that evening, before the party even started. She certainly got very animated; but as the party went on a long time, and everybody else got very animated too, it didn't matter. Having to drive home, and not feeling very social, I drank very little, and this was one of the very few times in my acquaintance with Jill that she had definitely drunk more than I had. In the car coming back I said, 'Well, ma'am – you looked very pretty and were very much the life of the party this evening. I can't help thinking that being a bad girl agrees with you in some ways.'

She said, 'I say, I've drunk too much. Does it show?'

'Only in an entirely charming way.'

'I hate women who get drunk.'

'You're not drunk. You're only cheerful. Everybody was.'

She said, 'Doc was. I've been talking to Doc. About the Pearce business.'

'Why?'

'He brought it up. I didn't. He asked me how Elsie was and said it was a damned shame. I agreed with him.' She giggled slightly. 'I've been talking to Elsie, too. I've had a lovely day. Are you drunk, too?'

'No.'

'Well, that's fine because you won't hit anybody going home. We don't want another, because that would be *too* complicated. I wish Elsie didn't squint so. Doc says her mother's dying.'

'That's probably just as well, poor old thing.'

'Yes. One more less mouth to feed for Elsie. For you. Elsie's as strong as a horse. I couldn't do what she does. But then I shouldn't try. I never do try. That's the thing about me, I don't try.'

I said, 'You know the nice thing: "The man says, 'I cannot.' His friends say, 'He will not.' The physician says, 'He cannot will.' " '

'I say, that's awfully good. I've never heard that before.'

'You've heard me say it scores of times.'

'Have I? I don't remember. I'm rather drunk, darling. Anyhow, Doc thinks it's a damned shame. I agreed with him. You know I know he doesn't care a damn about me, don't you?'

'Who? Doc? He's very fond of you.'

'No, fool. Bill. He doesn't care a damn about me really.'

I said, 'I should think he's just about as fond of you as he's capable of being of anybody.'

'Oh yes. But he isn't going to sell the house. Not unless I make him. I could make him, but I shan't. It's all very funny really. Did you go to bed with Loo?'

'No.'

'Why not?'

'I didn't want to.'

'Don't be silly – everybody wants to go to bed with Loo. That's what she's for. Besides, you must have *somebody* to make love to. Otherwise you won't like it.' She looked at me with anxious solemnity. 'I'm worried about you, darling, not having anyone to make love to.'

I said, 'I dare say I'll manage. You *are* tight, aren't you?'

'Yes,' she said simply. 'Very. But it's a good thing really, because then I'm not afraid of you. Shoo!' She flapped at me with vague carelessness.

I said, 'Why are you ever afraid of me, Jill?'

'I'm not afraid of you, it's what you'd think. I've never got drunk with you before. That was because I was afraid of what you'd think. I don't care what *he* thinks. It's all very funny really.'

We drove in silence for a few minutes. Then Jill gave a slight giggle. 'And the funniest thing of all is that it's all about that really. The whole thing.'

'About what?'

'About killing Joe, and Elsie and the police. That's all it's about. Not anything to do with Bill. Damn Bill. It's about that.'

'What is?'

'The trouble. Us. That's what you can't forgive me, and never will. Making you do that for me. Not owning up. That's it, isn't it?'

I said, 'You know I honestly don't think so. Lots of times I've completely forgotten about it.'

'You may think so.'

'And anyhow you'd started with the Honbill before it ever happened.'

'Doesn't matter. You'd have let me have that. It was the other thing. You've never wanted me since that, and never will...' She turned to me. 'Why did you have to do that?' she said miserably. 'I knew at the time what it'd do to us. I wanted to tell, and you wouldn't let me. You stopped me. Why did you? I wanted to tell them.'

There were tears in her voice. I said, 'Come on – cheer up.' Somehow I particularly didn't want her to cry when she was drunk.

'Anyhow, I couldn't help it,' she said almost angrily. 'Honest, I couldn't. I *wasn't* going fast and I *wasn't* drunk. I am now, but I wasn't then. And I *can* drive that car. It would have been just the same if it had been this one, and you driving. And then it wouldn't have mattered, and everyone would have said it was an accident. And anyhow I didn't know I'd hit him. Honestly...'

She trailed off into silence. After a moment she gave a sort of shuddering wriggle and said, 'I wish Elsie didn't *squint* so. I never know what she's looking at.'

I said, 'What were you talking to her about to-day?'

'Oh, I was being sweet. Elsie likes me. I was being sweet to her. I always am. She thinks I'm kind and nice and rather wonderful. It's very funny. I wanted to say, "And give the green bathroom a special do, and anyhow I killed your husband and so what?" just to see her face.'

I said, 'Darling, you've had too much gin and you're being a bit dramatic. You never wanted to do any such thing.'

'No, that's quite right. I've only just thought of it. But don't you think it's a nice idea?'

'No.'

'But don't you really, darling? After all, it'd save so much trouble.' She suddenly leant away and stared at me. 'Supposing I did?' she said in a low voice.

'Did what?'

'Went and told her. And Eddie. And everybody. Went and said it was me. Would you have me back if I did that?'

I said, 'Don't be silly, Jill.'

'But *would* you? Tell me.'

I said, 'Look, my dear, you're talking nonsense, so stop it, there's a good girl.'

'But then they'd send me to prison and after that you'd like me again. That's what it all is. You think I ought to be punished. You always think people ought to be punished. Me. And you. And Bill and everybody. I don't see why you think that, when I didn't mean to.'

I didn't say anything and there was a long silence. I glanced at her out of the corner of my eye as I drove, and saw that she was leaning back with her eyes shut. After a while she said carefully, 'I say – I hope you're not taking any notice of this. I do seem to be remarkably drunk. Sorry, partner.'

I said, 'That's all right. Be home soon now.'

We were only about ten minutes from home then, but she went to sleep at once, and when we stopped and got out, she seemed practically normal.

I hadn't intended to bring the business of Philippa into this; partly, I suppose, because it isn't a thing I am very proud of, but mainly because I didn't feel that she was really very much concerned with the story I am trying to tell. I meant just to say baldly that about this time I

223

acquired a mistress, that she was a good person who was very kind to me, and that I was grateful to her but never loved her, and leave it at that.

But I see now that this won't quite do, because there is no doubt that Philippa made a tremendous difference to my life during the next three months, and but for her I should probably have acted very differently.

I have already said when and how I met her. She was a war-widow of about thirty, and my first reaction to her was that she was intelligent and amusing, and moderately physically attractive without being strikingly so. She was a rather tall girl with nice grey eyes and very beautiful silky black hair, but the rest of her face wouldn't have been called pretty, and she had a big, full-lipped mouth which she always painted so as to make it look even bigger. She used a lot of make-up, and, considering that she was very hard up, managed to dress rather well. She made some sort of living by journalism, writing pretty shocking articles for women's magazines with great facility and considerable cynicism. When we first met I thought she was pretty hard boiled, though good company.

It was purely because I had this impression that I ever got in touch with her after that first meeting. I was very much in need of company, I thought of Philippa, and it seemed that she was just the person to have a drink with. I remember that I was shy about ringing her up like that. I have never been able to realise that any moderately attractive woman is ever lonely and in need of amusement. In fact, as she told me later, when I rang her up at about six o'clock one evening, the immediate prospect before Philippa was to wash her hair, and then go to bed with a bun, some coffee, and a book.

We had a very pleasant evening, and after that I took her out several more times in quick succession. We got on very well together in a rather peculiar and, to me, unusual way – a sort of deliberate and conscious refusal to go much below the surface of everyday things. From the outset it was a deliberately limited relationship – by me because I wasn't prepared to transfer more than a part of my loyalty from Jill; by Philippa because she realised this. What she gave me, she gave me because she wanted to give it; outwardly, at least, expecting nothing in return. She was one of the most unselfish women I have ever met.

And she gave me a great deal. She was a very cheerful person, with a knack of finding everything that happened to her slightly comic, and her own actions in the matter mildly absurd. After a long period of seeing myself as a pathetic – almost tragic – figure, this attitude was very refreshing. I had some bad patches after I met Philippa, but never quite again those orgies of self-pity that used to leave me feeling almost physically sick with myself.

She knew my position, and about Jill, from soon after we met, but we seldom talked about it. She never offered any opinion or advice, and never criticised Jill, though I noticed that she sometimes spoke of her with a slightly one-sided smile. I don't think she ever had any doubt, or even pretended to have any doubt, that Jill and I would join up again, and that that was what I really wanted. In the meantime, it was none of her business. Characteristically, she allowed me the best of both worlds. 'All you want, darling,' as she once put it, 'is somebody to sleep with while you're being faithful to your wife, and I don't see why you shouldn't have it.'

I said, 'And how about you? I must be damned irritating, to put it mildly.'

'Darling, you're completely maddening. But in rather a sweet way.'

I always had a conscience about Philippa. I have one to

this day. She is the only person in my life from whom I have deliberately taken more than I could give back. But she was a queer person, and knew this, and was proud of it.

During the last two week-ends before we left Crossways, Jill and I were both a good deal better and steadier than we had been – I because I was less lonely; Jill, I think, simply because she was looking forward to being with Bule. She stopped crying about everything, and we even contrived to have some quite practical discussion. Once Crossways was gone, it wasn't very complicated, except that we couldn't quite see what to do with Claude. I knew Jill didn't want him, and I could hardly have him in a furnished flat in Clarges Street. In the end, I decided to send him to board with the man who had bred him, who was used to having large masses of dog about the place. I remarked that if we'd had four children to dispose of instead of one mastiff it would all have been a good deal more difficult. Jill said, 'If Claude had been four children, it all wouldn't have happened anyway.'

The rest was fairly straightforward. We didn't have to saw the dining-room table in half, or anything of that kind, as I believe people who break up sometimes do; because, for the time being at least, nobody wanted a dining table – nor any of the rest of the stuff. The only thing we had any dispute about was money, where Jill decided to be proud and say she wouldn't take anything from me. But I pointed out to her that, whether she was living with Bule or not, I was legally liable to maintain her until we were divorced, and that anyhow I didn't wish her to be entirely dependent on Bule. In the end she agreed to take twenty pounds a month. From my experience of Jill, that wouldn't get her very far. But it was all she would take.

*

It had been arranged that on the day of the move Jill should go off in the morning, and that I should stay and see most of the furniture out, and go up to London in the evening. This was rather a good idea, because it meant that Jill would, of course, be rather late for her train, and could be bundled off at high speed almost without noticing that, if there was a definite moment when we were parting, this was it. Anyhow, she went off without a tear or a protest, and seemed, on the whole, to mind more about leaving Claude than about leaving me. Perhaps it was because Bule was meeting her at the other end.

About four o'clock most of the stuff was on board, and there didn't seem to be any point in hanging about any longer. I went out to the kitchen. The Lewises and Elsie were there, clearing up. I remember that for some reason the place was full of wasps, though it was only July. Jill had left out a bottle of sherry so that I could have a drink at lunch time, and it was still about half full. I said, 'Here – we can't leave that behind. We'd better drink it.' All the glasses had been packed by then, so we had to drink it out of some old kitchen teacups which were still about. Mrs Lewis giggled, as she always did when you gave her a drink. Elsie was very shy about it. Lewis said, 'Well – here's good luck for the future.' I thought he said it with a trace of impudence, and that both he and his wife looked at me slightly oddly. I think they probably knew a good deal more about why we were leaving than we realised. I had meant to say something to Elsie, to confirm what we had arranged about going on with her allowance. But it was awkward with the Lewises there, and it was all understood; so I just shook hands and came away.

I wasn't taking the car. She was getting on in years, and I didn't want her in London. I had arranged to sell her to a garage near the station. So I now went on a sort of delivery round. I had a crate of geese, and the cat in another box, and Claude. They all had to go to different people, and it took me nearly an hour to drive round and drop them and say good-bye. After that, there were only the car and me.

It was a beautiful evening, and going across the ridge on the way to the station I suddenly realised that everything was now disposed of, and that I had a tankful of petrol and plenty of money, and there was really no reason why I should go to London at all. There was no reason why I shouldn't turn off and go anywhere else in England – or out of it. I even stopped the car on the ridge and sat and played with the idea vaguely. But there was nowhere I wanted to go, and in the end I just drove on, and left the car at the garage, and went to the station.

The train was practically empty, and I had a compartment to myself. I had nothing to carry, and I put my hat on the seat beside me. It was a rather unpleasant brown hat that I had always disliked. Somehow it seemed absurd to have that as the only thing I had to cart away from Crossways, so I threw it out of the window, and when I arrived in London I had nothing with me. It was very strange to see London, when one had this peculiar feeling of having nothing. I walked slowly from Charing Cross to the Club, tasting this sensation, and I still don't know whether it was good or bad.

By walking very slowly, I managed not to get to the Club until half-past six, which meant that there were some people there to have a drink with and talk to. But you need to be in the right mood to enjoy the talk in the bar of your club, and, after half an hour of it, I went and sat down and read a magazine. I had a feeling that if I could get through that evening somehow, life might begin again the next day, and that I might find something to take away this peculiar feeling of emptiness and blankness. The one thing I was sure about was that I must not go back to Clarges Street until as late as possible – until I could go in and fall straight into bed, without ever having to look at the place. If I had had any sense, I might have guessed beforehand that this would be a bad evening to be alone, and have arranged to go to the theatre or a concert. But I hadn't, and the Club wasn't helpful. The place was very empty, and only a handful of people were dining. I tried ringing Philippa, but she wasn't there, and by ten o'clock there was nothing to be done about it but to go back to the flat. On the way there, I even went into a pub and sat and drank beer by myself for a few minutes until turning-out time, which is a thing I don't think I have ever done before, and don't much want to do again.

My bedroom was immediately inside the door of the flat, and I had meant to go straight into it without ever going into the living-room. But as soon as I opened the front door, I saw a light under the door of the living-room, and knew. I went in, and Philippa was sitting on the floor by the electric fire, reading. Judging from the number of cigarette butts in the ash-tray, she had been there some time. She looked up and smiled and said, 'Hullo. Sorry about this.' I kissed her and said, 'Bless you.' It wasn't a very adequate remark but it was exactly what I meant at the moment.

Philippa said, 'I thought you might possibly turn up with your wife, or a bit of your love life or something, which would have been awkward. But it seemed worth chancing.'

I said, 'I haven't got a wife. Or a love life. Or a house. Or a dog. Or a car. And I've thrown my hat out of a window, and if you hadn't been here I should probably have thrown myself out of another. As you probably guessed.'

'I guessed that you'd either go and get drunk and riot round the town with a blonde, feeling very free, or else you'd get back here feeling fed up. Being you, the chances were that it'd be the second.' She looked round the room for a moment and then said, gently, 'You know, I don't really think you'd better stay here. It's rather an awful dump. What do you pay for it?'

'Twelve guineas a week.'

'My God.'

I said, 'I don't mind that. It's having to come here as well that gets me. Usually, if they fine you, they don't make you go to jail too.'

Philippa got up and said, 'Well, it's a lousy place. Let's go somewhere else.'

'Where?'

'My flat. It isn't as grand as this, and the geyser's a peril. But it's less like the set for a Russian tragedy. I've got a spare bed, though the mattress is a bit odd.'

It was just off Church Street, Kensington, up about six flights of stairs, and it had been the attics of a tall, narrow house, with a grocer's shop at street level. Philippa had bought practically everything in it from junk furniture shops, and the only thing on the floor of her spare room was a rubber bath mat. There was a bath, but it was in the kitchen, or else the gas cooker was in the bathroom, depending upon how you looked at it. There were odd garments of Philippa's practically everywhere. She was not a tidy person. We sat by the gas fire and drank tea and talked until about three o'clock the next morning.

I never went back to Clarges Street.

15

I suppose this period when I stayed at Philippa's flat can't really have been more than six weeks or a couple of months; but it always seems to have been longer. Perhaps this is because we fell at once into a certain rhythm and design of life, so that whilst I can remember hardly any specific incident, the pattern of the thing remains very clear to me. Philippa had a life of her own, and she neither altered it, nor expected me to alter mine. I lived in the place, and worked from it. If I wanted her company she was usually there. But she never allowed me to feel that she was depending on me, or expecting me to spend time with her that I might have wanted to spend in other ways. She knew I was fond of her, but not in love with her. She knew that she was seeing me through a bad patch; and she preferred it to stay at that. I have never been so close to a person in some ways, whilst knowing so little about them in others.

I think I should have got to know her better, and perhaps have been more generally conscious of what was going on around me, if it hadn't been for Jill. The sensible thing would have been for us to stay completely apart. But I had promised her that I would always let her know where I was, and, once she knew my telephone number, she was always finding some reason for ringing up, and suggesting that we should meet for a drink or a meal. I never used to ring her, or make any advances. But there were a certain number of things that had to be settled, and we met at least once a week.

I hated these meetings with Jill, and Philippa once told

me that it always took me about two days to get back to normal after one of them. Yet somehow I could never bring myself to tell Jill bluntly that I would rather not see her.

There was no doubt that she was having a bad time. She always professed to be delighted that I had left Clarges Street and gone to Philippa, and I think this was probably true. But she herself was coming up against all the obvious difficulties. In fact there was something peculiarly exasperating to me in having foreseen it all so accurately, and in having to watch Jill slowly and painfully finding out what anybody could have told her beforehand. She didn't complain about Bule. In fact she usually talked about their relationship with a sort of cynical, almost desperate, gaiety. But she left me in no doubt of the way things were going.

The truth was, of course, that Bule had never wanted to become involved in anything as complicated or important as this. All he had wanted was a pleasant love affair with no catches in it; and to find that his life was positively being affected and interfered with apparently left him with a sense of grievance. Not that he was letting it be interfered with much. As far as I could understand, he was just going on doing whatever he wanted to do, and leaving Jill to fit in as and when she could. On two of the occasions when I saw her, he had gone down to his house, and since she couldn't very well go there, she was left alone in London. I think she suspected that he had other love affairs going on too, though she never said so.

I hated all this; in theory, I didn't mind Jill's nose being rubbed in it. She had not only asked for trouble, but more or less insisted on having it. But it is never much fun to see a gentle and generous person being hurt and humiliated; and even less fun when she has been your wife.

Yet there was nothing I could do. She was still in love

with him. She used to talk sadly about us, and about how she hated being away from me, just as she had done it when we were at Crossways. But I knew quite well that if I had her back, Bule would only have to snap his fingers and it would all start again. In fact, she hardly bothered to deny it now.

And of course the effect of it all was to tear me to bits. I pitied her, and despised her, and hated her, and, I suppose, loved her too, in a way. But the worst part of it was that this mix-up of feelings came out as a sort of furious irritation, so that I couldn't be with her for ten minutes without losing my temper. I knew that she was in an utter mess, and that what she wanted from me was some sort of comfort and gentleness and friendliness and sanity; and sometimes for a few minutes I could give it to her. But sooner or later, the sheer blank silliness of the thing, and the sense of utter waste and folly came back to me. And then I would sneer at her and try to hurt her, and go away and wish I were dead. I remember once when I was in this mood she said something about 'really being too old for this sort of thing.' I looked at her, and she was looking tired and drawn and I knew she was miserable. And I said, 'Oh, no, darling. A rose in bloom. Getting just a *trifle* brown round the edges of the petals perhaps, but still . . .'

Yet she would go on arranging for us to meet. I still don't see why I let her.

In the end, I began to realise that it couldn't go on much longer, because it was quite obvious that Jill was going to break up. She had become very thin, and she looked five years older than she had done when they came back from Spain. I told her to see a doctor, but she always insisted that she was quite all right – quite all right, and jumping violently at any sudden noise and with her nails always digging into the palms of her hands, and looking as though she hadn't slept for a week.

The last time I saw her must have been about two months after we left Crossways. I think it was three days later, on a Saturday, that I was called to the telephone at the Club some time before eight o'clock, and found it was Bule. He said: 'Sorry to bother you, James, but do you happen to have Madam?'

I said, 'They don't let females in here. Why? Have you lost her?'

'Not exactly lost. Just mislaid for the moment. I thought she might have been in touch with you.'

He said it all a bit too casually and I was frightened. I said, 'What's happened?'

'Oh, nothing important. I'm sorry to have bothered you.'

'Why did you think she might have been looking for me?'

'Well, my dear man, she quite often is.'

I said, 'Look – you know the state that girl's in. If you've had a row or something, for God's sake tell me, because . . .'

'Not exactly a row. It's just that she was a bit upset and I thought . . .'

I said, 'Get into a cab and come round here. And fast, before I come and break your neck.'

He hesitated and then said curtly, 'All right,' and rang off.

I had been right about the casualness. Something had shaken him badly. He looked very green and seemed glad of a drink.

I said, 'Now tell me. She's walked out on you, has she?'

'For the moment. I imagine she'll come back.'

'Why did she walk out?'

'Oh – a bit of mutual stupidity – mainly mine.'

'What about?'

He hesitated. 'Really, James, I don't think there's any point in going into it. I assure you that it was quite a minor thing.'

I said, 'I've done my best to be reasonable in all this, and I've tried to be fair to you. Now play fair back. What *happened*?'

He sat and looked at his cigarette for a moment and then shrugged his shoulders. 'All right. If you put it like that. We'd been going down to Cornwall this week-end. I found I'd made a double date and couldn't go. And she was disappointed. That's all.'

'You've been down at your place. When did you get back?'

'To-day.'

'And where's your other date?'

'Rye.'

'Where she couldn't go with you?'

'Yes.'

'So after leaving her alone in London all the week, you came back to-day and were going straight off again?'

His lips tightened slightly. I said, 'I'm not accusing you. It's not my business how you treat your mistresses, but I must know the facts.'

He nodded. 'Yes. Well, that's what it comes to. It was a pure piece of forgetfulness and I realised that she'd be disappointed. But she ... went rather surprisingly off the handle.'

'And told you what you were?'

Bule hesitated. 'Well, no. That's rather the point. If she had, I shouldn't have worried. But she got rather hysterical, and talked very wildly.'

'What did she say?'

'Oh, you know the sort of thing women do say when they're in that state.' He fidgeted with his cigarette. He might have heard women say these things before, but he hadn't liked hearing them this time.

I said, 'What you mean is that she said she'd kill herself?'

'No. As a matter of fact I don't think she did. She said she wished she were dead. But it was all very incoherent. One thing she kept saying was, "I wanted to, and you wouldn't let me, and now it'll never come right." *What* particular thing she's wanted, I've no idea. But it was something I'd stopped her from doing. Coming back to you, presumably.'

I said sharply, 'Say that again. What she kept saying?'

'I can't be sure of the words, but it was something like "You wouldn't let me, and now it'll never come right." '

I sat and thought for a moment and then the penny dropped. I jumped up and said, 'How long ago was this?'

'About half an hour before I rang you. I tried to calm her down. Then I went into the next room to the telephone, and when I came back she'd gone.' He looked up at me in surprise. 'Why? D'you think you ... ?'

I said, 'Unless she's put herself in the river, which I don't think she has, I've got a hunch that I know where she's gone. And what's more she'll probably have got the half-past seven and it's too late for us to get it.'

'Half-past seven to where?' said Bule irritably.

'To Maidley. But it's a slow one, and it only gets there a few minutes before the eight-ten, which we can just get if we run for it.'

I made a dive for the street. The big Lagonda was standing outside. I hadn't realised that he'd got it there. We piled in and I said, 'Eight o'clock. You can just do it.'

'Charing Cross?'

'Yes.'

As we started he said, 'I don't get it. You mean you think she's gone to my place? Or to Crossways? And anyhow why should she?'

I said, 'If she's gone anywhere there, it'll be to Elsie Pearce. Or Eddie.'

'Oh . . . I see . . .' he said slowly.

'That was what you "wouldn't let her do." I know, because she said the same thing to me once – that we wouldn't let her own up when she wanted to. She's got it into her head that – that all the trouble started from there, and that nothing would ever come right for her until she'd told Elsie. My bet is that she's gone to do it.'

Bule thought about it for some moments in silence. After a while he said, 'You could be right. But it's a very long shot, surely?'

I said, 'My dear man, I've known Jill as many years as you have months.'

When we stopped at the traffic lights in Trafalgar Square, the clock on St Martin's said eight-five. Just as the traffic began to move, Bule suddenly said, 'Damn!' and instead of going straight across, barged over to the right, across the stream, and shot down towards the bottom of the Strand. It was a dangerous thing to do, and there was a lot of horn-blowing.

I said, 'Here – where the hell are you going?'

Bule went across on the last moment of the amber light into Northumberland Avenue, and went down it like a scalded cat. He said gently, 'It's Saturday, sweetheart. No eight-ten on Saturday. No nothing until nearly ten.'

'My God, you're right. I'd forgotten it was Saturday.'

'In . . . which . . . case,' said Bule, as he whipped in and out on to the Embankment, 'the question is whether . . . I can get us there . . . before . . . the . . . seven-thirty, which

... depends on ... how much I'm held up by ... the bloody traffic between here and New Cross. What time does that train get there?'

'Nine-fourteen.'

He glanced up at Big Ben as we turned over Westminster Bridge. It was six minutes past eight.

He gave a slight shrug. 'Well, I *have* done it in an hour and a quarter. But it takes a bit of luck, and we don't seem to have a lot of that about at the moment. Still ...' He hitched the driving seat forward another notch so that he was sitting right up to the wheel, and I saw his elbows come in to his sides, and the curious look of blank concentration come on to his face that I had noticed that night when they drove me home from the station.

I must have done that drive out of London hundreds of times. Usually one is so resigned to crawling along in traffic practically all the way to Bromley, and doesn't much notice whether the going is unusually good or unusually bad. I doubt if it was particularly bad that night, but of course it felt like it. Bule had his own theories about the route, and we spent a lot of time shooting down empty side streets, round three sides of a square and back on to the main road like a taxi in the rush hour. The Lagonda accelerated like an aeroplane in a power dive, and Bule drove her as though he was driving in some peculiar sort of road race, with his eyes flicking down to the rev. counter before every gear change. I don't think he used top gear for more than a few seconds all the way from Westminster to New Cross. As long as we were in traffic he talked to himself all the time in a jerky undertone, swearing at other drivers and reasoning with policemen and traffic lights, keeping time with what he was doing with the car. It was a curious effect, though I only remember one thing that he said. Just as we went away from some lights, a woman ran across the road, and we nearly got her. Bule muttered, 'My dear lady ... my dear silly old cow ... don't do that ... or you'll join the lamented Joe ... and then we shan't be able to stop because we're ... in a hurry and then ... there'll be an even bigger mess.'

As we finally got clear, he turned on to the A20, the Dover Road. I said, 'You know it's a lot farther this way?'

He said, 'It's five miles farther and I can average another ten miles an hour. I don't come this way unless I'm in a hurry, but if you've got the knots and don't mind using them, it's quicker.'

He lit himself a cigarette very quickly and deftly and settled down to it. I don't know what the car's maximum speed was, but it was something very high, and I doubt if he ever went within ten miles an hour of it. But he kept her moving in her very fast stride, so that the effect was of one smooth rush, yet always with the feeling that the car was what a horseman would call 'collected.' And in a run where he was driving a fast car very fast, he never, in the first hour, took a serious risk. Whatever else he was, he was a magnificent driver.

Bule stopped the trick of talking to himself as soon as we were clear of traffic and for a long time we drove in silence. Then he said suddenly, 'I never knew she felt like that – about Pearce.'

'She never told you?'

'Not a word. Anyhow, *did* she want to own up and *did* I stop her? I don't remember that particularly.'

I said, 'It wasn't you. It was both of us. At least that's what she said to me. Anyhow, it's a nonsense. The thing was a complete Jill-manœuvre.'

'What exactly do you mean by a Jill-manœuvre?'

'A method of getting somebody else to insist on your doing what you want to do anyway.'

'Yes,' said Bule thoughtfully, 'I see what you mean.'

'She always does it. Then somebody else carries the responsibility.'

'Yes. She doesn't do that with me, because carrying responsibility isn't my strong suit. Hand it to me, and I just drop it. But I can well see that she would do it with you. And of course you like it.'

I said, 'Do I? I doubt it.'

'Oh, come – the father-figure to end all father-figures. But anyhow, why should she suddenly do this?'

'She feels she hasn't really got you. She thinks she really lost me because I hated all the wangling over the Pearce thing. And she's got a bee in her bonnet that until she's owned up and been punished I shall never like her.'

'I see,' said Bule thoughtfully. 'And is she right?'

I hesitated and then said, 'No. She isn't. I *didn't* like it and resented having to do it. But I don't hold it against her particularly.'

Bule changed down for a roundabout, and took the car round it with her offside wheels about three inches from the concrete curb. As he snicked top gear in again he said, 'I only ask because, assuming for a moment that we get there in time and also assuming that your guess is right and that she *is* on the train, what exactly are we going to do about it?'

'Stop her and tell her not to be an ass.'

'But you're sure she's *being* an ass?'

'How d'you mean?'

'James, my dear man, let's be quite clear about this. To me there's no problem here. There never has been. I don't feel strongly about Justice and Fairness and all the other abstractions. I don't think life is a just or fair business, and I see no particular reason why it should be. On the other hand I intensely dislike fuss and inconvenience and discomfort. So my sole-reaction to this mess was how to get out of it as conveniently and pleasantly as possible. At the time, in spite of anything she may say now, I think Jill agreed with me. But you're a very different sort of person who *does* mind about justice, etcetera, so it came rather hard on you. If Jill didn't like what we did, it was purely because she thought you wouldn't.'

I said, 'I think that's probably true.'

'Yes. Well, here's the point. Jill's been married to you for years, and for years she's been assuming that what you said and thought was the Voice of God, so to speak. I've come across this in scores of little ways with her. In a lot of them, I've laughed her out of it. But it may be that this Pearce business feels to her like a mortal sin against God – *i.e.* you. And in that case the girl may be quite right – she never *will* be happy until she's owned up, and thereby put herself right with God – *i.e.* you.'

I said dully, 'It was my choice. I could have made her go to the police. I didn't, and there it is.'

'Oh, quite. Unlike the normal God you may conceivably have made a mistake. But if you did, then you mustn't stop her from trying to put it right. And if you didn't, then you must tell her that you stand by your previous decision, and that you don't disapprove of her for acting on it.'

'I never have.'

Bule smiled at the road. 'Oh, yes you have, James, and oh, yes you do. Witness what you said a moment ago about a Jill-manœuvre. You want it both ways. You want to be a chap who loved his wife, and was prepared to say, "To hell with Mrs Pearce and everybody else but her." But you also want to make it clear that you're a good, socially minded citizen with a feeling for justice, who thoroughly disapproves of doing a thing like that.'

I said, 'I think both those things happen to be true.'

'I dare say. I'm not interested in your conflicts. But in effect what you've done is to say, "I will prevent my wife from going to prison. But I don't mind her being in a mild hell." And Jill, poor sweet, being a reasonably direct and simple person, finds this rather confusing. So do I.'

I said, 'You're implying that I've worried her about the Pearce affair. It's quite untrue. I never have.'

'Maybe not in so many words. But she's been cast out of the Divine Presence ever since, hasn't she?'

I said, 'Well, my God . . . ! That really is pretty cool, even for you! So I cast her out, did I? Do you realise . . . ?'

Bule's eyes never left the uncoiling road. 'Don't let's argue about it, James,' he said rather wearily. 'Who left who, and which came first, the chicken or the egg, and all that stuff. The point is that if she has come down here, it's in a last desperate attempt to do what she thinks you want. For God's sake, make up your mind what you *do* want, and make it clear to her, or she'll go crazy. I'll do anything anybody likes. I don't understand either of you – and particularly not you. But I only want everybody to be happy. So I'll keep quiet, or go to the police, and give evidence, true or false, or any damn thing that I'm told. But you're the boss on the moral front so, for the love of Mike, let the men in the ranks know their orders.'

I said slowly, 'I think she's got to be stopped. It's too late to own up now. It wouldn't do any good. I see what you mean, but it isn't on.'

'Right,' said Bule promptly. 'Now we know where we are.'

You turn south off the A20 about fifteen miles from Maidley. As we did so I looked at my watch and said, 'Five to nine. Nearly twenty minutes . . .'

Bule thought for a moment and then shook his head rather dubiously. 'It'll be a near thing, James. If it were a decent road from here on, it'd be a pushover. But I wouldn't guarantee to average forty-five over this bit in anything – not without an odds-on chance of breaking our necks, which wouldn't help much. Still, we'll do our best. Any chance that the train will run late?'

'It's usually fairly good. Never more than a few minutes behind.'

'Well, it had better be a few minutes behind to-night. What's the good of having the railways nationalised if you can't have a train a few minutes late?'

He scared me on that last fifteen miles. He was still driving beautifully, but the roads were narrow now, and in order to keep moving fast now he had to take chances. For a while I thought we were just going to do it, but the last bits get gradually more and more difficult. At ten-past nine we were still only at Lifley, five miles away.

I said, 'We shan't make it.'

'I know, damn it. Sorry, James.'

'I've never seen a better piece of driving.'

'What shall I do? Go for the station anyhow? She might be late.'

I thought and then said, 'No. If we go to the station and it isn't late, we're sunk. Whereas if we go straight to the village and it *is* late, we're all right anyway.'

'But if we don't get her at the station we may miss her. She may go to Eddie, or Elsie, or even my place.'

'Make for Tarrant's Lane. She'll go to Elsie.'

Bule turned off and said, 'You seem very sure about the whole thing. It'll be rather funny if she's sitting in the flat doing a bit of knitting and listening to the radio.'

I said, 'In that case I shall have pleasure in paying you for all this petrol. But she'll be on that train, and she'll go straight to Elsie.'

Bule said, 'I sometimes think that you know practically

everything about Jill except anything that matters. If the train's in time and she gets a taxi at once she'd be there by nine twenty-five; and so shall we, as near as damn it.'

I said, 'We'd better be there first. She won't waste any time.'

It was twenty-six minutes past nine as we turned into Tarrant's Lane. As we did so a car came along it. We were travelling too fast for that narrow place and there wasn't time to stop. Bule said 'Hell!' very softly, and went over so that his hub caps cut a piece out of the bank, and a bush brushed the side of the car. We got by without touching, though there can't have been three inches in it. Bule said calmly, 'Sorry again, James. We're sunk.'

'Why?'

'That will have been Madam's taxi coming away, my dear. I told you we needed luck, and it isn't a thing we've got in the shop just now.'

16

We went the remaining four hundred yards down Tarrant's Lane and round the slight bend. The road was at its narrowest just there, and Bule had to go on a few yards, past Thorn Cottage to the garden gate, if the car wasn't to block it entirely. The light was going fast. We had been driving on the spotlight and for a moment I had an absurd idea that Joe would come shooting out from the darkness of the garden with his bicycle, right under our near wing, into that glaring light.

I jumped out almost before the car had stopped, and went back. There was a light in the front window of Thorn Cottage. Somebody was standing silhouetted against it at the window. That would be Elsie, and I remembered that she had gone to the window to look at every car that passed, and that she had said the car that killed Joe would come again if she went on watching. I had knocked at the door before it occurred to me that, after all, Jill might not be there, and that then I should have to have some excuse for coming. Under my breath I said, 'Hullo, Elsie, I was just passing and I thought I'd drop in and see how you were.' But nobody passed to anywhere along Tarrant's Lane at night. That had always been the difficulty.

The door opened, and as soon as it did I knew Jill was there. I said, 'Good evening, Elsie.' She said, 'Oh . . . good evening, sir . . .' and looked past me, and I realised that Bule had come up behind me. I had forgotten about Bule. Elsie stepped aside and said something. I expect it was 'Won't you come in?' I went past her and saw Jill standing there by the fire, where the old woman used to sit. She was wearing a very smart black town suit, and it looked odd in that room. I suppose it was what she had on when she had the row with Bule. She was very pale, and all her make-up showed in patches against her skin. When she saw me she suddenly put her hand up and drew her fingers hard down her cheek and gave a sort of shudder, and her lips said something, I think it was 'No,' but it may have been 'Hullo.'

I said, 'Hullo, darling. You are here, then. I thought you might be.'

I turned to Elsie and said, 'I wasn't sure if my wife would be here but I thought she'd almost certainly drop in to see you as we were in the village.' I was looking at her carefully, and I thought it was all right – that she didn't know. But with that queer, squinting, bony mask, you couldn't be sure. So I covered up with my second idea and said, 'She hasn't been frightfully well, and we're going back to town.'

Elsie said, 'I bin saying to Madam that she looked poorly.'

I was certain then. I said, 'When did you get here, darling?'

Jill just stood there and stared at me. Elsie looked at her and waited and then said tentatively, 'It wasn't more than a minute, was it, Madam?'

Jill shook her head and muttered, 'No. Not more than a minute.'

Bule said, 'How are the children, Elsie?' He said it absolutely naturally and easily. She hesitated for a moment and then slowly turned, with her head up, and squinted at him and said, 'They're very well, thank you, Mr Bule'; and it was as though she had slapped his face. I couldn't see why for a moment, and then I realised that she must know

246

about Bule and Jill, and remembered that she had loved Jill and had liked me. Bule saw it too, but he just went on smiling and said, 'Good.'

Elsie turned to me and said in her awkward way, 'Won't you sit down, sir – I'll move that...' She whipped the usual mess of children's clothes off a chair, '... and perhaps Madam would like a cup of tea? I've got the kettle on. Won't take a moment...?'

I said, 'It's very good of you, Elsie, but I really don't think we ought to stay. We've got to get up to London to-night and I don't want my wife to be late.' I made a slight confidential movement of my head.

Elsie said, 'Of course not, sir...' She hesitated and looked doubtfully at Jill.

Jill was still staring at me. I don't think she had ever taken her eyes off me since we came in. She said in a low voice, 'I've sent for Eddie.'

I hadn't thought of that one. I expect Elsie thought I was puzzled. She said almost apologetically, 'Madam said she wanted to see Eddie, sir, so I sent Maureen round for him. He won't be a minute I don't expect, but of course if you...'

Bule said, 'Look, Jill, I really think we ought to get on back. You can see Eddie next time you're down.'

Jill turned her head and looked at him for a moment and then turned back to me without a word. Elsie said gently, 'Or if there's any message I could give him, Madam...? I'll be seeing him to-morrow?' She said it almost coaxingly.

Bule said, 'Anyhow, surely Eddie's usually out at this time in the evening, isn't he, Elsie?' I think he wanted to make sure about the slap in the face. She turned to him exactly as before and said, 'I couldn't say, Mr Bule,' and after that he can't have had any doubt about it.

Jill had closed her eyes again. She swayed slightly and

put a hand out to steady herself. Elsie and I both moved forward quickly. I put a hand under her arm and said, 'Come on, old lady – I think bed's the place for you.' Elsie said something to me in a low voice that I didn't catch, except for the word 'poorly.' She was squinting at Jill with her head slightly on one side, and an expression of deep concern.

Suddenly I felt Jill's arm tense under my hand. She pulled away and turned and looked at me and said, 'You wouldn't stop me now. You wouldn't do that to me, darling . . .' She was asking for mercy and I couldn't go on looking at her eyes. I looked away and said very gently, 'You'd better come home, Jilly. You've got everything a bit mixed up.'

She said, 'No!' in a sort of angry wail. 'No! It isn't mixed up. *You're* mixing it up again and I had it all clear . . . Jimmy, don't you see it was this that did it to us and I must get rid of it otherwise I – I can't go on. You *must* see I can't.'

Bule said quietly, 'Jill, you're talking nonsense.'

She took no notice, and never even looked at him. She said, 'You didn't believe it was right. I knew you didn't. If only you'd stuck to what you believed, it would have been all right. But you swung round and said the other thing, and that we must be sensible. And then I got confused, because then there – there wasn't you any more.'

I said, 'I thought I was giving you – what you wanted.'

'I know – I know,' she said wretchedly, 'but you oughtn't to have cared a damn what I wanted. I wasn't worth much, anyhow. And you paid too much for me. More than you could afford. And after that you always hated me and – and wouldn't have me. And so I didn't care what happened . . .'

I suddenly remembered that Elsie was standing there

squinting from one to the other of us with that anxious watching-by-the-sick-bed expression. I managed to smile and said, 'Well, look, darling – isn't it a bit mean to do all this on Elsie? Hadn't we better go home and talk about it?' The fear came back into her eyes and she said, 'No!' just as she had done when we came in.

'But . . .'

'No,' she said desperately. 'If we go away you'll never let me come back and do it, and it'll never be right and we shall go on and on . . .' She turned to Elsie and said, 'It was me, Elsie.'

Bule took a quick step forward and said very calmly, 'Come, come, Jill – you're forgetting your grammar. You should say, "It was I." And you should also now come home because . . .' He was moving as though to take her by the arm. Jill shrank back from him slightly and looked at me. I thought, 'She's dying, and what she's asking me to do is to finish it for her.'

Bule was saying, '. . . so come along and . . .'

I said, 'Shut up!'

I turned to Elsie and said very carefully, 'What my wife is trying to tell you is that she was responsible for Joe's death.'

There was a moment's pause. In the silence, Bule murmured gently, 'Oh, James – James – a bad general. You never let the man in the ranks know . . .'

Elsie said stupidly, 'For what, sir?'

'For Joe's death.'

Elsie looked at Jill for a moment and then said in an odd voice, 'She doesn't know what she's saying, sir. She's poorly . . .'

Bule said, 'Of course she doesn't. She ought to be in bed.'

Elsie whipped round sharply on him. She was a very big,

gaunt woman and she looked terrifying. She said, 'No, Mr Bule – she doesn't know what she's saying. But there's some could tell about that, if they had a mind to. Or so Eddie reckons.'

Bule was smiling slightly. He said gently, 'Well, well – and what does Eddie reckon?' She took a step towards him and pushed the hideous mask up at him. 'He reckons you was driving down the lane and sneaking up to Mr Manning's back gate after Madam, and that's how it happened. And now you know.'

Bule said, still with the slight smile, 'Eddie's a hell of a good detective. That's exactly what *did* happen, Elsie. And now *you* know.'

The colour had gone from Elsie's face leaving it mottled with tiny red veins. Jill said wearily, 'It's not true, Elsie. It was me. He was there, but I was driving the car.'

Elsie turned and looked at her. Then she said in a quick mutter, 'No, no, Madam. It was him. Eddie knows, see? Only he can't prove it.'

Jill said doggedly, 'I killed Joe.'

'No,' Elsie said with the same frightened urgency. 'It was him. Eddie, he *knows*. Besides you wouldn't do that – not drive on and leave him there, Madam. You've always been good to people. You wouldn't do that. It was him. And that's his car. I see it come to-night like it did . . .'

Jill said, 'It was that car. But I was driving.'

Elsie turned to me and said, 'Mr Manning, Madam doesn't know . . .'

I said, 'I'm sorry, Elsie, but what my wife is saying is true. It was Mr Bule's car that hit Joe, but she was driving it.'

She stood there for a moment stock still. Then she said almost in a whisper, 'But he *said* he done it.'

'It isn't true. He was only trying to protect my wife.'

Elsie's head turned very slowly to Jill. She said gently and with wonder, 'And you never *said*, Madam . . . ?'

Jill said, 'I didn't know. Oh God, I didn't know I'd hit him . . .' She put her hands over her face. I grabbed her and for a moment her weight was full on my arm.

Elsie said quickly, 'She's going off, sir . . . she ought to lie down . . .'

Jill stiffened and said, 'And then after I was frightened and – and they wouldn't let me . . .' Her voice rose. 'But I *did* tell you. And now we can tell Eddie and they can do it to me and then . . .'

She covered her face again. Bule said quietly, 'You see what happened, Elsie, was that Mrs Manning was driving past just as Joe came out and . . .'

Elsie said, '*You* . . .'

He stopped when she said that, and tried to smile. But she wasn't an easy thing to smile at, and all that happened was a rather ghastly parting of his lips. She spoke quite quietly, almost breathlessly. She said, '*You* . . .! You – coming sneaking round after Madam when Mr Manning wasn't there. Trying to come between them that loved each other, and she that was always good to people and Mr Manning too, with your car and all your la-di-da and Honourable and the rest of it. And rushing about and running over my Joe and not caring. You ought to be hung. An' you *shall* be, because Eddie knows. He knows it was you and . . .' She stopped suddenly and an expression of utter bewilderment spread slowly over her face. She looked in a startled way from Bule to Jill and back again. Then she turned to me and said almost in panic. 'But what are we going to say to Eddie, sir? Eddie's coming. What are we going to *say* . . .'

Jill said, 'I'm going to tell him.'

'No, no, Madam,' said Elsie in terror. 'You mustn't say

that to Eddie. Otherwise he'll ... he'll ... See, if you tell *him ...*'

Jill said wearily, 'But I did it.'

'Yes. But you never meant it. You didn't know. Otherwise you'd have stopped. But, see, if you tell Eddie he'll be angry and being in the police ... He can be awful, Eddie can. So you mustn't ...'

Bule said, 'I think what Elsie's saying is that it would have been much more convenient and satisfactory if we assume that *I* was driving. Which, I would point out, is what I've said from the beginning.'

Elsie was saying, 'See, Madam, if you was to tell Eddie that, he wouldn't understand, not knowing you like I do, and he'll never take any notice of me when I say anything ...'

Eddie came in without knocking. After all it was his sister's house. I never knew what happened to Maureen, who'd been sent to fetch him. Perhaps she came in by the back door or something. They were odd, rather self-effacing children. I fancied that Eddie had a queer glitter in the hot blue eyes and I thought, 'He's spotted the car outside.' I said, 'Ah, hullo, Eddie. Here you are,' and shook hands with him. He said, 'Good evening, sir. Good evening, Madam. 'Evening, Mr Bule.' He looked at Elsie inquiringly and said, 'Maureen said Mrs Manning wanted ... I 'spect it was Mr Manning really but she *said* Mrs Manning ...'

Elsie said quickly, 'Well, Eddie ... see Mrs Manning's been taken poorly so ...'

The hot angry eyes went to Jill. They were puzzled. Whether they were suspicious, I couldn't tell.

I said, 'It was just that we dropped in to see Elsie, and thought we'd like to say hullo to you, Eddie.'

'Oh,' he said slowly, 'I see. Only Maureen said ...'

Elsie said, 'I just told her to come and get you, that's all.'

He nodded. His eyes were on Jill. He said, 'I'm sorry you're not well, Madam.'

Jill opened her lips but nothing came out.

I said, 'Elsie only told you that because we'd been saying that we must go. We've got to get up to town to-night.'

Eddie said, 'Ah. Well, I'm glad you didn't go without seeing me, sir.' He paused and added gently, 'Going up in Mr Bule's car?'

'Yes.'

He nodded again. 'Nice car. I was looking at it when I came in.' He turned to his sister. 'You seen it, Elsie? Mr Bule's car? You come and look at it.' He took her gently by the arm and led her over to the window. She hesitated for a moment and then let him take her. Eddie said softly, 'You have a look at it out of the window. 'Course you can't see it much without the lights on . . .'

Bule said, 'Come outside and have a look at it, if you like.'

Eddie slowly shook his head. 'No, thank you, Mr Bule. Don't bother. I dare say Elsie saw it when you came. Didn't you, Elsie?'

She said, 'Yes,' in a low voice. Eddie said, 'Ah . . .' and seemed to be waiting for something. But she stood there and looked at him in silence and fear. A slight frown came over Eddie's face and he glanced swiftly round from one to the other of us, like a man who is trying to see who are his friends and who are his foes. With his eyes still on Bule he said quietly to Elsie, 'It's a lovely car. I doubt you ever seen one like it before, have you, Elsie?'

'I seen Mr Bule about in that one,' she said huskily. Bule had produced a packet of cigarettes. He took one and then, like one who had forgotten his manners, offered the packet with a smile and said, 'Sorry, Eddie . . . ?' Eddie pushed his chin forward so that the scar showed vividly and said rather loudly, 'No thank you, Mr Bule.' He turned back to his sister and said, 'But not down here I'll lay. You've never seen Mr Bule's car in this narrow place before?'

She squinted at him with the same expression of fear and said tremulously, 'No, Eddie. No. I ain't.'

There was a long pause and I saw her shrink back a little as he stared into her face with the white-lashed, unwinking blue eyes. I said, 'How's the pig, Eddie? Killed him yet?'

He had to turn, and as he turned something of the tension went out of him. He said, 'Last week, sir.'

'What did he go? Nine score?'

'Near on ten, Mr Manning . . .'

He looked round again in that suspicious inquiring way, and I realised that, with those white lashes and the pushed-forward snouty face, he looked himself like a puzzled and angry pig, trying to nose its way through some obstruction. He had pushed his snout against Elsie and she had stood firm, and now he turned and pushed in another direction. 'I couldn't understand it when Maureen came. She didn't say anything about you being here, Mr Manning. She said, "Mrs Manning's with mum and she wants to talk to you." I thought to myself, "Now what will that be . . . ?" '

I said, 'It was rather mean to fetch you out like that, wasn't it, Jill?'

It was taking a chance and I knew it was taking one. But she had looked at me like that, and said she was dying and in pain, and asked me to finish it, and I couldn't gang up with anybody against her any more. She looked at me now for a moment, and I tried to show her that I was with her whatever she did; and then she suddenly smiled slightly at Eddie and said, 'Yes. It was an awful shame. But we did want just – just to see you. As we were down here.' I knew that that was the answer, as long as Elsie didn't crack; and I didn't know, and don't know now, whether I was glad or sorry.

Eddie said respectfully, 'Where are you living now, Mrs Manning? We haven't heard much about you since you left Crossways?'

Jill said, 'In London. We're ... in London.' Her hand went up to her cheek and she drew her fingers hard down it. I could see she hadn't got much left. Elsie saw it too and said, 'Madam's been poorly ...'

Something in the way she said it must have angered him. He was strung up and suspicious, and he was an irritable man. He swung round on Elsie and said, 'Oh, shut your mouth!' There was something brutal about the anger in his voice. I said quietly, 'Eddie.' But he had let himself be angry now and he had to go on. He pushed his chin out at me and said, 'Yes, *sir*?' loudly, like a man who is looking for a fight. I said, 'I don't think you should be rude to Elsie.'

'No, sir. Maybe not. But I was brought here, told that Mrs Manning wanted to talk to me; and if she does, Mrs Manning can speak for herself, without Elsie here keep saying she's poorly as soon as I speak to her.'

Bule said, 'I don't think Mrs Manning's in a fit state to talk to anybody.'

'No, Mr Bule, I don't suppose you do.' Eddie's face was red with fury now. 'And I can very well see why not, too.'

'What exactly do you mean by that?' said Bule coldly.

'You know what I mean, Mr Bule. There's something going on here and it's my duty to find out what it is. I know you wasn't here when Mrs Manning sent for me.'

I hadn't thought of that. Of course Maureen had told him. 'Well?' said Bule calmly.

'Well, sir, it could be that Mrs Manning wanted a word

with me when you weren't here, and then doesn't when you are.'

I said quietly, 'I don't quite see what's biting you, Eddie. My wife only wanted to say hullo to you.'

He whipped round and said, 'No, sir. I don't reckon so . . . ' and then as we looked at one another the fire seemed to die out of him. His chin came down, and he shook his head, and said with sudden helplessness, 'I don't see, Mr Manning. Not what it is.' The blue eyes were not angry now, only puzzled. And then suddenly his lips came open slightly and his eyes went to Jill, and I heard him draw his breath in sharply. If he had asked me then I should have told him. But he didn't. He muttered something under his breath that sounded like, 'All right, then . . . ' and took a pace so that he was standing right in front of Elsie. 'Els,' he said very gently, 'that car of Mr Bule's. You say you never seen it down here before?'

'No,' she said quietly.

'You sure of that?'

'Yes, Eddie.'

He half put out his hand as though to take hers and then drew it back again. He said in a low voice, 'Els – a car came down here one night. It killed your Joe, an' it left you a widow an' by yourself, an' the kids without a father. Them that was in it didn't care an' didn't so much as stop. I been looking for that car ever since, see?'

Elsie's lips said 'Yes.' Her face was deadly pale and twitching violently. 'You saw the car that killed your Joe. You saw it go by. Was it anything like that car out there?'

She seemed to hesitate for just a moment and Eddie said, 'They killed your Joe an' drove on an' left him lying there and . . .'

Elsie said, 'No. No – it wasn't. Not like it.'

'Why not?' he said quickly. 'Why wasn't it? It was a big car you said, and . . .'

Elsie's voice was a croak. She said, 'Wasn't like that. Not – not so big. An' different . . .'

He pushed his face forward so that it was only a few inches from hers, but she didn't flinch from him now. He said, 'You're sure?'

'Yes, Eddie. Yes, I am.'

He turned away from her with a sound that seemed to be half a groan and half a snarl. There was a moment's dead silence. Then Eddie's shoulders went back and his chin came up. He said quietly, 'Awright. Then I see how it is, an' I can't do no more.' He picked up his cap and went to the door. With his hand on the latch he looked round and said briskly, 'Good night, Mr Manning. Good night, Madam . . .' Then he turned and looked full at Bule and, still looking at him, said gently, 'Good night, Els. I done my best for you an' Joe, see?'

I said, 'Good night, Eddie.'

Nobody else spoke as the door closed quietly behind him, or for several seconds after. Bule lit another cigarette, and the match cracked sharply in the silence. Elsie was standing with her head slightly bent squinting down at the floor. Without looking up she said in a flat voice, 'Madam ought to go home an' – an' go to bed. She's poorly.'

Bule said, 'I quite agree.'

'That's right,' said Jill bitterly. 'Madam ought to go home and be put to bed and wrapped in cotton wool . . . *Damn* madam, the selfish bitch.'

I said, 'Oh, come, darling. You . . .'

She took no notice of me, but went over to Elsie, who was still staring at the floor. Jill said almost curtly, 'I'm sorry. But you see, I'm no good.'

Elsie didn't look up but her face twitched. I think she was trying to smile. She said, 'You never meant it.'

'Elsie,' said Bule quietly, 'I know you don't want me to talk, but there's just one thing. Eddie will have another go at you, you know. To see what he can get out of you . . .'

Elsie's head came up as it always did when she spoke to him.

'Don't you worry yourself, Mr Bule,' she said proudly, 'I won't talk.' Then the flash of pride was gone and she muttered again, 'Madam ought to go home and . . .'

I said, 'Yes, you're quite right. We'll go now. Take her out to the car, Bule. I'll be with you in a moment.'

Jill hesitated for a second looking at Elsie. Elsie did smile this time. She said, 'Good night, madam.' Jill turned suddenly and stumbled towards the door without a word.

Bule said, 'Good night, Elsie,' quietly, and put his hand under Jill's arm, and they went out.

When they had gone, I said, 'Why did you do that?'

'Do what, sir?'

'Why didn't you tell Eddie?'

She raised the squinting eyes to mine in simple surprise. 'Eddie would've bin angry. He'd've . . .'

'You didn't want her to get into trouble?'

'Madam's always been very good to me, Mr Manning. An' . . . an' . . .' her voice cracked. 'He wouldn't have wanted it.'

I said, 'No. Perhaps not.'

'No – he wouldn't. He was always good to people. Too good to them, he was, and there was those that took advantage of him . . . but . . . but she never meant it.'

I said, 'I want you to know that it was I who stopped her from owning up in the first place. I'm sorry, Elsie.'

She said, 'Yes, sir,' dully. But I don't think she really

took in what I said. After a moment she said again, 'I won't tell.'

I said, 'I don't like leaving you here by yourself. Couldn't you . . .'

'I'm used to it now, sir,' she said simply and without bitterness. 'You ought to go and – and take Madam . . .'

I said, 'Yes. Then good-bye, Elsie. And thank you.' I held out my hand, and saw her wipe her palm quickly down the side of her skirt before she took it. Her hand was cold and clammy. As I turned away she said, 'Mr Manning . . . don't let her have to do with him. He ain't no good.'

I said, 'No, I'll see to it.'

Bule was standing beside the car. He had put Jill in the rear seat and she was sitting with her head thrown back and her eyes closed, as though she was asleep.

Bule said quietly, 'It is now half-past ten. What would you like to do – come back to my place? Or do you want to get back to town?'

I said, 'I'd rather go back, if possible. I want to get her . . .' I was going to say 'home,' and then I realised that there wasn't any home, and that I had nowhere to take her. Bule saw, and said quickly, 'You'd better take her to my flat. She's got all her stuff there. I can see you in there, and go to the Club.'

'You won't get into your Club by the time we get up.'

'Then I shall go to a pub or a Turkish bath or something. Anyhow, let's get on back.'

He opened the back door of the car. It was the one that had had the scratch on it. I got in and said to Jill, 'We're going back to town now, Jilly.' She opened her eyes and said 'Yes.' She didn't look at me but stared straight ahead. Bule started up and switched on the big spotlight and we slid away down the lane. As we did so Jill turned quickly and looked through the back window for a long moment. Then she turned again and sat with eyes on the road in that blank, almost sullen stare. I put my arm round her and she leant wearily against me, but neither spoke nor looked. We must have driven for half an hour like that, in silence, seeing the white road rushing to meet us in the brilliant lights of the car. Then I saw her eyelids beginning to droop, and she went to sleep.

We were nearly there when she woke up again, and she seemed a good deal more with us. She said, 'Where are we going?'

'To Bill's flat. He's going to drop us there and go to his Club.'

She frowned slightly. 'Do we have to do that?'

'Not if you'd rather not. We could try a hotel. But it's a bit late.'

She said, 'No. It doesn't matter. I'm extremely sorry about that performance.'

'Never mind. We'll talk about that later. What you need now is bed.'

She said, 'Bed – what a heavenly thought . . .' She was quite in control of herself now, and when we got to the flat she said briskly, 'Well, if nobody minds, I shall go straight to bed – merely saying that I'm very sorry to have been such a bloody nuisance to everybody.'

Bule grinned and said, 'It was a pleasure, Madam.' He took her hand and kissed it and said, 'Good night, Jill. Sleep well.' She smiled back and said, 'Good night.' I think it was the only word she spoke to him directly all the evening.

When she had gone Bule said, 'I'm not quite sure whether I offer you a drink or you offer me one. But anyhow I shall have one small one, and then go. I think you'll find everything you want, and Jill knows about ordering breakfast and so on.' He went and got us drinks and said, 'That woman Elsie is quite something.'

'She is indeed.'

'Poor old Eddie. He's done such a good job on this, trying to arrange for *somebody* to be run in. And no one will help him.'

I said, 'No.' I didn't want to talk about it to him. He saw this and drank up quickly and said, 'Well, I'll clear out now. Regarding us, I think it's all fairly clear now, isn't it?'

I said, 'I'd like notice of that.'

'Oh, I think so, James. I think the erring daughter has come back to daddy all right.' He cocked an eye at me. 'I assume daddy will have her?'

I said, 'If she wants him.'

He shrugged. 'She always has. She always will. In some ways at least.' He stubbed out his cigarette and rose. 'Anyhow, it all fits rather well, because I've got to go away in a few days and I shall be away some time, which is probably a good thing.'

I said idly, 'Where are you going?'

'Switzerland.'

'At this time of year?'

'Why not? Autumn in Switzerland's pretty spectacular. Good night, James.'

17

Jill seemed all right the next day – rather surprisingly all right. She was a trifle grim, and she didn't smile much, but she was entirely sensible, and unusually business-like. We agreed that it was going to take a bit of time to get going again, and that meanwhile the best thing was to forget what had happened, and concentrate on the practical things like finding somewhere to live. I told her Bule was going away, which apparently she hadn't known, and she agreed that that made it easier, but said that she had known she was through anyhow, for some time. She said, 'You may not believe it, but there are limits to the extent that even *I* can be an ass.'

It was odd and uncomfortable being about in Bule's flat – though less so, perhaps, than I should have expected. Two days later I found a furnished place in Knightsbridge and we took that for three months, while we sorted ourselves out.

The nasty job was telling Philippa I was going. I rang her up the day after we got back, and said I wanted to talk to her that evening. I didn't say what about, but I think she guessed. She had always said it would happen sometime, and I had realised that I was just exploiting her. But that didn't make it any easier.

I had a key to the flat, and, as I went up those interminable stairs, I suddenly realised that I should probably never go up them again, and I was sorry, and afraid of something. Philippa was sitting on the floor, just as she had been that night in Clarges Street. She had a drink in her hand, and that was unusual, because we seldom drank in the flat. She didn't get up, but just smiled at me and said, 'Hullo, darling. Come and have a drink.'

I took a drink, and realised that she had already had two or three. I didn't like that because I thought I knew why.

Philippa was looking at my face with a broad grin. She said, 'How's her ladyship?'

I said, 'Well – that's what I've come about.'

'Big get together, eh?'

'How did you know?'

She laughed and said, 'Because you're looking so po-faced, darling. And anyhow you sounded po-faced on the telephone, if you *can* sound po-faced on the telephone.' She poured herself out another large gin and shook her head and said, 'You are a darling old sucker, aren't you?'

I said helplessly, 'Flip – I don't quite know what to say to you.'

'You don't have to say anything, my dear. It's all quite clear and always has been. You just give me one chaste kiss and remember to leave your keys, and that's that.'

'I think you've been kinder and more generous to me than anybody I've ever met.'

'Sure,' she said flippantly. 'There's only a few of us left. Have you slept with her yet?'

'No.'

'That was nice of you. There'd be something peculiarly insulting about a person being unfaithful to you with his own wife. Her ladyship pleased?'

'I think it's what she wants.'

'Well, my God, I should hope so!' She shook her head. 'I wish people would let *me* do that sort of thing and get away with it. Pity I've never met her. She must have something like genius, that woman.'

I said, 'Flip – I've no right to ask you, but do you mind not doing it? You never have before and . . .'

She took my hand and said, 'I'm sorry. I'm a bitch. You mustn't mind.'

I said foolishly, 'You will let me see you, and . . . ?'

She laughed and said, 'No, ducky. That I will *not* do. Stone dead hath no fellow. You're going to have another drink, and then we'll pack you up and off you go.' She looked at me for a moment and then said very softly, 'It's all right, fathead. Of course it is. It's all going to be fun – having your Jill back and starting again and . . .'

I said, 'Yes . . . yes! But how about you?'

She smiled up at me and said, 'Swank! Think I can't live without you, hey? Drink up that drink and have another.'

She came down to the door with me when I went. I kissed her and she offered me her cheek. I said, 'Oh God, Flip, it isn't right – it isn't fair.' Her lips trembled, but she smiled up at me and said quietly, 'It *is* right, and it *is* fair, and it's what I always wanted for you, and now bless you, darling, and off you go.' She gave me a gentle pat behind and I turned and went down the street without looking back. I never saw her again, or knew what happened to her, except that she moved from the flat soon after.

I suppose really that that ought to be the end of it – the neat, rounded end, after which you can reach under the seat for your hat, feeling that everything to follow can reasonably be inferred. And so perhaps it might have been but for the purest chance. Or perhaps not. I have never known, in this whole story, whether everything turned on these small chances; or whether it was all quite inevitable, and that chance never determined what happened, but only the way in which it happened. The chance here was a fat man named Burrell. I was at school with him, and I think I have met him three times in the twenty-odd years since then. We disliked one another at school, and when we have met since we say hullo, and ask one another if we have been down to the old place, and neither of us ever has; and we ask one another if we have seen so-and-so, and neither of us has ever done that either; and then we part – with relief. That is how well I know Burrell; and I met him for the fourth time in twenty years, just about a month after that night when I said good-bye to Philippa.

I don't know quite what to say about that month. It was a bit odd and strained of course. It was bound to be that. After all, Jill and I had been apart for months, and we had lost the habit of one another to some extent. We were shy of one another, when we thought about it. But we were so used to one another's ways, that most of the time we could get along *without* thinking about it. Jill, on the whole, seemed better than I had feared she might be. She didn't mope, as she had done before we left Crossways, and she didn't crawl and apologise for her existence. It was as though, from the time she went to sleep in the car coming back that night, she had put on some curious sort of armour; and the armour made her at once tougher, and more difficult to get at. She would talk readily enough about what had happened. But she always spoke of it briskly and sensibly, and without emotion, as though it had all happened to two other people. It would be absurd to say that we had fallen in love all over again, or went on a second honeymoon, in the way people are supposed to do sometimes. I don't think either of us felt like that. We knew that we had come uncommonly near to making an absurd mess. We knew that it would take time to put things right. And we both very much wanted them to come right. We had to go slow and have patience. At least this is what we always told ourselves, and I think it was what we felt.

One thing that worried me a good deal was Jill's insistence that we should go back to the country. I knew now that she had never really liked it – that it bored her and she felt buried alive. To start all that again seemed absurd. But she insisted that we ought to do it. 'You know you like it and need it. You hate living in town. And anyhow I could do it now. The only reason why I couldn't do it before was that I was always kicking against the pricks. I shouldn't do that now.' She often said things like that – things that implied that she had changed, and would always see life differently in future. But she always said them with a curious detachment as though it was a thing to be neither glad nor sorry about, but just a fact. On the house-in-the-country business she was very insistent; and in the end, rather against my better judgment, we started to look for one in a rather vague way. It was after one of these expeditions that I met Burrell.

We had been down to look at a house somewhere in the Chilterns. It was a week-end, and we stayed with one of my co-directors, Angell – practically the only one that Jill ever liked. The house we went to see was hopeless, but their place was very pleasant, and it was arranged that Angell and I should come up to town on Sunday night, and that Jill and Judith Angell should follow on Monday. So on the Sunday night I went to dine at the Club, and there at the bar was Burrell. Some member had brought him in, given him a drink, and then pushed off to telephone.

There were very few people in the bar, and I had to talk to him. His mouth was still loose and slobbery, and he was fatter than ever. We ran through the usual formula, and agreed that we hadn't been back to the old place, and hadn't seen anybody. He then reminded me, with roars of laughter, as he always did, about the time when I beat him for throwing water over somebody else's bed. I could never remember this incident, but he always brought it up, so I suppose it must have impressed him. I hope so. Then he suddenly said, 'Seen Bill Bule lately?'

I said, 'Not for some time. Why? Is he a friend of yours?'

'Oh, Lord, yes. Known him all my life. Great friend of my brother's. He lives near you, doesn't he?'

'He did. Or rather I did. I've sold the house that was near him.'

'Oh – have you? I haven't seen him for a while, but he did mention that you were close together.' He looked towards the door and said, 'Ah – here's my host...' and then, almost as an afterthought, as he turned away— 'Very bad luck that, isn't it?'

I said, 'What is?'

'About Bill.'

'What about him?'

'Oh, haven't you heard? Very ill apparently. In the London Chest. My brother told me. Well, cheerio, old man. Nice to have seen you.'

Bule was lying in bed looking ghastly. That striking ivory pallor had turned to glass completely now, and his face and neck were very thin. Even his hand, as I shook it, seemed nothing but bones. He grinned the charming boyish grin and said, 'Well, well, James, this is very civil of you.'

I said, 'What on earth have you been doing to yourself?'

'Well, that's the rather maddening part of it. If this were all the result of drink and dissipation, I wouldn't mind. But for years they've told me I must be rather careful of my chest, and I've been rather careful of it – *rather*, not very. And this is the result.'

'I thought you were going to Switzerland?'

'I did. But it didn't work very well, so they brought me back.'

'It was because of this that you went?'

'Yes. As a matter of fact, I'd heard that I must go, the day before our Dick Turpin's ride to York in the car. How's madam?'

'She's fine. Away at the moment. Back this morning.'

'Good. All going well?'

'Yes.'

He smiled and said, 'I'm very glad, James.'

After a moment I said, 'Why didn't you ever say anything about this?'

'None of your bloody business, my dear man. And quite irrelevant anyway. Besides . . .' He hesitated for a moment.

'Besides what?'

'Well, come, James – things were complicated enough for madam without the party of the third part upping and saying, "Oh, and by the way, I'm probably going to pass up my checks."'

I said bluntly, 'Are you going to pass up your checks?'

'That appears to be a fine medical point. The docs say that broadly speaking, and all other things being equal, they cannot absolutely guarantee to be responsible for the outcome. Which is big of them.'

He lay surprisingly still, only moving his eyes and his mouth. I said, 'What happens now?'

'To me? Well, I've got one lung deflated, and presumably getting better. But now the bug has got at the other, and since I shouldn't be much good with *both* deflated, this is regarded as a poor show. They're messing me around a bit here and then shipping me back to Switzerland. Oh – by the way, I've sold the Lagonda.'

I said, 'Pity. She was a lovely car.'

'Yes, but if I'd had the use of my brains I should have sold her immediately after she slew Joe, instead of going on motoring about the district in Exhibit A. I can't imagine why we never thought of it.' Bule turned his eyes towards the window. 'How does madam feel about that business now?'

'She's hardly mentioned it. Personally, I doubt if it was ever as important to her as she made out.'

'I check on that. But there had to be some reason – some *simple* reason – for the mess. So she fixed on that.'

I said moodily, 'I don't think about it much myself. I suppose Elsie's all right; but I've done nothing but go on paying her two pounds a week. It's amazing what you can let people give you and still go on living with yourself.'

He smiled. 'James – I congratulate you.'

'On what?'

'On having at last made that discovery. You must *always* let people give you things. It's unkind not to. After all, they like being Grand Guys too.'

I said, 'You think that goes for Elsie?'

'It goes for everybody.'

'So there's no kindness – no generosity? Just different sorts of selfishness?'

'People do what they want to. They act as they are. Sometimes it works out well for other people, and that's unselfishness. And sometimes it works out badly for other people, and that's selfishness.'

'And there's no choice in the matter? People can't rise above – above what they want, or make themselves better?'

'They can't rise above what they are.'

I got up and walked to the window. The leaves off the plane trees were already making a hell of a mess. I said, 'I don't believe it. And if I did believe it, I'd rather be dead. It's that damned cynicism that made this mess for all of us.

The truth lies somewhere between you and me. I've always known it did. Between my priggishness and desire to be a Grand Guy, and your cynicism and desire to be a bounder. It's so easy for you to laugh at me over these things. But if my philosophy gets me into trouble, where does yours get you? Don't you see I might very well laugh back?'

He said gently, 'But I never stopped you, James. I never expect to be taken seriously.' I turned and looked at him, and nearly said, 'Not even now?' He saw it in my face and grinned and said, 'In fact I'm seriously thinking of inverting the performance of Addison, and sending for my friends to show them how facetiously a non-Christian can die. Not that I have any intention of dying, unless the doctors insist on it.'

Without moving his head he turned his eyes to the clock beside the bed and said, 'I'm afraid they'll throw you out in a minute.'

I said, 'Yes. I must go. How long will it be before they ship you off?'

'Don't know exactly. Two or three days.'

I said, 'I'll come in again soon,' and picked up my hat. Bule said, 'James . . . ?'

I turned. He was lying there looking at me with a slight smile.

'Yes?'

'Just before you go, may I be impudent and offer a small bit of advice? Or even make a request?'

'Yes.'

'Don't go home and tell madam all about this.' I didn't say anything.

'I say that because it would be very like you – and don't *do* it, James.'

'Why?' I said stupidly.

'Because if you do you'll hurt yourself. And it's quite

pointless.' I said bitterly, 'You think she'd come back to you, eh?'

'I don't say she would. But she wouldn't like it. And then once again you'd feel hurt and betrayed ...' He frowned slightly. 'You ask too much of people, my dear chap.'

'Maybe.'

'So I should be obliged if you'd give me your word about that. It's so convenient to be dealing with somebody whose word is his bond.'

I hesitated and then said, 'All right. If that's the way you want it. I won't tell her.'

'Thank you, James. I'm sure it's the best thing. After all, it can't be too easy for either of you anyway, and it would be futile to complicate it any more. Well, God bless, my dear chap. Drop in again if you have time.'

I went back to the office and sat at my desk for a while. But that was no good, so I went out and wandered into Berkeley Square and sat down in the gardens. It had been raining, and that had brought a lot more leaves down, so that everything was very wet and slimy. I hadn't noticed before how late in the season it was getting. One never notices these things in London. There was a very handsome young man, dressed like a tramp, sitting on one of the seats near me. He was just sitting staring in front of him. He was there when I arrived, and still there when I went away, and the whole time he hardly moved.

It was nearly five o'clock, and I knew that within an hour I should have to go back to the flat, and that Jill would be there, and that I must make up my mind. But I wasn't thinking about that for the moment. I was thinking about the truth lying half-way between Bule and me. That had always been the difficulty. I had always seen their point of view – his and Jill's. Or part of it. But I always had the feeling that they didn't see mine at all. It was all so simple. 'People are like they are, and in the end they do what they want to. Therefore . . .' It was true up to a point. And yet . . .

And then I remembered the curious little smile on Bule's face and saw what it was that he had really been saying to me. 'It would be very like you, James.' It would be very like me to tell her. I saw the challenge, and understood the wry comedy of making me promise not to tell her. He was offering me his way out – the way he would have taken. Just keeping my mouth shut. I could accept it; and that was defeat utter, complete and final. Or I could refuse it, and do it my own way, and take my chance. As soon as I realised that, there was no longer any question, because I had nothing to lose by telling her that was worth keeping. And if I didn't, I had lost anyhow, and no longer existed. Bule was lying there now, with that slight grin, waiting to see whether there was any such person as I; or whether it all vanished in a cloud of vague good intentions as soon as there was a puff of cold wind. I grinned to myself and said, 'The old basket . . . !' with something like affection, and got up and went home.

Jill was there, and, as I kissed her, I thought I saw something in her face that I hadn't seen for a long while, and I remember thinking, 'It's going to be all right. We've just made it.'

I said right away, 'Look, Jilly – I've got something to tell you. I'm breaking a promise by doing so, and I'm probably being a lunatic too. But I think you've got to know . . .'

She said quickly, 'What? Something . . . ?'

I took a deep breath and said carefully, 'The Honbill has TB'

'TB?' she said stupidly.

'Yes.'

'Badly?'

'Yes. He's in hospital. They're shipping him off to Switzerland in a few days.' I took out a cigarette and lit it. My hands were shaking badly. I said, 'I didn't know whether to tell you or not. He made me promise not to. But we've never done things that way.'

She put her hands over her face and said, 'No,' in a low voice. I said, 'I've been to see him to-day – I only heard last night. And I just want you to know that if there's anything I can possibly do, I shall. Not that there will be.'

Jill said, 'Where is he?'

'London Chest Hospital.'

She was silent for a moment and then she jumped up and stood staring at me and said breathlessly, 'I must go to him.'

I said, 'No, darling. That's exactly what you mustn't do. He knows it. I know it. You know it. You . . .'

She said, 'I must. You wouldn't stop me from that, Jim. I must go.' I looked at her for a moment, and as I did so I knew all about the suit of armour, and the house in the country, and the rest of it, and realised that there was nothing left to fight for.

I said, 'It's still like that, Jilly?'

She said hopelessly, 'Oh, darling – don't you see it *must* be – with this happening? What else can I do? Otherwise it's – it's an utter betrayal.'

'Of what, darling?'

'Of him. Of me. Of everything I've ever done or said . . .'

'And if you do go, it's an utter betrayal of us.'

'But I could just go and see him,' she said piteously. 'I *must* do that . . .'

I said, 'And then in a few days' time when he goes to Switzerland . . . ?'

She stood and looked at me for a moment in silence and then dropped into a chair and took her face in her hands.

There was nothing left to do now but to help. I said, 'It's all right. If you're foresworn, that settles it. I hoped you weren't, but I knew you might be, and if I hadn't been prepared to chance it, I shouldn't have told you.'

Without looking up she said again, 'You wouldn't not let me see him.'

I said, 'No. I wouldn't do that. Not if you must. But you must face what it means, darling.'

She looked up at me sharply in a frightened way. I said slowly, 'You see I haven't any more to give. If I had, you should have it. But I haven't.'

'What d'you mean, Jim?'

'If you go now, you must go altogether. You can't love two people at once.'

She said desperately, 'But I can – I *can*!'

'Not when I'm one of them, darling. You see I can't manage with – just a part of you, when I've had it all.'

She said, 'Not if I just went to see him and – and then came away and . . . ?'

I laughed and said, 'You run true to type, don't you, darling?'

Jill was silent. I said, 'You're still in love with him, aren't you?'

'Yes,' she said quietly. 'In a way.'

'And if you go to see him, and he's – in that state, and going away and has to be looked after? How could you come back and live with me and – and work to get us started again . . . ?'

She said, 'We're utterly caught. You had to tell me. And

274

if you told me I had to . . .' She beat her clenched hands together and cried, 'It's all must, must, must . . .'

I caught her to me and said, 'It's all right, Jilly. There must be some sense in these things somewhere.'

She was crying. She said, 'There isn't – there isn't. It's not fair to make me be a bitch when I don't want to be. I never meant it to happen. I didn't want to hurt . . .' And then at last the cry I had been waiting for – expecting, and hoping, and fearing – 'Why did you have to tell me?'

After that it didn't matter, and I laughed and said, 'Self-preservation, darling. A man must live.'

That was nearly a year ago. They went to Switzerland a week later, and have been there ever since. But Bule is a good deal better, and they have some hopes of coming back to England, so it's time to get the whole thing cleared up. Jill has never said so, in so many words, but I think they want to get married, and if any girl can get the Honourable William to marry her, it's a shame to stop her. Wherefore your petitioner the said James Langton Manning will humbly pray, and the machinery will work, and it will solemnly be established that the said Gillian Manning has committed adultery with the Honourable William Bule, and the statisticians will add one to the column headed 'Decrees arising from wife's infidelity between tenth and fifteenth year of marriage (childless).' All of which may help to establish something of sociological importance. Or again, may not.

I said when I set out to write this that I was doing so because there was something that I didn't understand, and that writing it might clear the thing up for me. I think it must have done so, because the longer I have gone on, the more monotonously and blatantly like themselves I have felt people's actions to be. I think it was not realising this that puzzled me, and I know it was being puzzled that hurt. I seem to have expected Jill to wear trousers and to have been to a good public school, and to have my sort of honour, and my sort of principles, instead of wearing a skirt and having her own. When Loo tried to tell me, I wouldn't believe her because I didn't want to. And when Bule told me the truth about himself, I never believed him, but told myself that he was a poseur who was talking for effect, and that underneath he must see it all as I did.

And above all, I misunderstood and overestimated me. It was, after all, an easy thing to do. It had all been so simple before this happened – the easy loyalty, because one had no wish to be disloyal; the excellent principles that were never tested; the calm assumption that life was a simple thing of rule-of-thumb right and wrong. Yet in the end there was so little certainty there; and if truth and faith and honour and courage didn't pay a thumping dividend in five minutes, one was squalling with self-pity, and ready to throw them all out of the window.

I see now that it is more difficult than that; that in the end there aren't any dividends; that the only reward for keeping faith is keeping faith; and that if a man wants to be God, he had better remember that being God can be a very painful business, and one better left, if possible, to somebody with more experience of the job. I used to think that what had hurt me was that Jill had destroyed my image of her. I know better now. What she destroyed was my image of myself – that lovely shining, hollow image, so ingeniously made in Birmingham, which lies now in a thousand pieces. She was always breaking things, was Jill. And when I was in a good temper I used to say, 'Never mind, honey. It was a lousy thing anyhow and we're well rid of it.'

Wherefore your petitioner will humbly pray . . .